THERE'S
ALWAYS
A PRICE

A NOVEL

JEN SINCLAIR

Copyright © 2024 by Jen Sinclair
All rights reserved.

wjb press
12220 Atlantic Boulevard
Suite 130, #1331
Jacksonville, Florida 32225

Printed in the United States of America
First Printing, 2024

Library of Congress Control Number: 2024915240

ISBN-13: 978-1-965014-00-4 Paperback
ISBN-13: 978-1-965014-01-1 eBook

Copy edits: LZ Edits

To Mom, my hero, who used to soothe me and tuck me in by singing, *Tell me a story.* Thank you for believing in me. I love you.

Chapter One

Cassie

C hoices have a funny way of screwing everything up. Or at least they did for Cassie.

The fallout from those choices sat on her lap now, reminders of decisions she could not unmake—calamitous remnants of wrongs she could never right.

The dead right hand that couldn't hold a paintbrush.

The foreclosure notice pinched between unsteady fingers.

The phone with the single saved voicemail.

Cassie's head swirled as she sat on her stoop, regarding the fall foliage. October hues that once spoke life into her, awakening awe, and inspiring the brush of color across canvas, now simply fell flat.

She moved her gaze from the colorless world of her Queens front yard down to the papers. A light breeze tickled the pages and freed a few tendrils of light brown hair from the bun at her neck. According to the document, her husband Jason hadn't paid the mortgage in two hundred and thirty-six days. When the process server first handed it to her, frustration thundered through her chest. Flashes of anger followed. But numbness quickly returned her to the default setting to which she'd become accustomed.

Jason should have told her things were this bad.

He should have sold that damn business a year ago like he promised.

She should have paid closer attention to things after what happened with Frank.

Frank.

At the whisper of his name, she picked up the phone perched on her knee. Cassie hit the familiar sequence of buttons and lifted it, the weight of it shaking in her left hand. The automated voice rattled through her ear, announcing a date and time eternally etched in her mind. And then...

"Hi, Cassie. It's Frank. It's, uh, been a while. But...I didn't know what to say before. Listen, I hate to do this to you. Especially with what happened...to you. Your hand. The, uh, other stuff. I just...Jason is like a brother to me, and I trust him to do what's right. I hope you'll forgive me for doing it this way. Maybe when this invention gets a patent and makes millions. It will, Cassie. I know it. And Jason knows it, too. This is for the best... For everyone. I'm sorry, Cassie. For everything." She dropped the phone in her lap.

A gust of wind whipped through the yard, wrenching leaves from branches and sprinkling them through the browning grass.

The voicemail. The reminder of a choice she had made with the ultimate consequence: it had killed a man.

The phone alarm pinged. Dread filled her for the neurology appointment to come. Peeling her body from the stoop, Cassie moved through a haze of regret. She ducked back into the house and displayed the foreclosure papers on the foyer table next to their wedding picture to greet Jason in the unlikely event he arrived home before her. These days, he didn't cross their threshold until well after nightfall.

Walking outside to catch the bus, Cassie shuddered against the crisp air and the prospect that this would not be the last secret time would reveal.

***

The leather squeaked beneath her as she shifted side-to-side in the chair. Cassie's jitters ran rampant at every doctor's appointment, even a neurology follow-up that didn't require an exam. It wasn't always like this, but after years of medical appointments for one thing or the other, Cassie's nerves spiked whenever she entered a medical building.

Her anxiety combined with the fact Dr. Penchant was forty-one minutes late increased the vise-like pressure gripping her chest. She busted her ass to get here on time, every time. This rushing to wait was common, and she was sick of everyone else's time being more valuable than hers.

She rubbed the fingers of her right hand, bending and stretching them as her physical therapist instructed. While she still couldn't close the gap between her thumb and index finger to hold things, the tips were nearer to touching than they had been at her last check-in six months ago.

Even without full function, Cassie's arm had come a long way from when it dangled at her side. Back then, she had kept it in a sling to stop curious glances. An arm in a sling didn't draw much attention; people assumed the condition was temporary, something that would heal. A noodle-limp arm, however, screamed permanent damage.

"Sorry to keep you waiting, Cassie." Dr. Penchant rushed in, never making eye contact.

She nodded, familiar with the drill. The apology was a necessity, not a genuine sentiment.

"I have the results of your latest nerve conduction study. Let me take a quick peek to refresh my memory." Translation: he hadn't bothered to look at them yet.

Cassie fixated on the bare spot at the crown of Dr. Penchant's head as he bent over the tablet. The doctor was fourteen years older than her, the same age as Jason. That's where the similarities between the men ended. Dr. Penchant fell short of Jason's six-foot frame, more at Cassie's height of five-foot-nine. The doctor was wiry, pale, and delicate with the smooth hands his profession required. Jason was meaty, ruddy, and rough with calloused hands molded by three decades in construction.

Then there was the hair. In addition to the expanding bald spot, Dr. Penchant was totally gray. Even at fifty, Jason could still boast a full head of black hair highlighted by a dignified sprinkle of gray at his temples. Except for the lines deepening across his face, no doubt accelerated by the events of the last year, Jason didn't look his age.

"Right, so here's what we have." Dr. Penchant put the tablet down and swiveled to face her. He removed his glasses and folded them into his jacket pocket. "I don't see much change between this study and the last."

He may as well have slapped her. The sting in her face was the same.

"But my range of motion."

"It's possible there are tiny improvements that seem big to you. But they're too insignificant for the test to register." He looked at her with the sympathetic tilt of his head she usually found comforting. Cassie didn't want sympathy, empathy, or anything other than proof she was getting her hand, her *life,* back.

Granted, she hadn't been painting like she should have when she could. Instead of honing her gift and embracing her individuality and identity, she spent so many years avoiding it, pushing it down, until all that remained was mediocrity.

It wasn't until the doctors said she would never use her hand in the same way again that the regret crushed her from every side. If only she had spent more time remaining true to herself and following her path, then maybe the loss would have been cushioned by accomplishments she could claim.

She wanted to make a fist. She wanted the pinch of nails digging into her palm to sting the harder she squeezed. She wanted her knuckles to melt from red to pink to white. And then Cassie wanted to crash her fist into the side of Dr. Penchant's head, knocking that fake sympathetic bullshit look right off his face.

None of this happened. None of this could happen. No matter how hard Cassie tried or how much she wanted it, her fingers stayed miles apart.

"I know this is disappointing," Dr. Penchant muttered.

She looked up through tears blurring the man's face. Shutting her eyes locked them inside. Swallowing the anger, the sorrow, the *everything* that pushed against her chest evaporated any chance of more tears forming. She refused to allow any to fall in this sterile and stale room.

She cleared the remnants out of her throat. "What about Dr. Patella, that surgeon in the city whose procedure repairs nerve damage?" Cassie lifted her gaze to seek some answers—some hope—in his. His slow, shaking head killed what little she had left.

"We've talked about that. It's only in clinical trial phases, and you're high risk."

"But why? I'm healthy except for this."

"Because you didn't have a normal reaction to the medication that led to this damage, the insurance company deems you high risk. They'll deny anything in clinical phases, especially a surgical procedure."

"But what if it works?"

"Cassie, if it fails, you will lose all the progress you've made. It could mean permanent paralysis from the elbow down. Is it worth that risk?"

Dr. Penchant had been her doctor for three years, ever since she woke up in the hospital with no feeling in her right arm. As frustrated and angry as she was with him right now, the man had been an ally in this fight to regain what she had lost.

She bowed her head, nodding her understanding, hating every single second of the bitterness. Her whole life had been shaped by loss, and this season would be no different.

***

"I refuse to believe that doctor is right," Jess called from the kitchen while Cassie sat cross-legged on her couch.

"I don't like it either, but it's time to figure out what to do next."

Jess returned to the living room, wielding two large steaming cups of coffee and shaking her head.

The two were matched as roommates during their first year at NYU, but that was the only thing they had in common. Cassie had been an art major, and Jess had studied biology, intent on medical school. They first met on move-in day when Jess showed up with her parents and two older brothers. Jess was the "est" in her family—the youngest, the blondest, the tiniest, and the boldest. The family was a rowdy bunch, bickering with thick Boston accents on full blast.

Then there was Cassie, an only child, raised by her widower dad since birth. She was timid, introspective, and sensitive. Standing next to her dad and two suitcases, Cassie had been happy to let Jess decide what went where and direct the organized chaos unfolding in the two-hundred-square-foot space.

Cassie had predicted the two wouldn't make it through the week.

Now eighteen years later, she looked across the room as her best friend plopped down in the chair and couldn't imagine life without her.

Jess sighed. "I'm sorry, Cass. I hate this for you."

"I know."

Jess's empathy for others and her inability to stomach the sight of blood deviated her from medicine and toward her doctorate in psychology.

"Jason go?"

Cassie shook her head. "You know he didn't."

Jess looked down at her cup. Before her twins were born and Jess was a practicing psychologist, Cassie knew she had perfected her therapist face, a mask Jess slipped on to prevent patients from reading her feelings during sessions. But now, more than three years removed from practice, Jess's features were an accurate and instant reflection of her thoughts. Including the one she gave Cassie right this second.

Jess opened her mouth to speak, but then took a sip of her coffee, blocking whatever commentary fought to escape her lips. She supported Cassie in every way, including her thirteen-year marriage to Jason. But from the very beginning, Jess had cautioned that she and Jason were moving too fast. The fourteen-year age difference would become a wider chasm to bridge than Cassie's romantic mind could comprehend at twenty-three.

"Will he support your art career? Does he know about Paris?" Jess had asked the night Jason proposed. Cassie hadn't been able to answer, dismissing the questions with an of-course-he-does wave. It wasn't exactly a lie, she justified back then since he did know most of it.

A pang vibrated in Cassie's chest, shaking her back to the present. She told Jess everything, not filtering a word that ran through her head. But she decided on the way here Jess didn't need to know about the foreclosure. The omission cranked her nerves as high as an attempt to lie.

Telling Jess about the foreclosure would lead to a whole other conversation Cassie couldn't mentally or emotionally handle right now. She wanted to give Jason the benefit of the doubt and let him explain what was going on before Jess launched a deep dive into all the things wrong with it.

The first question Jess would ask, why would Jason hide the debt, would be followed by the bigger one: what else was he hiding?

Cassie shook the thoughts out of her head. She didn't have the bandwidth to consider anything other than what was happening right now.

"Maybe you should finally open your trust fund. Use it to take that trip to Paris," Jess said as if she had cracked a window into Cassie's thoughts.

She peered down at her hands. Her nails were so clean, the skin of her fingers unstained by color. Three years had passed since she swept a brush across a canvas. Three years since her fingerprints bore the permanent tinge of paint. It was so long ago; the details were beginning to slip away like it had been someone else's life and not hers.

"What good would come out of Paris now?" Cassie said.

If only she had known it would be the last time.

If only she hadn't put that brush down and picked up that last syringe.

The familiar sting nipped her throat and tears pooled behind her heavy lids. Letting herself ruminate on these if-only scenarios plunged her deeper into the abyss. Back to the fertility clinic, the doctor's advice to stop, the one last shot she gave herself in secret because *she knew* her body would do what it was supposed to that time.

If only it had worked.

If only it hadn't left her broken inside and out.

The abyss swallowed her, choking her with grief. A primal cry erupted from her chest, unleashing the sorrow, the pain, the torment Cassie had kept bound with shame. If only she had made the right choice and let go of that quest to become a mother, the paint would still be embedded in her skin.

Jess's arms pressed around her, holding without condition. The arms of a best friend. The arms of a mother. The arms of someone who understood what came next for Cassie was the acceptance that nothing she wanted—creating art and life— could ever happen.

It was the end of the hope Cassie held of returning to her previous life. The art she once created, the dreams she once chased... All of it was gone. They were out of reach, somewhere she could never touch again. All that remained were pain and regret—and the fear of what would or wouldn't come next.

Chapter Two

Jason

J ason stared out his office windows as the factory floor fell silent and the last of the workers pulled out of the parking lot. He started every day at these windows when the sun's first rays pierced the horizon, the orange fire licking the black sky from deep purple to lilac. Then, at night when the work was finished and his body and brain were depleted, he'd watch darkness reclaim the sky.

In these moments, Jason let himself think about Frank, and the years they spent swinging hammers, breaking their backs, shooting the shit, all to climb closer to that top rung of the ladder. Make a name for themselves and have people working for them instead of the other way around. Garner all the respect that came with success.

"Damn it, Frank," Jason hissed into the dingy panes of glass.

Fifteen years into their partnership, Frank pulled out of their construction company and bought the plastics factory. Why? Because Frank wanted to do more than crack the construction business; he wanted to break into corporate America and have a shot at greatness and a legacy.

Frank got greedy and abandoned him. So, Jason vowed never to set foot in the factory.

Yet, a decade later, here he stood on both feet, waiting for a call that would grant him a reprieve or fast-track his ruin. He looked between the darkness and the phone, wanting to get it over with but also willing it to stay silent.

He sighed and took the five steps to the desk. He lowered to sit, using the armrests to help defer the weight from his back, but the muscles screamed anyway. Jason got himself situated and opened the drawer. Fishing out the ibuprofen, he tossed a few back as the phone lit up.

"Hey, Bill, so how'd it go?" The purgatory of the pause gripped him.

"It's a no, Jason. Not enough equity. Too much debt. You'll have to shut down."

Jason let the weight carry his head forward to the desk. "I can't do that." He clenched his eyes shut; Frank's face flashed across his dark lids.

"You're broke. You won't make payroll next week without a bailout."

He had run the place on next to nothing for the year since Frank died. Jason was prepared to keep going because he believed in the plastic proto-type. Just like Frank.

"You said there was another group of investors. A last resort or some-thing." Jason forced the regret from his head.

"They only want the land."

"But they'll give us a cash deposit up-front while they do their due diligence, right?" Jason knew the substance in development would be a game changer for the plastics industry. He only needed to buy his team time to finish.

"I'm going to need to give them more details about the plastic prototype if you want a shot."

Jason let his head fall back while he contemplated how much he was willing to share with potential investors. He didn't want to reveal how close they were to full adhesion of the substance Jason believed would give consumers a comparable plastic product that was also environmentally friendly. But Bill was right. These high rollers needed more than bread-crumbs to sink their teeth into.

He huffed into the phone. "We need to stay afloat for the next six to seven months, long enough to get that patent. So don't give anyone details unless they call with real interest."

Once Jason had that patent, the tables would turn, and all the investors who turned him down would be banging at the door begging for a piece.

"I'll see if I can find someone."

Bill ended the call with a sigh. Jason was pushing the man, but he had to. The consequences if this didn't work...

His cellphone screen remained lit with the smiling face of his wife. Cassie begged him to change that picture, but it was one of his favorites. Taken years ago, it showed her first thing in the morning, drowsy smile raising her flushed cheeks under pine-green eyes. Her long brown hair was pulled back, messy, and light-blond sparks shot from the rim of her face. A streak of faded yellow paint crossed her chin.

It was the way she used to look at him, the way he used to see her before everything went to shit. Before she crumbled under the weight of more loss than even Cassie—who had been born into it—could bear.

If this last-ditch effort to save the factory didn't work, what would he tell her?

Jason threw his phone on the desk on top of the growing piles of overdue warnings and collection letters. He needed to fix things before Cassie found out how far down into their finances he'd dug trying to save this place.

Why did he do it? The chance to leave the blue-collar world of Queens and achieve success and acceptance in a world beyond the sheetrock and sawdust of construction certainly drove him as it did Frank. That drive had bound them from the first day they met.

That same tie had been severed the night Cassie begged Jason to ignore his phone, and Frank swallowed a bullet instead of his pride.

***

Jason wound through the darkness of the tree-lined street and pulled the truck into his driveway at ten thirty. Nighttime enveloped this block, more so since the streetlamps blew out weeks ago and hadn't yet been replaced. He sat for a moment, letting the spasm in his back ease before heading into the dark house. Only the foyer table light remained on, giving him all the light he needed to make his way inside.

He popped off his boots and threw his keys at the foot of the lamp on the table. Something caught his eye, a piece of paper propped up on their wedding photo. His fingers retrieved it. Not a piece but several pages. He held them under the bulb to try and make out the writing.

"The bank is taking our house," Cassie said from the living room. Jason's head moved in her direction, the document crinkling in his sudden grip.

He walked over to her. The half-moon trickled in through the window, and the contrast in light and shadows kept her tucked away.

"So, you aren't surprised," she continued. "At least that makes one of us." She tilted her head, and half of her face dipped into the single beam of light.

"Let me explain," he said.

She crossed her arms, and her lips snapped shut.

His mind raced with questions and answers and uncertainty. How much did she know?

Enough. She knew enough.

"I'm handling it. Bill—"

Cassie scoffed. "This is your explanation. That you're handling it with Frank's old financial adviser. The one that got him in the red in the first place?"

"Honey, can you just listen for a minute?"

"I'm trying, Jason. But you need to actually talk for me to be able to listen. Something you haven't done in a very long time. How can you when you're never here?"

Jason sucked in courage. He had to come clean. Right now. If he didn't... "I couldn't shut the factory down. Not when we're so close to that patent. It's what he...what Frank would've wanted."

Cassie brushed the side of her face, the moonbeam catching the glint of a tear. "Frank is dead. Whatever he wanted shouldn't matter as much anymore. It shouldn't" —her voice cracked and broke. The implications punched him square in the gut. "It shouldn't matter more than me. More than us."

"But, Cass, this prototype will change everything," he said. He shook the pages toward her. "And these papers won't matter. We'll have plenty of money. We'll have everything we ever wanted!"

Her sniff echoed out of the shadows. "All I ever wanted was us. You and me. And all these years, I've waited. Sat on the sidelines while Frank pulled your strings...made promise after promise to get you to give up your time, your clients, your money, because of some great new idea of his. And every single one put you...put *us* further in a hole."

An irritation, like a pebble stuck under his tread, crept up from his stomach. It snowballed and rolled into his chest. Frank had his faults, but he had been Jason's oldest friend. Like a brother. Now, Frank was gone. Dead in the worst possible way.

"He's been dead for a year, and he's still working you like a puppet." Her words hissed through the air between them.

Jason turned away. The bitterness in her voice coaxed out the anger simmering in his chest. He swallowed hard, bit down against it, and did what he could to contain the fire threatening to break free.

Cassie didn't have the right to spit all over Frank's memory. The muscles in Jason's arms squeezed. Cassie was wrong. She was so *damn* wrong. He wanted to make this product happen, not just for Frank, but for himself.

"Jason, please just tell me what's going on," she whispered. Her breath struck the back of his neck. "I don't want to be mad at you, but they're taking our house. And Frank...I don't want to keep revisiting it. I can't."

Her words were tinged with sorrow and guilt. He could tell her it wasn't her fault. Frank was always going to do what he did, whether Cassie let Jason pick up the phone that night or not. Jason could tell her he never blamed her. Not for any of it. Even though when Frank came asking for help again, Cassie drew a line in the sand. Made Jason choose. It was either her or Frank.

So, he told her he would always choose her. He loved her. He needed her.

If Bill didn't come through in the next couple days with the high-risk capital, Jason would lose everything. At this very moment, Cassie and the hope that this factory could be the thing that got him the recognition he deserved were all he had left.

He turned and met the gaze of the strongest person he'd ever met. If he told her now how bad things were, how deep that hole he'd dug really went, part of the weight crushing in on him would ease.

"I'll fix it, Cass. I promise. We aren't losing the house. Or us." He spoke the words into the grief-doused air mingled with the jasmine shampoo radiating from her. Her chest sank as she exhaled before nodding and turning away. Just like that, the moment to confess all he'd taken came and went.

Jason closed his eyes.

As long as she blamed herself for Frank's death, even a little, she would cut Jason enough slack and give him time to fix things.

But if she ever found out he chose Frank over her, that he took everything she'd been holding onto from her father, she would never forgive him.

Chapter Three

Three days. Seventy-two hours, more or less. That's how long it had been since Jason heard from Bill. He'd been warned months ago this group of high-end investors was their endgame should they hit brick walls with traditional routes. Jason stayed busy at work overseeing the latest production samples, watching as the sheets of biodegradable plastic rolled off the line. The samples weren't perfect, but each one they tested gave them more data to make the next better. He caught bits of sleep either on the couch in his office or the guest room at home, but his anxiety didn't afford him more than thirty minutes here or there.

Jason's phone pinged with a text.

Cassie: Will you be home for dinner?

It was already half past four. The crews in the factory were cranking the heat to get this latest sample to bind. Steam wafted through the air, carrying a burning oil and rubber smell that clung to Jason's clothes. Even his office didn't provide much of an escape. The echo of the grinding gears thrummed through his head. But he wanted to stay to make sure it held, which meant it would be at least six-thirty before he left.

He typed back: Probably not.

He leaned back in his chair and propped his feet up on the credenza behind the desk, stretching his back. The mental stress and lack of sleep weren't helping his muscles, and the spasms had brought him to his knees more times over the past three days than he cared to admit. He thought again about going back to see the doctor who prescribed him those painkillers years ago, but the last thing Jason needed was another issue to add to the growing pile. He promised Cassie when he kicked them the last time he would never go back. He promised her a lot of things; he didn't always follow through.

He stared at the framed wedding picture on the corner of the credenza. She wore a simple white dress with a long zipper down the back. He inhaled the memorized smell of lilies in her hair and recalled Frank's slap to his back after the Justice of the Peace declared Cassie his wife.

His fingers clutched air, recalling the feeling of the dress as it came apart and how creamy smooth her skin had been under his hardened hands. She was his from that night on. Or so he'd believed. He was so proud of her—of having her—of the fact she chose him, an older blue-collar guy from Staten Island, when she came from such a different world in Park Slope. His buddies couldn't get over how lucky he'd gotten, and really, neither could he.

The ringing phone tore his thoughts back. Time was running out, and the only thing that could save him now would be a miracle. Didn't he deserve something to go his way? With everything that had gone wrong for him, he believed he was worthy of some kind of divine intervention.

"Here we go," he said to the empty room. He put the phone to his ear and tried like hell to keep his voice steady. "Hey, Bill. What's the word?"

"I called in every favor I could think of and left nothing off the table," Bill answered.

"And?"

"I got one reply. Arthur Chopin. We used to work together at Finley a decade or so ago."

"Okay."

"And you aren't going to believe who he works for now. You ready?"

Jason said a silent prayer. "Go for it."

"Dalton Enterprises."

Sitting back in his chair, Jason took in a full breath of air for the first time in days. "Seriously? Dalton?"

"Yes. Arthur said he'd be open to meeting with you. Said the prototype sounds interesting."

Jason's heart hammered his ribcage, a reminder he was still here. There was still hope. "What's the play?" he asked.

"They want a meeting tomorrow morning. Can you get there by nine?"

"I'll be there fifteen minutes before that."

"Jason, this really is it. If you don't pitch Dalton a softball down the middle, he won't swing and—"

"I know, Bill. It's game over." Without another word, Jason hung up the phone and lowered his forehead to the desk. He filled his lungs with the stale odor of rubber and gas as the factory hummed around him. He relished in the sweet smell of possibility as a smile graced his face for the first time in months.

***

Jason spent the night at home holed up in the spare room downstairs, going over the production, marketing, and consumer data, and then writing, rewriting, and re-rewriting his pitch. He needed to know every number inside and out. Every ingredient. Every part of the bonding and production process. The uses for the prototype were virtually endless. He needed to drive this point home more than all the others.

It had to be perfect. He had to be perfect. If he couldn't convince Lucas Dalton of the viability of the product they were creating, the factory was done. So was he. Since Dalton had a reputation for being a man not easily impressed by anything or anyone, Jason needed to take extra care in the details. They would either make his presentation or break him into a million tiny pieces.

Jason was dressed before the sun came up, which wasn't out of the ordinary. But as he rounded the bend into the kitchen, he stopped short at the sight of Cassie leaning against the counter. She was rarely awake this early anymore unless she had a doctor's appointment or plans to babysit Jess's twins.

"You're up early. Got big plans?"

She turned and handed him a steaming cup of coffee. "No. I wanted to see you before you left." She reached out and adjusted his tie, straightening the knot he'd been fighting with for the past five minutes. She looked up at him from beneath her long lashes. "This is what you need to do to fix things, right? To pay the mortgage?"

He nodded. "If I can land this, it'll solve all our problems."

"Then you'll make it happen." Her hands lingered on his chest, pumping extra blood into his heart before she turned back to the coffee pot. He admired the curve of her hips and the way her black leggings clung to every inch of her long legs. Taking a scalding sip from his coffee, he burned the lust away.

"That's the plan." He cleared his throat. He couldn't sound nervous or distracted with Lucas Dalton. The man was a shark and hadn't gotten as far as he had without smelling blood in the water.

Dalton was a business prodigy and financial genius. When Walter Dalton died nine years ago, he had named his grandson the successor to his financial empire. So, at twenty-nine, Lucas Dalton became one of the youngest CEOs in the country. Some were skeptical of the man's ability to continue what his grandfather started. But Dalton had proved anyone who doubted him wrong. Under his leadership, Dalton Enterprises went global, swelling its net worth into the billions.

"Who are you meeting with?"

Cassie's words cut through and rattled in his head. "I didn't tell you?"

"If you did, I was asleep."

"It's Dalton."

Her brows lifted. "Lucas Dalton? The playboy?"

Jason chuckled. "That's him. He also happens to be one helluva busi-nessman, Cass." He moved around the kitchen, too anxious to eat, but needing to take something with him. Cassie plucked a banana off the stand and stacked it on top of his coffee tumbler.

"I know, but all Jess ever talks about is whatever flavor of the month he's dating."

"Well, let's hope he thinks I make a good flavor." He winked, and she smiled, something he hadn't recalled her doing in a very long time.

***

Dalton Enterprises was headquartered in the Rooney Building, one of New York's newest skyscrapers, on Manhattan's Upper West Side. The sun glinted off the steel and windows on the eastern side overlooking the Hudson as Jason entered the lobby. At seventy-seven floors, the Rooney boasted some of the most unique and forward-facing office spaces in the city, full of high-tech and modern features. The atrium was adorned in steel and aluminum fixtures fashioned into works of art, like the chandelier of stars bursting from the high-rising ceiling over his head. He wondered what Cassie would think of the design.

Dalton Enterprises was a flagship tenant, occupying the three top floors, and as Jason emerged from the elevator, he did his best to keep his shoulders back, his posture rigid, and the crown of his head reaching toward the ceiling. He checked in with the receptionist and took a seat. Three other groups were here, duos or more. Each whispered and leaned into each other, no doubt here for the same reason he was. An endorsement from Dalton meant something to the rest of the business world.

Bill had only ever encountered Dalton once, but he'd given Jason a few last-minute pointers on the phone that morning.

Always maintain eye contact, even when it seemed impossible.

Don't stutter.

And never, under any circumstances, admit you don't know the answer to a question.

A woman called his name from the hallway. "Mr. Reynolds?"

He stood and, like an idiot, raised his hand. He dropped it, embarrassed at his childish response. Her heavily made-up face never registered anything other than courtesy.

"Follow me, please." She led him through a hallway lined with men and women perched behind cookie-cutter desks. These people served as the first line of defense outside imposing doors that led to the high rollers of Dalton Enterprises. Jason wiped his brow and willed his heart to stop its relentless hammering.

They stepped into an all-glass conference room with a black lacquer table encircled by at least a dozen chairs. The woman gestured for Jason to sit. His hand lingered on the back of the chair at the head of the table before he resigned himself to one on the right.

"May I get you something to drink, Mr. Reynolds?"

"No, I'm good. Thanks."

When the woman left, Jason swallowed the latest round of nerves that rose from his stomach. He contemplated unpacking his briefcase, afraid of making any kind of misstep that would sink his chances. Instead, he leaned back in the chair and unbuttoned his jacket. He wasn't a suit guy, and the starched collar scratched his neck. He fought the urge to loosen the noose squeezing his throat.

"Jason Reynolds?"

He jumped up at the sound of his name and met the extended hand of a man about his age wearing a suit that probably cost three times as much as Jason's had.

"Arthur Chopin, vice president." He rolled out the chair at the head of the table. The move triggered an extra tick of Jason's heart.

"Thanks for coming in on such short notice," Arthur continued. He brandished an iPad and tapped at the screen. "You own the plastics factory in Queens that you're trying to raise capital for."

Jason stared at the reflection in Arthur's thick glasses. "That's right." He glanced back at the closed conference room door. "Are we waiting for anyone else?"

Arthur looked up at this query and wrinkled his brow. "No, it's just us."

"Didn't Mr. Dalton want this meeting?" Jason asked.

Arthur set the iPad down and clasped his hands on the table. "I thought I was clear with Bill yesterday. I was intrigued by the concept and wanted to hear more about the process. A substance as strong and durable as plastic, but environmentally friendly is intriguing. I told Bill that if I found the data viable, I would bring it to Mr. Dalton."

The blood rushed out of Jason's head.

"But," Arthur said, "after consulting with the head of R and D over some of the details in Bill's email, I won't be bringing this to Mr. Dalton. I'm sorry."

"That email was only the basics. I've got all the data here." Jason gestured to the briefcase at his feet.

"It just isn't for us. But I wish you the best of luck."

Arthur stood, the salt-and-pepper goatee framing his lips barely moving against the courteous smile.

Jason shot up and re-buttoned his coat. The sweat pooled under his armpits; the starch clung to his back. "So, Mr. Dalton was never going to listen to my pitch?" he asked without needing an answer.

"Again, I apologize for the miscommunication."

He scoffed. "Like you're doing me a favor? You could've at least heard me out."

He snatched up his briefcase and walked to the conference room door, opening it like it was made of paper. He was about to leave when the gravity of the situation stopped him. This was it. His last shot to stop the bleeding. He needed to fight like his life depended on it—because it did.

He looked down both directions of the hallway, trying to figure out which way led to Dalton's office. He envisioned the building schematic and assumed Dalton would want the best view. That would put him on the south side, to the left.

Jason made the quick turn.

"Mr. Reynolds, the exit is this way," Arthur called from behind.

Jason took long strides toward a set of double doors looming ahead. The sound of quickened steps behind him confirmed he had made the right choice. But before he could reach his intended destination, an older, impeccably dressed woman stepped in front of him.

"Mr. Reynolds," she said. "The exit is back that way." She was the picture of calm, her tone soft but firm.

"I had an appointment with Mr. Dalton I intend to keep." He would make a stand here if that's what it took. He would not back down. Not willingly. The woman looked over his right shoulder and nodded. Jason clenched his teeth, feeling the skin tightening along his jawline.

"Of course." She stepped aside. "By all means, go ahead."

The sudden shift and access sunk Jason's stomach. He hesitated, anger fizzling. Standing tall, he took the final steps through the door that would either lead to salvation or damnation.

Chapter Four

"Jason Reynolds," Dalton's voice beckoned from the far corner.

Jason stood in the doorway, dwarfed by twelve-foot floor-to-ceiling windows on two sides. The square footage of this room equaled half of Jason's house.

"Mr. Dalton." Jason smoothed his jacket and squared his shoulders. He locked his knees and stretched the crown of his head toward the gold chandelier dangling above.

Lucas Dalton was twelve years younger than Jason and it was clear, even in the shadows before he emerged, that he stood several inches taller. Bill's description of Dalton's size was not exaggerated. He had warned Dalton would make Jason feel small, and this proved accurate, even with thirty-five feet separating them. Jason, though, was never intimidated by the stature of a man since his own had been sculpted by decades of manual labor. But Dalton definitely loomed large and imposing.

"What can I do for you, Jason?" Dalton asked. His deep voice held just the right amount of bass and grit to meet the expectations of his size.

Jason's mouth dried up. The frothing created by anger was gone in an instant. "Yes, Mr. Dalton. I wanted to speak to you about my factory." Jason dropped his tone, trying to make it lower, more commanding. Now that it was out, he regretted it, sounding more like a teenage boy in the throes of puberty than a man in charge.

The narrowed icy blue stare and subtle head bob confirmed this suspicion, and Jason gritted his teeth to keep them from chattering.

"Plastics, right? Queens," Dalton said. "That shit show." His lips curled into a smirk.

"With all due respect, Mr. Dalton, that's not true. We have studies. Real data. We're going to get a patent in the coming months for a composite plastic substitute that performs as well as the real thing but decomposes quicker."

"No, you won't." Dalton slid his hands into his pockets.

"We will. We hav—"

"You won't because you'll be out of business in, what, a week? Maybe two?"

Arthur had implied Dalton didn't know anything about the factory. Jason's point in pushing his way in was to pique the man's interest, but Dalton's revelation shattered his plan like glass thrown against a wall. Jason wasn't sure how far Dalton was going to let him go before kicking him out. But he hadn't yet. If he could give him a scaled-down version of the pitch, it might get him just far enough.

"I wanted to give you...your company an in on the ground floor. Before we get the patent and the stuff...takes off. Because when it does, it's going to completely change the plastics industry by giving manufacturers a strong and sturdy biodegradable product."

"That's why you're here, to give me some sort of advantage?" Dalton wrinkled his brow as skepticism poured from him. "You may want to reconsider how you frame this, Jason. You need me. Not the other way around."

Dalton's face didn't betray his intentions, his square jaw set in stone. If Dalton was playing him for a fool, Jason had to play along.

He inhaled and swallowed hard against the pride in his throat. "You're right. The truth is, I need your help. My former partner killed himself and left us...me in a real bind."

He hadn't put it out there like that before, what Frank did. Jason always left it vague, saying that his best friend died unexpectedly, giving those who asked nothing more than that.

But this moment seemed bigger, like Jason, for whatever reason, needed to tell Dalton the truth about Frank. Something about Dalton's face shifted, like a chisel slipped out of a woodworker's hand rounding the corner of a square. Jason jumped at the unexpected blemish.

"We've got a shot at creating something big. All I need is the money to keep things up and running through the patent—which I expect in six months."

Dalton's posture and expression reset to default. "How much?"

"Five million."

Dalton scoffed and shook his head. "That's steep for a chump operation, Jason."

"We'd get by with half for the next few months," he said.

Dalton shifted his gaze to the right. Jason quelled the hope springing from his gut.

"Leave your proposal with Stephanie on the way out." Dalton turned his back and retreated behind the desk. The door opened and the woman who had stood guard now waited for Jason to join her.

The meeting was over. Jason could do nothing else except pray.

***

Back at the factory, Jason traded his suit for his work clothes and spent the day on the floor. Working alongside those on the line, putting his hands on the materials, on the products, molding and shaping and testing alleviated some of the trepidation oozing beneath the surface. The work provided an outlet to burn the stress.

The phone remained silent, except for Bill's three calls asking for updates and Cassie's texts wondering the same. At the end of the workday, he returned to his office and pulled the phone from the back pocket of his Levi's. Nothing from Dalton, though, just debt collectors and bankruptcy attorneys. Jason ran his grease-stained fingers through his hair. Ten hours had passed since he walked out of Dalton's office. The silence that swallowed him was all the answer he needed.

The next step, Bill counseled, was liquidation. It would move quickly because firms would jump at the chance to pick up a prime piece of real estate at a fire sale price. But the debt would take every last penny, leaving him with nothing to pay his personal bills.

He cleaned up some of the paperwork on the credenza, eyes landing on that picture again. Guilt gnawed at his gut. He'd blown through a great deal of money trying to save this place. This was going to end them. Of that, he was certain. Then what? He would lose everything—his wife, the image of success he had worked hard to curate, his reputation—all of it.

A noise caught his attention, but he dismissed it. The factory was an old brick and metal warehouse. It often howled, especially when empty.

"I hope I'm not disturbing you." The deep voice spoke from the doorway.

Startled, Jason turned. The air rushed into his lungs as his senses fired a million miles a minute.

Lucas Dalton slid into the office still dressed in the same suit from that morning. He didn't look a bit weathered after the long day. Even his dark blond hair remained stylishly slicked from his forehead.

Jason tried to wipe some of the grease from his hands. "What are you doing here?"

"Mind if I sit?"

Jason feebly gestured to the metal chair in front of his desk. Dalton sat, his frame even more imposing in this smaller space. He scanned Jason's office, and Jason took a moment to try and see anything redeeming about the tattered space. But the man's expression gave nothing away. Dalton unbuttoned his jacket and settled back.

Jason sat. What could this visit mean? He didn't want to give rise to false hope, but this had to be a good sign.

"Can I give you some advice?" Dalton started, crossing an ankle over his knee. "Your proposal was basic at best. I know you probably put a lot of work into it, but your lack of business sense is evident."

"You're not investing?" Jason's spine rounded with the weight of defeat. "Not a chance."

A rush of heat surged from Jason's torso and soaked the back of his shirt. His stomach plummeted, sending a lump up into his throat.

"Then why are you here? You could have told me that on the phone."

"I didn't have to tell you at all, Jason." Dalton appeared comfortable, confident, and rigid, while chaos swirled inside Jason.

"Then why?"

Dalton smirked and clasped his hands in his lap. "I wanted to get a look at the land."

So that was it. Dalton wanted first dibs. With the inside information Jason handed him, Dalton now expected the sale to follow sooner rather than later.

"You were never going to give me that money." Jason couldn't keep the contempt from cutting his words. He had spent the last year treading water, believing it would all eventually pay off. The last hope Jason had sat here with a lifeline a billion dollars long, but Dalton refused to throw it.

"The deal is no good." Dalton stood and meandered around the office; hands shoved in his pockets. "You said your partner killed himself. Why?"

Jason shifted in his chair, peeling the sticky shirt away from his back. "I'm not sure," he said. "He didn't leave a note if that's what you're asking."

Something flickered across Dalton's face. "Most don't. But you really have no idea?"

Jason planted his feet and hefted himself out of the chair. The ache in his back was nothing compared to the hammering in his head.

"He owed a lot of money to people he couldn't pay."

Three days after Frank's funeral, Jason had gotten a visit from one of the creditors. A man with greased black hair, a gold chain around his neck, and the butt of a gun peeking out from his waistband. Jason cleared out the business account to keep him from making a return visit.

"Interesting. Now you're in the exact same spot."

"Not exactl—"

"What matters most to you? Is it the money?"

Jason's mind raced to keep up with Dalton's train of thought, but as of yet, he was falling short and losing ground by the second.

"My reputation. This factory. The people who work here. They're good and don't deserve this."

Neither did he. Not after all the time he put into building a better life. Not that Dalton would understand what it meant to struggle or sacrifice a damn thing to get where he was today. Certainly not his pride. Dalton grew up in a world of privilege where everything, including a company, was handed to him. He never lost anything he didn't want to lose. Never felt responsible for another person's life—or death—like Jason.

Dalton stepped toward the credenza. His icy blue stare trained on the only picture in the room.

"That your wife?"

"Yeah."

"How long have you been married?"

Jason shifted his weight. "Thirteen years."

"Any kids?"

"No." Jason crossed his arms across his chest.

Dalton remained fixated on Cassie for a few more seconds, then he turned his back and strode to the windows.

"Most men would say their family meant the most to them."

Jason scoffed. What would Dalton know about family? "What do you want?"

Dalton reeled around. "Does she know?" The two men stood six feet apart, but only one of them was composed, relaxed. Casual. Jason clenched his fists and gritted his teeth. The air between them heaved with hostility.

"What do you mean?"

"That you stole her money. That she has nothing." Dalton's icy eyes reduced to slits. "Not only did you blow Frank's life insurance money, but you mortgaged your house. You opened three credit cards in your name. And when you couldn't get a fourth, you opened three more. In *her* name."

Jason's heart stalled mid-beat. The blood rushed from his head. Lights popped all around like someone was flicking a switch on and off in rapid succession.

"But that wasn't enough. So, you took the last valuable thing of hers you could find." Dalton stepped forward. "Does she know?"

Jason's legs wobbled. He stumbled and clutched the desk for support. How did Dalton know all this? The foreclosure was public record, but the credit cards...

Cassie's trust fund.

Dalton tilted his head. "Oh. She doesn't."

His tone. The bravado. All of it was a taunt. Jason fell heavily into his chair, and his weight pitched him forward in a crash-ready position.

Collecting himself just barely, Jason rasped, "What do you want?"

"To help." Dalton walked back to the metal chair and resumed his casual seat. "I'm willing to give you the five million dollars."

Jason catapulted upright like his seatbelt caught before his head hit the steering wheel. "You said you weren't investing."

"I'm not interested in the business."

"Then what's the money for?"

Dalton flicked his eyes to the shelf behind Jason. "The thing that wasn't on your list."

Mind whirling round and round, Jason tried to unravel what Dalton meant. He turned and tracked Dalton's stare. Piles of folders and papers... Beyond those... His wedding picture...

A cold chill poured over his head and settled in his chest.

"I want you to introduce me to your wife," Dalton continued.

"Is this a joke?"

"I never joke about money."

"Why do you want to meet her?"

"To decide if I'm going to help you."

Jason's ears rang, and the cold in his chest turned white hot. "What does she have to do with this?"

Dalton dipped his head and took his time before bringing his eyes back up to Jason's. "If she still looks like that"—Dalton paused, trickled his fingers down his tie—"I may want to pursue her."

"*Pursue* her?"

"Things come too easy for a man like me." Dalton clasped his hands in his lap. "Bedding a woman, for instance, loses its thrill when they just lie down. But"—Dalton shifted forward—"chasing your wife may prove more challenging."

Jason caught his breath and tried in vain not to stutter. "You want to pay me five million dollars to chase my wife?"

"I'll pay you half that to pursue her."

Confusion clouded Jason's head.

"You get the rest," Dalton continued, "after I seduce her."

The office melted away, leaving Jason in darkness in every direction. He shook his head to clear it and drive out the heaviness. He clenched his jaw, his fists, and his legs tighter. And tighter.

Five million dollars. To seduce his wife.

Jason's every cell raged. Dalton had tossed his offer out like a lit match inches away from a leaking gas tank. Jason exploded to his feet. "Get out!"

Dalton's gaze drifted to Jason's fists, then back up, but the man's voice was as calm as still water. "I'm giving you one last chance to save yourself. You think she'll stick around when she finds out what you've done?"

The dig hit squarely. Yes, Jason had made mistakes and suffered setbacks in his business dealings in the past, and though Cassie was upset by these, they had made it through.

But this time was so different. She would never forgive him for lying, for hiding the money he had funneled to Frank before he died. For digging them deeper and deeper into the pit. He'd had the chance the other night to unburden himself, but he hadn't because he had wanted to give this business one more shot.

The business. Dalton's words. *Most men would say their family meant the most to them.* Voices screamed in his head. Throw this bastard out. Go home. Confess he ruined their life. Beg her to forgive him. Cassie loved him, and she needed him; they needed each other.

A smaller voice whispering gave him pause. Jason could get two and a half million dollars without doing anything nefarious. What was the harm to Cassie?—to them?—if Dalton liked what he saw and paid Jason for it? She was devoted and loyal. She wouldn't fall for whatever bullshit this guy would throw at her. No matter how unhappy she'd been.

Firmly, he shook his head against that voice, even as it reminded him this was his absolute last chance. He turned his back to Dalton, focusing on their picture and the smile of the woman he had vowed to love, honor, and protect at all costs. Could he pull her into shark-infested waters? All to save himself from drowning?

Turning back slowly, he whispered, "What do I have to do?"

"Bring her to my apartment tomorrow night. I'm having a small get-to-gether before the place is remodeled." Metal scraped the floor as Dalton rose from the chair. "It'll give me a chance to see if I'm interested. I'll wire the money by midnight if I am."

"And then what? You get the rest of her life to try and have sex with her?"

"Six months. You won't make it beyond that without the rest of the money."

"She'll never agree to this." He said, "Not in a million years."

"Of course, she won't. That's why you aren't going to tell her." Dalton looked at his watch. "Do we have a deal?" He thrust out his hand.

Jason stared at that hand. If he took Cassie to the party and didn't get the money, he would come clean. He would tell her everything. Tell her he had given Frank their money against her wishes. He'd tell her about the credit cards, the trust fund—all of it.

Unless he didn't have to.

Two and a half million would buy him time. He could catch up on the mortgage, and even pay some of their other bills. Plus, he could give the factory a few more months to get that patent. Even if things with Cassie and Dalton never went any further.

Jason took his hand. Dalton's grip was strong, and his blue eyes flickered like a pilot light reignited.

Chapter Five

Cassie

C assie returned from her run and stopped short. Jason's truck was in the driveway. Odd. He had been gone when she woke up, and she assumed he would be spending another full Saturday at the factory. Irritation immediately prickled her skin. Other than a few vague texts proclaiming things were promising, Jason still hadn't filled her in on yesterday's meeting with Lucas Dalton.

She walked into an empty kitchen and set down the bag from Peg's containing her coffee cake, a reward for running five miles this morning. Her unrelenting nerves and frustration gave her plenty of fuel to make the miles fly by at one of her fastest paces in the year since she'd started running.

She peeled off the compression hoodie as she walked to the bedroom and stopped short in the doorway. Jason was passed out face down and diagonal across the bed still fully clothed. It reminded her of their early days when he'd work double shifts. He'd come home too plagued by exhaustion to bother getting undressed. She'd often wake in the middle of the night to find him asleep on the couch, feet hanging over the arm, work boots still on.

His job was different now; their whole life was. Back then, she had her art restoration career to help when things got tough. Now, any financial burden was his alone. Without any income from her, it all fell on his shoulders, so while Cassie wasn't about to excuse his misappropriation of their mortgage payments, she was willing to be patient and let him try and make things right. For now.

She sighed and quietly closed the door. Moving carefully to avoid the creaky plank on the other side of the threshold, she showered in the bathroom downstairs. Cassie stood under the water, letting the warmth wash over her skin. Her dad used to say a hot shower was a good way to wash the weight of the world away. If her easel or sketchpad didn't do the job, the rush of water certainly would.

If only she could grip a pencil.

When the full use of her hand didn't return after six months of physical therapy, Jess had suggested Cassie try using her left hand to sketch. She said creatives often found ways to work around the loss of their main tool.

For months, Cassie slogged through grade-school letter formation worksheets using only her left hand. She made some progress and could now write semi-legibly as a lefty. But anytime she picked up a piece of charcoal or tried to put a Faber-Castell pencil to sketch paper, it slid through her fingers like grains of rice—like so many opportunities through the years.

She gave up trying to make her left hand do something it wouldn't. Her art had never been forced. It used to flow through her, so doing it any other way was unfulfilling.

She stayed in the shower until the water beating her skin turned cold. After dressing, she consoled herself with the coffee cake. She warmed it and the scent of cinnamon and sugar filled the kitchen, working its magic before her fork ever touched it.

"I can't believe I slept like that." Jason thudded down the hallway. He came up behind her chair and squeezed her shoulders. When his hands lingered, for a moment Cassie wished he would drop his lips to her skin like he used to. Instead, he gave her a gentle pat before withdrawing his touch.

"You needed it."

"Apparently," he said. "That smells good. Peg's?"

"Of course."

Jason cut himself a piece and popped it into his mouth. He looked refreshed, almost invigorated.

"How did the meeting go?"

Confusion clouded his face, and his eyes grew distant for a split second. Alarm coursed through her. Was that another lie?

"Yesterday?" she asked. "Didn't you go to the city to—"

"Dalton, yeah. That was yesterday morning." He bobbed his head.

"And how did it go?"

"Good. Great even. Which reminds me, do you have a party dress?" He moved to the fridge and grabbed what was left of the orange juice, chugging it straight from the bottle even though he knew she hated it.

"A what?" she asked.

"A dress. Not super fancy, but one you can throw on for a thing tonight." Jason tossed the empty carton in the overflowing recycle bin and made his way over to the table.

"What thing?"

"At Dalton's place." Wood screeched against the pine floor as he took a seat. "He invited me—well, us—yesterday."

He acted like he was going through some rehearsed scene, but she didn't have the script. "You got invited to a party at Lucas Dalton's house?"

He nodded and tossed another piece of cake into his mouth. "Email says it starts at six."

"And you're just now telling me?" She jumped up from the chair. Jason's strange behavior triggered an avalanche that crumbled the last of her sanity, sending it cascading into her gut.

Anger pumped with every quick beat of her heart. This didn't seem like the kind of thing you could just throw on any dress for. A party at Lucas Dalton's called for planning and preparation, both physical and mental, especially if it meant the investor would help Jason with this latest financial debacle.

"Babe, I'm sorry. I meant to tell you, but I crashed. I know it's rushed, and if you don't want to go, we won't." He stood and put his hands on her shoulders. His eyes, big and brown with little flecks of gold at the corners, had caught her attention all those years ago. That and his easy smile.

"Is he investing?" she asked.

A shadow glanced across his face. "I think so. I'll find out at the party, or maybe after. He isn't an easy man to read."

"So, this is important to you?"

"It's important to us, Cass. Yeah." The sparkle in his eyes was duller these days. "But I don't want to force you."

She took him in. The wear of his worries was evident. He no longer had that easy smile. Since Frank died, he rarely cracked so much as a grin. The shock and sadness of the loss swallowed Jason in a way none of their other tribulations had. He had promised to sell the factory, blaming it for Frank's demise. But a month later, Jason changed his mind. He believed the plastic substitute Frank's team had been working on was so promising he needed to keep it going so someone else didn't benefit from Frank's work.

If she'd stood her ground and said no, they might not be here. But Jason's guilt over not answering the phone outweighed hers. The choice she made—to tell Jason to cut ties with Frank and let him figure out his challenges on his own—was the reason Frank took his life. It was another weight to the load on her shoulders.

The pain etched in the dark circles under Jason's eyes pulled at her empathy, and she made a choice. "I'm sure I've got something I can make work."

He wrapped his arms around her, and she stepped into him, letting his arms fold her against his solid form. He pressed her tightly, though, like she would slip through his fingers and fall away if he loosened his hold.

***

The elevator ride to Lucas Dalton's penthouse afforded Cassie plenty of time to second and third-guess her choice of dress, shoes, hairstyle, and everything in between. She had called Jess to help, and after a round of squeals and claps, Cassie refused to come over and pick up the sexy red dress Jess had begged her to wear. Instead, Jess talked her through some of the better options in her closet.

She had landed on an aubergine chiffon dress with an empire waist and cap sleeves. The scoop neckline was modest, and the skirt long and light down her legs. She paired the dress with black flats to minimize her height. At five-foot-nine inches, even though Jason was six feet tall, heels of any size often made Cassie the tallest woman in the room. She had no intention of drawing any attention to herself.

She had swept her brown hair into a low knot at the base of her neck and kept her makeup minimal, with a dash of gray above her green eyes, a sweep of mascara to accentuate her lashes, and a hint of pink gloss on her lips. Her bottom lip was fuller than the top, and any kind of lipstick made the inequity between the two stand out.

Jason had stepped back, clutching his chest when she emerged from the bedroom. She giggled and blushed at his dramatic and very slow whistle. The lengthy sweep of his gaze across her body caused a lost sputter in her core and her cheeks to blush.

Her unease rose with each floor in the elevator. Lucas Dalton was the closest thing to royalty New York City had. After Jason left for the meeting yesterday, Cassie had saddled up to the computer with her coffee and a full morning to burn. It didn't take long for her to get sucked into the black hole of Lucas Dalton's life. In business circles, he was described as ruthless, cutthroat, and incorrigible. When Lucas Dalton made up his mind about something, insiders listened. He rarely made mistakes and was not known to fail at any business venture he gambled on.

Jess always kept her up on the gossip about him. His personal life largely remained a mystery, but what was reported centered around his penchant for beautiful women. The paparazzi snapped plenty of pictures of him out and about the city, each time with a different woman, usually a model, an actress, or an heiress. The gossip columns took great care to note he was never seen with the same woman twice. Some pontificated he lacked the time or inclination for a relationship.

Jason squeezed her hand when the elevator came to rest. His clammy palm was unusual and twisted Cassie's stomach into knots. He was always good at acting confident even when he was anything but.

When they stepped into an ornate hallway, a man in a tuxedo greeted them with flutes of champagne and directions to proceed down to the open door. Cassie didn't decline the drink, hoping like hell it would take the edge off.

Jason led her toward the unadorned slate black door, one unsteady step after the other. The stakes were high, and if she could do anything to help ease their financial burden, she needed to do it, just as she had when she pushed her own art to the side and took that restoration job years ago.

Entering Lucas Dalton's penthouse was like stepping into another world devoid of color and light. Stark. So dark. So sanitary. The contemporary elements, all sharp edges and stone, were a mix of black lacquer and white leather. Cassie walked across gleaming black marble floors and pushed back the odd sense that the apartment mirrored the nature of its elusive occupant.

Jason whispered in her ear. "So much for it being a small party."

She shivered under the seduction of his warm breath and surveyed the scene. The crowded space dripped with all the trappings of fortune and high society. Not one person in here wore something off the rack. Except her. Even Jason's suit had been custom-tailored. A few months ago, he spent the extra money on a proper black suit he could reuse, and she had agreed, even though it cost a fortune.

They drifted from room to room, dropping in on conversations. People gave slight nods after looking her up and down. Jason paused to shake hands here and there, this brush with temporary fame energizing him.

Cassie preferred to recede into the background, especially in social situations where she didn't know anyone. Jason, on the other hand, was a natural schmoozer, his relaxed and casual banter flowed freely. He could talk to anyone about anything. Small talk had never been something she excelled at. It exhausted her.

"Jason Reynolds." A man with a graying goatee sidestepped to stop their forward progress. He held his hand out to Jason.

"Arthur, good to see you again." Jason took the offered hand and his all-business tone reverberated through his greeting.

"I'm glad you're here. Mr. Dalton mentioned I might see you around, and this time, you were invited." When Arthur chuckled, Cassie's stomach flipped as she found more concern than humor in his words.

"Cassie," Jason said. "This is Arthur Chopin, Mr. Dalton's VP and right-hand man."

"Yes, well, it appears I make a better businessman than a security guard, as you proved yesterday." Arthur adjusted his glasses. The ease of his voice and stance stood in stark contrast to Jason's rigid features.

"It's a pleasure to meet you, Mrs. Reynolds," he continued, offering Cassie his right hand. Her lack of mobility in her hand didn't allow for the firm handshake Dad had taught her was so important. Arthur either didn't notice or care, taking her hand in his own lackluster grip.

"Please, call me Cassie. It's nice to meet you, Arthur."

The man's smile was kind enough, but his comments to Jason and her husband's stiffening nagged her. Light reflected off the sheen of the bare spot on the top of his head, which gave way to a ring of gray and dark hair.

"Enjoy your evening, Cassie," he said and turned to Jason. "You too, Jason." He clapped Jason on the back as he passed.

Jason looked down at her and his features melted from fixed to annoyed, a response, no doubt, to the alarm on her face. He gestured toward an open door across the room. She followed and tried to push the familiar frustration out of her mind. The one that reminded her of all the times Frank had roped Jason into something that set them back and saddled them with some sort of debt. She sighed, hoping like hell he wasn't leading her toward another dead end.

Chapter Six

They stepped into a dining area. The massive onyx table and chairs at the center didn't bear the marks of frequent use. The dimmed chandelier, a twist of four golden rings, sent finger-like shadows creeping up the walls.

"What the hell was that about?" Cassie asked.

"My meeting yesterday morning was scheduled, but not with Mr. Dalton. With that guy, Arthur, the VP. When I didn't get anywhere with him, I sorta made my way to Dalton's office."

Cassie glanced around to ensure they were alone. "Like, forcefully?"

"No, nothing like that." He raised his right hand like an oath. "We wouldn't be here if I did."

He had a point. She shook her head and turned away, an attempt to beat back the frustration grumbling in her throat over his continued practice of keeping her in the dark. A set of wall-mounted picture lights at the far end of the room caught her eye and as she drifted closer, the irritation raking her sternum ramped back up.

"You've got to be kidding me," she said, more to herself than Jason.

She crossed her arms, examining the modest-sized canvas mounted in the center of the lights. The drips and chaotic style were the signature of Jackson Pollock. The fact that it was in the home of Lucas Dalton meant it was an original.

"That what I think it is?" Jason asked from her right shoulder.

"If you think it's a Pollock, then yes." Her answer was short and annoyed, matching her mood.

He scoffed. "Your favorite. Great."

She shook her head and inched closer to study the painting.

"It's awful. Seriously, how is that art? Who out there decided that a guy who threw paint from cans was inspired or talented?"

"Tell me how you really feel, Cass." Jason chuckled. He rubbed the middle of her back, and she shrugged off her irritation. Her MFA adviser liked to remind her that people with too much money would throw it away on whatever society deemed worthy and not necessarily on things that were.

"How much did he pay for this? Ten...eleven million?"

"More like fifteen."

Cassie stiffened at the gravelly voice. She turned to see a tall figure emerge from the shadows. Although she'd seen plenty of pictures, Lucas Dalton's presence sent heat surging through her.

"Mr. Dalton," Jason said.

"I was beginning to think you changed your mind." Dalton hadn't looked away from the painting and his half-lit profile was all edges. Cassie's legs shivered, and she thanked her past self for picking the long dress. Tearing her stare away from him, she turned back to the painting.

"My wife, Cassie, was just admiring the painting," Jason said from a million miles away.

Cassie winced at his choice of words. The air to her left shifted, sending a hint of cedar tinged with citrus her way.

"Are you an art expert?" Lucas Dalton asked.

Cassie shook her head slowly, still refusing to face the man.

"Oh, no. Just a fan." Cassie's throat clenched.

"Of Pollock?"

"Of art. In general." The energy racing through her set off by his proximity was unexpected and unsettling. She cursed her body. Lucas Dalton was just a man. One who could save her house from foreclosure and stop her life from crumbling more than it already had. The pressure intensified, pushing in on every square inch of her, threatening to crinkle her like paper.

"So do you like it?" he asked.

"The painting?"

"Yes. You made a comment about the price."

Oh, God, he heard.

Cassie attempted to clear the sand pouring down her throat, buying her some time to find a way out. She could keep stalling and avoid the question, hoping for a diversion of some kind, like the ground opening beneath her. She could also tell him she liked it and lie, which, historically speaking, she was awful at.

Then there was the truth.

Jason drew closer to her. His hand burning into her back made his opinion on the way she should answer loud and clear.

"Well," she started, drawing in a deep breath of the citrus-cedar air. She looked into Lucas Dalton's eyes for the first time and the azure pools swallowed her instantly. But not enough to lie. "I'm not a fan. I think Ruby the elephant from the Phoenix Zoo was more talented."

Jason groaned behind her.

Cassie was taken by Lucas Dalton's pinched gaze, the iciness in contrast to the heat emanating from it. She didn't look away as much as the forces between them willed her to.

No photograph could do him justice, unable to capture the totality of this man before her. The sharpness of his face and the few freckles that dotted his forehead and danced down his left temple made her feel like she might come undone. He was every bit the masterpiece he appeared in pictures, and then some.

Her eyes followed the path of his Roman nose to the deep pink lips beneath just as the corners ticked up a hair.

"So, you're saying I overpaid?" His dark blond eyebrows hugged the skin between them as he jerked his head toward the painting.

"By about fourteen million nine hundred and ninety-nine thousand dollars. Respectfully," she thought to add.

He nodded. "What do you think I should do with it?"

"Sell it. Get your money back, and go find some real art."

Out of view of Lucas Dalton, Jason moved his hand to Cassie's shoulder blade. He, too, probably wished a hole would swallow her.

"That's one opinion I've never heard." Lucas Dalton regarded her, then shifted his attention to Jason. "You two enjoy the party."

He turned and disappeared back into the shadows.

"Thank you, Mr. Dalton," Jason said after him. Once the man vanished, he added, "And thank you to my adoring wife who just sank any shot we had at getting his money."

She whirled around to the sight of Jason's pulsing jaw. His face was gaunt, lips pursed, glare dark.

"What was I supposed to do?"

"Not insult the man we need to save our asses, Cassie. You should have lied!" He ran his hand through his dark hair. His disapproval—his disappointment—deepened her dread. She had screwed up. Once again, she made the wrong choice, and the result may cost her everything.

"Jason." She stepped toward him and placed a hand on his arm. He shook it off. "I'm so sorry. I just... I didn't think."

"No, you didn't. And that's the problem, Cassie. You never do. Not about anyone but yourself." His harsh tone pushed her back.

"That's not true or fair, Jason," she whispered.

He stormed out of the room, leaving her insides as turbulent as the painting she despised.

Chapter Seven

Jason

A nger filled his chest. He didn't like to get like this, especially not with his wife, but he couldn't help it. All she'd had to do was lie. That's it. She wasn't good at it, but she didn't have to be. All she had needed to do was tell a stranger his painting was nice. But she couldn't do it. She wouldn't do what was best for them both when he really needed her to.

He made his way to the open bar set up across the apartment. If he was about to have the life taken out of him, he might as well indulge in some good scotch on Dalton's dime.

"Give me a Macallan. A double." The bartender went to work and quickly offered the drink to Jason's unsteady hand. He breathed in its rich scent. He should slow-play this and enjoy each sip. Instead, he tipped it back and finished it, letting the alcohol scorch a path to his stomach. He returned the glass to the bar for a refill.

This one Jason took and stepped away. The immediate buzz of the indulgent booze dulled his nerves for the moment. The night was shot. Now all there was left to do was figure out how to tell Cassie they were broke. Without the money from Dalton, not only was the factory gone, but so was everything else, including the trust fund.

He had no idea how she would react. That trust had been a surprise gift from her father she only found out about after he died. She had never bothered to look at its balance, not even when the estate lawyer sent the annual accounting. It was something she couldn't face and didn't want to have anything to do with, not even when they bought the house or went through fertility treatments. If he brought it up, she would say it wasn't the right time. He didn't push, but he had always wondered what would make the time right.

He surveyed the crowd and wondered if anyone else was auditioning their wives for a role in Dalton's sick play. He shook his head and drained the rest of the drink. He should go and find Cassie. She hated being stuck at a party where she didn't feel comfortable. He adored the way she clung to him, especially since heads turned everywhere they went. He loved it, and he was positive she would eventually catch on that he was taking her to gatherings all the time just to show her off. To let others in similar circles know he could get a young and beautiful woman while they couldn't.

"Another Macallan?" the bartender asked.

He hadn't realized he had drifted back to the bar. "Sure, what the hell," he said. His phone vibrated inside his jacket, but he ignored it.

He grabbed the refill and meandered toward the crowd. The vibration started again, and he reached in to fish it out. It was Bill.

"Bill? What's going on?"

Jason couldn't hear the response above the noise of the revelers, so he slipped through a nearby door and out onto the stone terrace.

"You still there?" Jason asked.

"Jason, what the hell did you do?"

"What do you mean?"

"Dalton. What did you say to him?"

Jason's chest sunk down into his stomach. "Not a damn thing that mattered. Why?"

"The two and a half million. I got an alert about a wire."

Jason inhaled sharply. It couldn't be. "Are you sure?"

"Yeah, and the crazy part is it came from Dalton's personal account. Not the company. I thought he was a no-go?"

Jason exhaled, a vapor of alcohol escaping his chest. That scene in front of the painting. Even with the insult, Cassie had passed the audition. His head reeled; every bit of his body wracked with the implication of it. This was just the down payment. There'd be another two and a half million if Dalton got what he wanted in the next six months...

"Did I lose you?" Bill asked.

"No, I'm here." His eyes landed on his wife inside the glass door. She always stood out in any crowd. Not just because of those mile-high legs or perfect figure; she had a way about her, an energy, a light that drew people to her. She had no idea she had this hold over people, and Jason was always grateful for that. "I guess he saw something that changed his mind."

His stomach soured when the reality of what he had done filled him. He had betrayed her. His agreement—his *permission*—to allow Dalton to play this twisted game was far worse than anything else he could have done. Even the truth of their financial situation may not have been as bad.

Then again, he now had a reprieve from the looming disaster. Even without the rest of the money, he could undo some of the wrong.

"What do you want me to do with the money?" Bill asked.

"You good to meet tomorrow?" Jason regained control over his racing thoughts. He had one last shot. He couldn't blow it now. There was no going back.

"That works. I'll meet you at the factory after ten o'clock mass."

Jason chuckled. "Say an extra Hail Mary for me, would ya?"

"Will do. And Jason," Bill said. "Well done."

His focus shifted from his wife to his own reflection. He smiled. He'd done it. He'd saved himself.

Chapter Eight

MONTH ONE

Cassie

C assie slapped her alarm clock to stop the incessant buzzing. The last thing she wanted was to leave the sanctity of her bed after two nights of almost no sleep. The haze of the morning hung about her, and the dark room's silence beckoned her to drift back to sleep. Life could wait. She snuggled back into her cave of slumber, alone and comfortable, warm and safe, relishing every second.

The fingers of her right hand tingled and she jerked it out from under the pillow. The pin-prickling shot from her elbow down her forearm, scorching every nerve and muscle as it raged through her palm and exploded through her fingertips. Sitting up, she clutched at her hand, squeezing her wrist as hard as she could and pushing her left thumb into the palm to alleviate the searing pain.

Every time she slept with her arm tucked beneath her pillow, she awoke to this same chain reaction of pain she couldn't stop. First came the needles stabbing from her elbow to her fingers. That gave way to a heat that felt like it would melt the tissue and split her skin. The whole thing lasted anywhere from seconds to minutes, until it finally morphed into a dull throbbing that could linger most of a day.

Cassie sank back into the pillows. The pain was more manageable than the emotions that followed.

If only she hadn't pushed the fertility treatment.

If only she'd given Frank the money when he asked for it.

If only she'd lied to Lucas Dalton Saturday night.

She shut her eyes, squeezing out the light, the despair, and the abyss hellbent on swallowing her.

The vibration from her nightstand worked its way into her brain and stopped the spiral. Cassie pulled her phone into the bed, squinting to read the text.

Jess: Are you on your way?

She blinked away the sleep. It was after eight a.m. *Shit*. Jess had an appointment in the city, and Cassie had agreed to babysit. She untangled herself from blankets that strangled every inch of her body and stumbled around, getting ready.

Seven minutes later, she locked the door behind her and booked it to Jess's. The walk on a normal morning took about twenty-three minutes, but today she jogged to get there five minutes sooner. The crisp fall air lacked the bite that would arrive soon enough, so she picked up the pace. The weather was ten degrees warmer than usual for this time of the year, and with the sun shining down, the sweatshirt she had thrown on kept her warm.

Jess burst out the door when she arrived. Purse slung over her haphazardly, she barked orders to Cassie as they crossed paths in the yard.

"Don't give them sugar!" Jess yelled as she dove into the waiting taxi.

Cassie waved and made her way inside. Nicholas and Abby were dancing circles around the living room while a guy wearing a weird orange hat and glasses cackled from the TV. She looked from the screen back to the energetic duo and realized she wouldn't make it without caffeine.

"Who wants doughnuts?"

***

A few hours later, the kids were fast asleep. Between the walk to and from the doughnut shop, and the dance-off to far better music (classic Bon Jovi), the kids lost steam and fell into their beds for nap time. Cassie challenged which of the three of them—Nicholas, Abby, or Aunt Cassie—would fall asleep first. In less than five minutes, the two tots drifted off.

She laid there amid the kaleidoscope of stars dancing across the bedroom walls and ceiling, the quiet broken only by the light snores of the kids and her thoughts. Moments like this used to stab her heart because, as much as she loved Nicholas and Abby, they were a manifestation of the life she could never have. The ache of longing was infinite, but early on in their lives, Cassie had reached a crossroads. She could harbor the anger of unfairness that she would never have children of her own and isolate herself from the twins and Jess to avoid the reminder. Or she could lean in and cling to them and throw herself into being the best aunt she could be.

Over time, her heart swelled more with unconditional love than hurt, and she dreamed of the days when she would regain her painting hand and adorn their walls with murals. The dreams kept her going during the many rough PT sessions and failed grip tests over the last three years.

Now, as she clicked on their monitor and escaped the room like a cat burglar, the reality she wouldn't meet that goal tugged heavy at her chest.

In the kitchen, Cassie found Jess holding the box of doughnuts and shaking her head.

"The old sleep contest works like a charm," she said, ignoring that she was busted for violating Jess's no-sugar directive. After all, she got them through the high before Jess returned.

"Only when Aunt Cassie does it," Jess retorted, taking an exaggerated bite from a chocolate doughnut, which Cassie beat back with an eye roll.

Jess cleared her throat and placed the doughnut box on the table. "Now that we're alone, I've been dying to hear about the party. Tell me everything." She sat down and patted the wooden chair beside her.

Cassie grimaced. "It was fine. Nothing great."

Jess scrunched her brow. "What happened?"

"It was a party full of super-rich people, and I wanted to leave as soon as possible."

"And?"

"And Jason and I had a fight. I think. I don't know if it was a real fight. It was more he got mad at me because..." Cassie eased herself down into her designated chair. "Well, there was this Pollock..."

"Oh, God you didn't throw your drink on it, did you?"

"No, but only because I didn't think of it at the time."

"Cassie!"

She crinkled her nose. "I sort of told Lucas Dalton that it sucked."

Jess's face froze, mouth suspended, brows lifted to maximum height. "You didn't," she rasped as the expression broke.

Cassie shrugged.

"It's Lucas Dalton, Cass! You can't go around insulting *that* guy."

"I'm aware, trust me. Jason said I ruined any chance that he would invest in the factory." Trailing off, she ran her fingers through the seam in the dinette. Once again, a bad choice had led to worse consequences.

"While we'll shelve the talk about how Jason's latest money fiasco is not your fault," Jess said. She stopped Cassie's third tracing of the table seam. "We *will* talk about what Lucas Dalton looks like up close."

Cassie smiled into her friend's eager eyes. Jess's celebrity obsession wasn't anything new, and Lucas Dalton remained one of her favorite targets. Anytime he was in the news, Jess wanted to talk about it—what he was wearing or doing or saying. Jess swore it was a healthy fixation, but Cassie teased she was borderline obsessive.

"Well," she started, and Jess inched her chair closer as if she could hear the news faster. "He's tall. Like way taller than I thought."

"He's six-three."

"I won't ask why you know that." Cassie chuckled. "He was wearing a nice suit—"

"Of course. Color?"

"Navy."

"Shirt?"

"Black."

"Oohh. That's a nice color combo for him." Jess took a sip from her cup and waggled her eyebrows over the rim.

"His voice is deep with a hint of grit in it. And he has freckles. Not a ton. But they kind of frame his face and trail down his jaw." She traced the pattern on her own face. Jess swooned against the back of her chair.

"I swear that man is so sexy. He can do whatever he wants to me."

Cassie giggled. It was comforting. Even though Jess was a thirty-six-year-old mother of two toddlers, she still harbored the same proclivity for men. Jess's teenage penchant for crushing on cute boys had transitioned into full-on romanticizing over handsome men. While Cassie certainly hadn't abandoned her admiration of a fine male form, she wasn't as vocal about it as Jess.

"Greg might have something to say about that," Cassie said.

Jess swatted the suggestion out of the air.

"Don't ruin the moment with reality. Leave me to my fantasies. They're all I have left."

Wide blue eyes and an attempt at a pouty face (her bottom lip too thin to accomplish the move) sent Cassie into a fit of giggles. She covered her face when Jess pleaded for details and rapidly fired more questions.

"Is his hair more ash or honey? Are his hands as big as they look in pictures? Does he smell expensive?"

Laughter squeezed Cassie's chest of breath. Absent any answers, Jess threw her arms up in surrender and exaggerated her disappointment with a very dramatic chin-in-hand move and corresponding sigh.

"It's like you don't love me, Cass."

"I'm sorry. I am. I promise I'll try and answer whatever questions you have, but know that it was dark in the room, and I was distracted by the—"

"Stupid Pollock. Yes, I know. I can't believe that damn guy ruined this moment for me."

Cassie smiled. "I've been telling you for years that he's awful like that."

"I know. At least now, I finally get it."

***

An hour later, Greg sent what he thought was a private text about getting home soon for a late lunch to water the cactus. Jess read it aloud and the two women fell out laughing, because "cactus" was Greg's code for sex since it was safe to say in front of two inquisitive toddlers.

Cassie made her way home, shuffling through the leaves littering the sidewalk. The crunch beneath her feet filled her head with long-ago autumns in the city with her dad, walking through the park on their way to the Brooklyn Museum or The Metropolitan Museum of Art. They had often spent time collecting fall leaves for collages or landscape studies. When she would finish her project, Cassie loved crumbling them, unlocking the magical moss and dirt fragrance between the cracks.

She had asked her dad how she could ever possibly capture all of this beauty in a painting. He would tilt his head ever so slightly up at the sky, and after a moment, he would tell her to feel her way through it: "Don't think too much. Just do what moves through you."

Her dad had encouraged her to act on the whispers that filled her heart. Even when things didn't fall into place—like the time she gave a painting to her middle school friend and was laughed out of her party—he had reminded Cassie that remaining true to herself was the most important act of art and love. She hadn't believed it then, and now, she was so removed from the practice, it all seemed impossible. In those moments when she did what she believed was right, it rarely worked out.

What would her dad say if he saw her now that she'd given up so much? The regret, the squandered opportunities, the poor choices, the life and people she'd lost littered the ground around her feet like the leaves.

She pushed away the memories with a rush of breath. Ruminating about bad choices, like the one on Saturday night, only led her back to the one where she declined her dad's dinner invitation—and never saw him alive again.

She rounded the corner onto Northern Boulevard, so lost in her head she didn't notice the man squatting at the curb until she had come dangerously close to tripping over him. She shuffled to the right and slowed when a trail of black plastic and electronic parts crunched beneath her feet, leading to a slick black motorcycle hobbled with a split tire.

But it was the man who caught her eye. His dark blond head concentrated down, his angular profile, familiar now that she had encountered it up close in his dining room two nights before. Her stomach curdled as she continued on her way, willing herself to keep going. He had someone coming to help. Do not stop.

She realized the pieces she was stepping on were what was left of his phone. Unless he made it a habit of carrying a spare, he couldn't have called anyone. Cassie turned back, trepidation shortening her stride. He didn't look up, his head fixed on the bike at the curb.

"Mr. Dalton, do you need help?" The words stuck to her mouth.

He swiveled his head toward her but remained silent, and his mirrored glasses failed to betray his thoughts.

"It appears I do," he said, standing and brushing his hands down the thighs of his black slacks. He rose to his full height and towered over her. It took a lot for her to feel tiny, but Lucas Dalton managed it in one swift move.

"Are you...hurt?"

"My pride maybe, but nothing I can't recover from." He kept his glasses trained on her and the growl of his voice sparked a flash of heat behind her ears.

His presence pressed down on her, and the exhaustion she had been feeling moments ago was gone, replaced by a surge of nerves rushing through her body.

Not a glimmer of him seemed to recognize her. *Thank God.*

"Mind if I borrow your phone?" he asked.

Embarrassment rippled up her neck in waves. "Yes, of course. Sorry about that." She patted the pocket of her sweatpants and then remembered she had tucked the phone inside the single pocket of her NYU hoodie.

This is a twenty-year-old hoodie. And sweatpants. With paw prints on them. And probably kid snot...

Cassie held the phone out without a word and avoided eye-to-sunglasses contact. She stared straight at the first clasped button on the midnight blue Oxford layered under the wide-open chocolate leather jacket. As Lucas Dalton reached for the phone, his hand swallowed her own, fingertips grazing her skin when he withdrew it.

The touch fueled the heat pulsing under the skin along her neck. Her hands went to the messy knot of hair she had swirled up when she ran out of the house that morning. She hadn't showered since Saturday, and now she wondered if she smelled. She stepped backward *just in case*.

This reaction was as ridiculous as it had been Saturday night. Lucas Dalton was an attractive man. Period. She'd been around them before. She was married to one. Her body needed to stop rushing and surging in his presence.

"Stephanie, I need you to get me a ride and a tow for the bike," he said into the phone, his tone more authoritative than harsh. "Have him get me at—where am I?" He separated the phone from his face, mirrored lenses trained on Cassie's face.

"Northern and 88th." She spoke to the patch of freckled skin directly above the first closed button of his shirt.

"Did you get that?" he said back into the phone. "And I need another phone." He kicked at the debris field around his feet. "Tell him to hurry. I've got a meeting and don't want to be stuck in this shithole any longer than I need to be."

The insult did little to detract from Cassie's current mission, settling on honey as the color of his hair. The top of it glistened as the sun's rays poured over him.

"Is there a place I can wait?" he asked after he hung up.

"There's a diner...Peg's." She gestured over her shoulder at the sign.

He returned the phone to her, and his warmth transferred to her hand, adding gas to the fire.

"Thanks," he said. "And sorry, that was rude. I don't like it when things don't go my way."

"Sure." It came out sounding far squeakier than she liked.

"So that diner."

"Right. Yeah. It's there." She nibbled at the inside of her lip. Now that her effort to help was over, she could put this whole thing behind her and continue her day.

The skin around the edges of his glasses crinkled.

"You should join me."

"Oh. Uh. I mean..."

"Or is there an offensive painting in there, too?" Lucas Dalton regarded her, his eyebrows lifting above the silver rims of his glasses.

Her heart paused its work and pumped no life through her for at least ten seconds. There's no way he remembered her.

Her chest tightened and she gulped down the embarrassment, too much to try and swallow.

"There is not." Her eyes jolted down to some imaginary point on the ground beneath her feet. Her ears burned and the sweat prickled her back.

"After you, Cassie."

Chapter Nine

T he late lunch crowd piled into Peg's. The chocolate brown tables and stools were filled with moms, grandparents, construction workers, and businessmen. Cassie spied the lone open booth in the back and made a beeline for it. Her brain rapid-fired reasons why she should not be sitting down at a table with the man whose multimillion-dollar painting she insulted days ago, the consequence of which had torpedoed any shot at financial relief.

"Afternoon, Cassie. Usual?" Diane brushed a damp rag over the table-top, shooing leftover scrambled eggs and pepper flakes onto the floor. As the older woman straightened, hand to her lower back, she took note of Cassie's guest. "Coffee for you too?"

"Is it fresh?" Lucas Dalton asked.

"Always."

He nodded and Diane moved away, but not before lifting her brows at Cassie, who sat down without acknowledging it. She settled in the sticky booth and noted Lucas Dalton waited before following suit. She would have to tell Jess he had very old-fashioned manners for a womanizing mogul. She would eat it up.

Diane reappeared and set down two steaming mugs of coffee along with a cluster of creamers, peeling two and setting them closer to Cassie's cup.

Cassie dumped the cream into her coffee and stirred. The brew here was at least twenty-five degrees hotter than anything she made at home. She was about to caution him, but before she could, he lifted the mug to his lips. He sipped it and gave no indication it was too hot.

"What do you usually get?"

Cassie wasn't sure he would eat anything on Peg's menu. It was a greasy-spoon kind of place, and she gathered a man like Lucas Dalton and his fitted shirts stayed away from butter-and-grease-soaked dishes.

She looked up from her cup and straight into his naked blues. His eyes had struck her in his dim dining room. But here in the light of day, they were damn near hypnotic.

"The muffins, if they have any left. They're baked every morning."

"Interesting," he mused without freeing her from the weight of his stare. She looked away, focusing instead on the specks of sugar sprinkled across the tabletop, the remnants from the previous occupants of the table.

Diane returned with a full tray of dirty dishes balanced in one hand. "Coffee cake, blueberry, and chocolate chip today, Cassie," she said, unprompted. She turned to Lucas Dalton. "Any questions about the menu?"

He shook his head. "She'll order for me." He took another sip from his coffee cup, tiny in his grip. Another detail to add to her report for Jess.

Diane raised her eyebrows again and made no attempt to hide the smirk teasing her lips.

"Caaa-sss-iee?" she asked. The singsong voice whisked Cassie back to her school days and those times a friend had caught her staring at a cute boy across the cafeteria.

Cassie cleared her throat. "One of each, please."

Diane went to retrieve their muffins leaving Cassie with nothing to say to the man across the table.

"Why did she open those?" he asked, staring down at the empty cream-ers. He returned the cup to the table and leaned back, fanning his left arm out across the booth, its length extending all the way to the end.

"She knows I can't," she answered. The intensity with which he regarded her made it impossible to look away. "What happened with the bike?"

"I don't ride it much, so I guess the tire pressure wasn't great."

"What about the phone?" she asked and tried extra hard not to stare directly at the widening gap between the buttons straining across his chest.

"That I threw because I was pissed."

Cassie appreciated his straightforward answer and the tingle in her belly courtesy of the slight raise of his left eyebrow. She willed her body to stop reacting this way. She was married. Lucas Dalton was a playboy. He hadn't gotten that reputation by being unattractive.

"You hone your discontent of Jackson Pollock there?" He nudged his chin toward her, casting his gaze down.

"NYU," he continued. "You graduate with an anti-Pollock degree?"

"Ah. Not exactly."

"Art history?"

Cassie slurped the coffee and shook her head. "Studio art. A bachelor's and master's."

His eyes went slack, but the skin between his brows arched.

"So, you're an actual artist?"

Cassie half bobbed her head, half shrugged. She should correct him. Tell him she used to be an artist, or maybe that she never really was. She stared into her cup, willing anything else to happen but this conversation.

"Tell me," he said, leaning forward onto what she could only imagine were perfectly sculpted forearms. "Why can't you open the cream?"

She hesitated. A man like Lucas Dalton didn't have time for her sad story, so she gave him the slimmed-down version. "I have nerve damage in my forearm. I can't close my hand to grip things."

He wrinkled his brow, staring at her hand. "Show me."

She didn't like displaying her damage for the world to see, especially when the one person watching was having such an unsubstantiated and intoxicating effect on her. She could refuse, but decided it was less of a hassle to comply. So, she held up her right hand and bent her fingers. His attention never wavered. Curiosity and then understanding painting his angular face.

He leaned back. "You right-handed?"

She nodded.

"Must make it tough to be an artist."

The pang in her chest echoed, chased by a rush of heat. Was he trying to get a rise out of her? The statement said in the same tone as everything else, didn't carry a hint of malice. But the way the intrusion raked itself across her sternum left her unsettled. A shadow passed across his eyes, impossible to read.

His face reflected no emotion. Either he wasn't capable of them, typical of a man in his elevated and unique societal position. Or he spent so long guarding himself that feelings no longer manifested in any outward way.

Cassie had a choice. She could continue to expect Lucas Dalton to be the mogul portrayed in the pages of gossip and business publications. A man raised by his equally cold grandfather from birth. A myth.

Or she could give him the benefit of the doubt: that none of this was a spectacle to him. That he had some benign interest in asking her about her hand, and there was more to him than met the eye. Perhaps he was being polite and making conversation with someone who had helped him out.

"It's impossible, actually. I haven't been able to paint in over three years, even though..." Why she was continuing this was beyond her. "I had stopped. I was restoring art for years before it happened."

His lashes dipped to the table. "That must be—"

Diane set down the plate of muffins.

Relief flooded into Cassie's chest, and she inhaled completely.

She shook away the shadows of those days and turned her attention to the fluffy goodies on the table. Cassie relished the sugar, cinnamon, and chocolate wafting from them. It took her back to the bakery she had visited with her dad every Sunday growing up. They would walk to the little shop, hand in hand. The older couple behind the counter greeted her with gusto and that day's special cookie. Her dad always let her choose two muffins: one to eat on the bench at the park across the street, and the other for dessert after dinner that night.

"You're drooling."

She moved her stare to his icy blue eyes. A flush rushed up her neck. "I'm not sharing if you're going to be judgy," she retorted.

"Don't let her fool you, she probably wasn't going to share anyway," Diane added, appearing from nowhere to refill their cups.

"Thank you for that, Diane," she said louder than necessary. The waitress left them with a wink.

Lucas Dalton leaned forward and plucked the coffee cake muffin off the plate. A piece of Cassie fell as he peeled the sticky paper away from her favorite muffin and squished the cake to bite it.

She willed her gaze away from his lips and grabbed the chocolate chip muffin, ripping a piece and savoring the gooey chocolate. She savored the warm, sugary sweetness filling her mouth, the moment interrupted when he reached for a piece from her plate. She relinquished it with an apologetic nod and watched him sink his perfect teeth into it.

"Maybe there's some redeeming quality to this borough," he said between bites.

"Why are you here if you don't want to be?" Her mouth was still half full of muffin—blueberry this time. Before he could return to finish off the coffee cake, she grabbed a chunk and dropped its crumbly mixture into her mouth. His eyes widened momentarily at her before settling back into his neutral stance.

"Meeting with your husband."

Cassie gulped down the cake that felt like a rock in her mouth. "Why?"

"He didn't tell you about our agreement?"

"No. I thought I screwed things up when I, well, you know." She quickly filled her mouth with another bite of muffin to stop further discord from tumbling out.

He rubbed his hands together to shake off the crumbs and pushed the plate toward her. There wasn't much left on it; the two of them had made short work of the sweet treats. She was surprised he had a sweet tooth. That he ate. That he was human.

"Insulted my painting? Jason tell you that?"

"He said I should have told you I liked it." She couldn't explain why this came out of her mouth with ease, like she was talking to Jess and not, well, *him*. She shouldn't be telling him anything, but something in the air between them made it easy and comfortable.

Lucas Dalton nodded. "Why didn't you?"

"I'm a terrible liar."

"You didn't even try."

"I figured you'd know," she said, her tone slightly heightened. "And I guess I didn't want you to have that impression of me."

The words tasted ridiculous leaving her mouth, because why would Lucas Dalton care enough about her to need a good impression? Jason needed to gain his good graces, not her. The weight of his gaze lingered even after she moved hers out the window, hoping his ride would appear and end her suffering.

When it was obvious her savior wasn't out there, she drifted back to him.

"I appreciate your honesty. It doesn't happen often." He checked his watch and looked over his shoulder at an interested Diane. He waved his hand and on cue, she lumbered over, flipping through the checks on her pad.

"I've got this." Cassie dug her debit card from her pocket and handed it to Diane. The woman looked back to Lucas Dalton, who shrugged and sat back.

"You know art. And you're honest. Those are two qualities I lack in my circle," he said while Diane slipped back to return the receipt and card to Cassie. "And then there's that. How many people do you think make a move for a check with me?"

Cassie again felt the weight of his stare as she shrugged. "You had a bad morning. I figured it was the least I could do, Mr. Dalt—"

"Lucas," he said, waving his hand. "And I want you to come work for me."

She flopped back into her seat like he had hefted a weight at her chest. The thud of her body hitting the back of the booth reverberated to the wall behind her.

"What?"

"Work for me. On my design team for my apartment reno."

"Mister, uh, Lucas," she corrected at his raised eyebrow. "That's nice, but I'm not a professional designer."

"You don't need to be. You just need to have good taste and be willing to tell me things I don't want to hear." The corners of his mouth hitched up a millisecond before he turned toward a black Audi pulling to the curb.

"Lucas, I can't."

"Why not?" he asked.

"I don't do that kind of thing." The temperature in the diner increased by at least fifty degrees. She wanted to melt onto the sticky floor without regard for what might be down there.

"You don't look at art? You don't decide if something looks good or not?"

"Well, I do that, but not professionally."

He nodded slowly and reached for his glasses. "After this project, you can't say that anymore." He slid out of the booth in one swift move and waited for her to join him.

She rushed to sign the slip and stand. He seemed taller now as if that was possible. Or maybe she was standing in a hole. The walkway narrowed with a large group congregating near the breakfast bar.

Lucas waved her by, which forced Cassie to turn sideways to pass him. As much as she tried, she couldn't avoid skimming his body. The scent of him encased their shared space with cedar and citrus mingled with the cinnamon from his breath. She passed quickly and made a break for the door like she was running from captivity.

"So, it's settled," Lucas said, returning the glasses to his face. "Come to my office Wednesday for a ten o'clock with the design team. My assistant will draw up a contract."

"Mr. Dalton, I don't know what to say."

He stopped abruptly and turned back to her on his heel. "It's Lucas. And I'll see you Wednesday."

He continued to stare down at her, unmoving, either because he was waiting for her to be grateful or because he sensed her uncertainty was winning the battle.

"I can't," she started again. "I'm not sure Jason will be okay with it." She stared herself down in his mirrored gaze. It was lame, wasn't it? Needing to ask her husband for permission to take a job that would help their financial situation. No, that wasn't it. Not exactly. It seemed fair to run it by Jason for multiple reasons, including that he was in business with Lucas, a detail Jason had neglected to tell her. Taking this job on the spot without regard for his feelings would make her no better than Jason. While she certainly wasn't without fault in the way their lives had turned out thus far, especially considering most of their mess was a result of her poor choices, she needed to be that much more careful about every other decision she made that had a larger implication.

How could a man like Lucas possibly understand any of this having never been married? He would surely believe she was as weak as she now felt. Her stomach dropped as the possibility he might rescind the job offer became more likely every second they stood there. Cassie wanted and needed the work. It terrified her, but at the same time, it excited her in a way she hadn't felt in a very long time.

"How about," he started, breaking the awkward silence, "I give you a ride over to the factory so you can run it by him."

His offer was so unexpected, she didn't know what to say. "I don't want to burden you. You're busy and so is he." She worried she might throw up if this exchange went on much longer.

"I'm going there, anyway. It's why I came here in the first place."

He resumed his walk to the car and the driver handed Lucas a cellphone. He stopped by the door and gestured for her to get in. After she'd said the wrong thing the other night, she couldn't figure out why he was being so accommodating and so nice. What choice did she have except to further insult the man who not only helped Jason's business but also offered to pay her money to pick out art?

She slipped inside the back seat, unsure of what Jason would think when they showed up—together.

Chapter Ten

Jason

T he day was humming along so well Jason didn't realize the morning was gone until half the crew got back from the first lunch break. He spent all morning on the line, whistling while they cut the newest batch of the compound. The atmosphere crushing down on him had all but dissipated, leaving him lighter for the first time in a very long while.

When he got word there were visitors, and one of them was Cassie, he started up to his office two steps at a time. She hadn't been here in months, so her presence unnerved him, but it wasn't until he reached his office that his stomach flopped.

It was one thing to find his wife waiting. It was quite another to find her waiting with Dalton.

"Sorry, I tried calling but you didn't pick up," Cassie said. But he didn't see her, could barely hear her. All his attention was tuned to Dalton.

"I've been downstairs working all morning," Jason said, eyes glued over his wife's shoulder as Dalton stoically looked back. "What's going on?" He crossed his arms across his chest, shielding himself against whatever was about to go down. He could not, would not, let this man get any kind of satisfaction over rattling him, which he obviously was here to do.

Cassie glanced back at Dalton, who moved his gaze away from Jason only long enough to nod at her.

"I ran into Lucas on my way home from Jess's. We grabbed a snack at Pe—"

"You did what?" Jason scolded himself for sounding so harsh. He couldn't give Dalton—apparently *Lucas* to his wife— a single shred of pleasure.

"We had muffins. I'll fill you in tonight, but the short version is he offered me a job as an art consultant. He wants me to go downtown for a design meeting Wednesday."

Her eyes were wide, her entire face lit with excitement. He hadn't seen that brightness in much too long.

Cassie had continued speaking. "...make sure that you were okay with that. Since he's your *business partner* and all."

He hoped Dalton didn't notice the deliberate way he was blinking or breathing. But if he didn't take these measures, he would be unable to stop himself from walking over and beating the living shit out of the man. Jason had known Dalton was ruthless before he met him, but this maneuver to get close to Cassie was despicable.

He swallowed hard and cranked his neck back and forth. The office dripped with tension, and Cassie being more intuitive than most, was certain to pick up on it at any time. She looked at him expectantly, searching for some measure of response. He had to act fast or else this whole deal would fall apart.

"Art consultant. Don't you have people that already do that?" He tossed his question to Dalton, who had yet to move a muscle or wipe that smug look off his face.

"For the business, sure. But not for my apartment. Cassie has a good eye, and I know she'll take very good care of me."

"I won't let you buy another Pollock at least." She smiled and shrugged, and if Jason didn't know any better; Dalton actually smiled back.

Jesus Christ, what had he done? This whole deal hinged on his belief Cassie wouldn't get close enough to Dalton to become caught up in whatever game he had planned for seducing her. Now here he was, barely two days after the down payment, offering her a job and *smiling*.

"Jason, are you feeling alright? You're so pale," Cassie said.

He inhaled and set his face right. "It's been a long few days, that's all. I'm good, honey." He made a show of stroking her back.

"Well, now that you two are in business together, things should start to ease up around here. Maybe you'll get some time off." Cassie stepped back and looked between the two men. Jason kept his face set in the most neutral position he could muster.

"That's the idea," he said.

Dalton's face remained fixed as well, but his radiated something else entirely. Clearly, Jason's discomfort amused him, reaffirming that this was all just some sick game Jason had agreed to play.

"Does that mean you're okay with me taking the job? It won't last forever. You said it would be for about how long, Lucas?"

"I'm not sure. About six months," he said. "If it even takes that long."

Jason gnashed his teeth. Of course, Cassie couldn't hear the taunting in Dalton's voice. Though he'd brought this on himself, Jason never would have made that deal if he had any inkling this would happen.

Her demeanor was so different in light of this new opportunity. Even if Dalton did have her straight in his crosshairs, it didn't mean he would be able to pull the trigger.

Jason straightened his back and softened his face toward her. "It sounds like the perfect job for you. You should take it."

Chapter Eleven

Cassie

C assie followed the click-clack of the receptionist's heels to a small conference room. The woman, whose slick bun clung to her head as tightly as her black dress hugged her body, ushered Cassie inside to join two others already seated.

The duo at the table regarded her with surprise and she forced a smile despite the nerves rattling around her insides.

"Hello," she managed and sat across from them. She recognized both from the design magazines in the supermarket checkout line. They didn't return the greeting with anything but continued confusion.

The receptionist set down a tray of empty glasses and water bottles—Fuji, Perrier, Avion.

"Help yourselves," she said. "If you need anything else, press zero on the phone and I'll be happy to get it." She nodded and left the room.

"Thank you," Cassie called after. Her voice stuck in her throat, and she reached for the closest water bottle.

The two designers across the table began a hushed conversation without acknowledging her any further. The gleaming crystal and gold clock on the faux plaster wall ticked down the last few minutes before ten. It reminded her of the one that had hung over the door in her dad's home office. Well, until the day Cassie got her acceptance letter into NYU, and she had flung open the door, sending vibrations through the wall and the clock crashing into the ground.

"Who are you?" the man across the table snapped.

She glanced between the two. "I'm Cassie Reynolds. Mr. Dalton—"

"What firm are you with?" the woman asked. Her short bangs barely dusted the midpoint of her elongated forehead and stopped a full inch above painted-on black eyebrows.

"I'm not with a firm."

This answer sent them back to their secret conversation. The only thing Cassie gathered was they were agreeing on something, by the frequent nodding and excessive blinking.

"Why are you here?" The bleached tips of the man's hair didn't move even as he emphasized every syllable with a firm shake of his head. She turned her attention to the man's face and noted his forehead also remained unchanged.

"Mr. Dalton hired me to curate the art in his apartment."

The man sat back in his chair. "We have all of that in our plan already, so," he said adjusting the thick-rimmed yellow frames around his eyes, "I'm sure Mr. Dalton didn't know that when he called you."

"Yes, we've got pages of pieces we've found," the reanimated woman added.

Cassie only shrugged. "You'll have to ask him when he gets her—"

"Say, where did you get that dress?" the woman asked. "It's very shabby chic." Her tone dripped with sweetness.

"Probably Target. It's where I get most of my clothes."

The woman's lips formed a large O with no sound, and she nudged her elbow into her partner's arm. He sucked his lips around cartoon-white teeth. Their not-so-silent fit of giggles confirmed it hadn't been a compliment. Whatever game they were playing, Cassie wanted no part of it.

She dropped her hands to her lap as heat built behind her ears. She hated being the butt of someone's jokes. She bit against her lip and pushed down on her knee to keep it from bouncing.

Sitting across from these two people having a good laugh at her expense—for reasons she still didn't understand—it dawned on her: she didn't have to be here. She didn't have to submit to their judgment or anyone else's.

She rose from the table with the straightest posture she could muster and left the way she came in, past the questions of the young woman behind the reception desk. She rushed inside the elevator and slammed the lobby button, falling against the wall into a welcoming silence.

***

The elevator did not give her an easy escape, though, and seemed to stop on every other floor. Everybody that entered pushed Cassie back further into the corner. When the too-tiny box arrived at the lobby, she emerged last, turning straight into a man outside the doors.

"Sorry," she mumbled, drawing her eyes up from the solid torso into Lucas's icy gaze.

"Don't we have a meeting?" he asked. His hands were pressed into his black trouser pockets and his suit jacket was open, revealing today's shirt and tie color combo: a Bordeaux red shirt topped with a charcoal and cobalt striped tie.

"This was a mistake."

"What was?"

"The meeting. The job. The people up there have it all figured out. You don't need me." She pointed straight up in the air.

"I see." He nodded and kept his head dipped for a second. His dark blond hair held a natural wave she'd failed to notice before. "You saw their plans?"

"Well, no. But they sai—"

"Come with me." He moved past her toward the back of the building.

After a second of hesitation, Cassie followed, hustling to keep up with his longer and effortless stride until they reached an unassuming door tucked in the back corner. Glancing around, she wondered if they should be here. But before she could raise her objection, Lucas flung it open and stepped inside. Her trepidation ceased once she realized it was a private elevator.

Lucas waited for her to enter before inputting a code that sent the lift up. A hint of pressure pushed her ear, but before it could squeeze too hard, they stopped.

The door opened somewhere inside Dalton Enterprises. Lucas waited for her to exit, then resumed his leading stride. Anyone standing along their path stopped whatever they were doing, nodding as he strode by, like soldiers paying homage to a commanding officer.

They entered the conference room she had left moments ago, and the two designers rushed to stand. Lucas closed the door, locking all four of them in the thick air. He gestured for Cassie to sit before he claimed the chair at the head of the table.

"Mr. Dalton." The man cleared his throat, casting a pained glance at Cassie. His partner paled considerably, no small feat since the woman's pallid coloring was corpse-like already.

"Cassie, have you met Hillarie and Antoine?" Lucas asked. He stared at the two, never lifting his gaze from them.

She wasn't sure what to do here. The air in the room choked her with tension and, by the looks of the two across the table, they felt it. "Yes."

"And what did you think of their plans for my apartment?" Lucas sat back, clearly awaiting her answer while remaining fixated on the designers.

The duo looked helplessly at each other and then at her. Their eyes pleaded with her to not out them. Heart thudding, Cassie said, "Lucas—"

He stopped her with a wave of his arm. "I know you didn't see the plans because they wouldn't show you. Why wouldn't they show you—someone I invited—the plans for *my* apartment?" He leaned forward on his elbows, the skin of his face pulling tight against his jaw.

Antoine sat straighter, clearly the braver one of the two. "Lucas—"

"Mr. Dalton," Lucas shot back.

Antoine's face twitched and his glasses bounced. He adjusted them with a shaky move of his hand. "Mr. Dalton, we were caught off guard, that's all. We didn't know who she was."

"Did you ask her?"

"She said she was here about the art."

Lucas nodded, a lone fingertip tapping the table.

Antoine blinked and ran his hand down his powder blue silk shirt. He clutched it toward the bottom and pulled it out slightly. Cassie guessed the gesture freed it from sweat. "She left before we got a chance, I guess, to get you."

Lucas tapped for another beat or two. Then three. Antoine's Adam's apple bobbed and sank.

"Actually, I went to get her after the receptionist told me she walked out."

The revelation surprised her. She had assumed his appearance in the lobby was simply a matter of coincidental timing. Why did he chase her? What did it matter? Her mind buzzed with questions she didn't dare ask.

"I don't know why she would do that, Mr. Dalton," Hillarie said. She tried to fake a confident lilt, but the break at the end gave away the deception.

Lucas didn't move his head to look at the woman, just his gaze.

"Really? You don't have any idea why she left?"

The two designers shared a glance indicating dread at the prospect of where this line of questioning would end. Antoine shifted. "We didn't mean anything about her dress. We were joking." He chuckled in an attempt to make it all right and support his assertion the insult had been entirely in jest.

The air dissipated from Cassie's lungs like a squeezed balloon. She should probably intervene and tell Lucas it wasn't serious. But instead, she stared wide-eyed at the pair across the table.

"What's funny about her dress?" Lucas asked. His tone was bolstered by an undercurrent of irritation.

Antoine's shoulders slumped. He stared at his partner who dropped her head. The color from his orange-sprayed face drained, and Cassie wondered if the beads of sweat mounting an attack at his hairline would trickle down leaving white stripes.

"Mr. Dal—"

"Cassie's a real artist, a painter with an MFA from NYU. That's something neither of you have."

The air went dead. The tenor with which Lucas spoke conveyed his position. It wasn't loud or angry. It was authoritative and confident, and it commanded every bit of space it took up.

Antoine nodded and his mouth opened, but nothing came out.

"I don't need to hear anymore." Lucas stood and buttoned his jacket. "You two can pick up your check on the way out."

That was it. Antoine reacted like someone had punched him in the face, and Hillarie looked like she might cry. It was done. The most popular design duo in the city had failed a test they didn't know they were taking.

Lucas said, "Cassie, come with me."

***

An older woman with chestnut and silver-streaked hair stood at the ready outside a set of soaring double doors.

"Stephanie," Lucas said still striding by, "Antoine and Hillarie are out. Get Jeffrey Tanner on the reno, and tell him I want him working with Cassie Reynolds, my art consultant." He disappeared through the open doorway. Cassie paused beside the pewter-gray desk with uncertainty kicking her gut from the inside out.

"Do you want him to come in this week?" Stephanie called into the doorway, and then she waved Cassie over. She complied and stepped inside.

Lucas was already behind his desk, eyes fixated on some papers crinkling in his hand. Cassie looked around, trying to rectify the warmth the sun's rays gave the space with the cold of dark wood and copper. Similar to the decor at his apartment, including all the harsh edges.

Lucas barely looked up as he answered Stephanie. "Send him the blueprints and set a meeting for Monday. I want Cassie to see him before that." Lucas leveled his gaze straight at her for the first time since she had run into him outside the elevator. "Do you have time this week?"

Standing in the middle of the room, hands intertwined, she willed her right leg to stop bouncing. "Yes, that should be fine."

The events of the last few minutes continued reeling through her head. While she had no idea what she had done to warrant Lucas's favor, this was a job she both wanted and needed.

Lucas sat and leaned back in the onyx leather chair and turned to the towering windows. The corner of his eyes creased. For a moment, his lids appeared to close. Then without warning, he sat up and turned to face her head-on. Any visible sign of discontent dispersed. His azure eyes crept up and down her body, creating a path of heat in their wake. He made no attempt to hide what he was doing, even when he paused on her hands before bringing his gaze up to her face.

"I'm sorry. I didn't intend for all that to happen." His voice was soft, the biting authority completely washed away.

"I'm sorry I caused you trouble. I know they're an exceptional design team." Her lips stuck to her gums and she gnawed at the corner of her mouth to stave off the unease stirred by his intensity.

"Those are a dime a dozen in New York. I'm not sorry they screwed themselves over by being mean to you. I don't tolerate that from anyone." He leaned forward and clicked the mouse. "I have to run, but take a look at the construction plans for the space." He stood then, holding his chair with one hand, beckoning her to take it with the other.

His magnetism pulled her over, and when she sat, he moved the chair—and her—toward the desk. He leaned down over her, one arm poised on the chair back and the other swallowed the mouse. His breath tickled the side of her neck. The air around her filled with citrus and cedar.

"Take your time. Stephanie will order lunch and get you whatever you need." He lingered for a moment and his scent hung around them. She was certain he could hear her heart hammer her ribs. When he bent closer for a beat, every hair on her neck stood up. She kept her eyes glued to the computer screen, afraid if she turned toward him, her cheek would brush against his.

Without further warning, he withdrew from her space and walked toward the door.

"And Cassie..." Lucas paused at the threshold. "There's nothing wrong with that dress. Or you."

He vanished through the door, taking his scent and all the air with him.

Chapter Twelve

MONTH TWO

C assie checked her watch again and started to make her way toward Lucas's building. He'd sent a text about thirty minutes before that he was running late from dinner. But she'd stalled long enough, wandering through one of her favorite art supply shops. She needed to stop fawning over art supplies she'd never use again. At least, not in the same way.

This quick meeting was the first time she would see him since last month. His demanding schedule made him hard to pin down on any given day, so most of their contact happened in texts or emails. He spent a lot of time out of town, which had been good for access to his apartment. They would need more of that now that construction had begun.

She hoped she could get through the few things on her list before Lucas left for his next flight. When she arrived at the entry to his building with a few minutes to spare, Ronnie, the doorman, greeted her.

"Good evening, Ms. Cassie," he said, tipping his graying head.

"Hi, Ronnie. I hope you don't get too cold out here tonight." The year-end had ushered in a bitter winter and daily temps hovered near freezing. The city buildings created a wind tunnel that brought the feels-like temp crashing into the teens.

She entered the elevator reserved for Lucas's penthouse and used the key card Stephanie had given her to unlock it. Having another man's key felt scandalous, and though it was only for work purposes, Jess's giggly ooooohhhhhss echoed through Cassie's head every single time she used it.

She called into the foyer. "Lucas?" She was met only with her own voice smacking into the plastic sheets hanging from the ceiling. With the blinds still shut, the large space remained cloaked in darkness. Cassie had been here so many times since last month she could navigate the shifting construction space with ease.

In the kitchen, she hit the button on the wall, retracting the living room blinds. When they opened, the city's twinkling lights laid out like constellations below the towering windows. She took a moment to admire the view of the sprawling city beneath her. She preferred spending time alone in this space as often as possible, though it only happened after the workday ended.

Since Cassie started working, her home life had taken a back seat. Some things improved—for example, the balance in the bank account she now paid attention to. Others had gotten worse. Jason's broodiness ebbed and flowed and his once passive comments often became aggressive or snappy. He'd say things like: *You're working late again. Is that what you wore today? Who is this Jeffrey you've been spending your time with?*

Other nights, she'd get home to dinner on the table and a smile making a rare appearance on Jason's face. Those nights, she found, were due to some win at work, not because of her.

She slung her bag to the counter and hefted out the three-ring project binder Jeffrey loved to tease her about. A tablet, he pointed out, wouldn't give her a hernia.

Aside from their differing opinions about technology, she and Jeffrey Tanner had clicked from the minute they met at Dalton Enterprises. Her trepidation was quickly erased the minute Jeffrey tripped across the doorway of the conference room. His olive cheeks blushed, and his amber eyes widened, but instead of the prima donna response Cassie expected, he curtsied and declared that making a lasting impression included a dramatic entrance.

A muted thud from somewhere in the apartment grabbed Cassie's attention. She turned toward the hall leading back to the bedrooms but was met only with silence. She flipped the binder to the section she needed Lucas to review, expecting him any moment.

A loud noise echoed through the walls. A rhythmic banging, like a hammer on wood. Was the crew still here? The building had a strict noise ordinance that didn't allow them to do anything that would disturb the peace between six p.m. and eight a.m., and Lucas forbade any other workers, besides her and Jeffrey, from being there while he was home.

Cassie took off in the direction of the sound to warn whoever was working to stop for the day. Lucas would be home any second; they were violating the contract. At this early stage, they didn't need to push things.

She followed the banging, now a consistent beat, toward Lucas's room. She stopped outside the cracked door, waiting to make sure it was coming from the other side. Had Lucas slipped in early? It didn't matter, though, because whoever it was started thrumming and drumming and smacking something harder and harder.

"Lucas?" she called. She thought she heard a voice, but the pounding intensified and drowned out anything discernible. Her stomach tumbled as she pushed open the door.

Lucas stood naked at the foot of the bed, head bent back as his hips thrust feverishly toward shapely legs that ended in red stilettos.

The woman cried out as his thrusting stopped.

Cassie jumped back out of view of the doorway and pulled it shut. The apartment grew dead quiet, and her heart lurched. After a few seconds of shock, she hustled back down the hallway, grabbing her bag, determined to get out of the apartment before they—before *he*—discovered she was there.

***

Cassie spent the elevator ride wrestling the binder back into her bag and her arms back into her coat. She pushed out of the lobby doors and didn't stop moving until she had put a full city block between her and the building. Her breath came in quick waves from both the shock of the scene and her quick getaway.

Now what? She paced up and down a slim slice of sidewalk, willing her heart to slow its hammering. The only logical thing she could think to do was call Jess.

"Aren't you in a meeting with my future husband?" Jess answered.

"Jess, you're not going to believe what happened."

"Lucas professed his undying love for you," she rattled back without even a beat.

"What? God, no!" Cassie shook her head as her friend giggled in her ear. "It's worse."

She wasn't sure what to say. She stopped pacing and scanned her surroundings like she was about to commit a crime, or worse, already had.

She put up her right hand to shield the phone in vain hoping to keep the words from sailing out and into the air around her.

"I walked in on him. You know..." Cassie waited for her friend's reaction.

"Getting dressed?" Jess asked in a similar hushed voice.

"No, not that..." She really didn't want to come out with it. The sound of the twins babbling in the background filled her ear. "He was doing it. You know. *It*."

"By *it* do you mean S-E-X?"

"Yes!"

Jess said something to the kids, likely attempting to escape somewhere out of earshot. The phone scraped against fabric. "Are you kidding?" she asked, whisper gone.

"No! Why would I kid about that?"

"How exactly?" Jess squealed. "Tell me everything."

Cassie looked around to make sure she could speak freely. Though everyone in the city remained in their own bubble and didn't realize anyone existed beyond it.

"I think she was bent over the bed, and he was behind her." A heat rushed up her neck.

"You saw them from the side?"

"No. From the back."

"Did you see that man naked, Cass?" Jess screeched.

"No. I mean, well, yes." She started pacing again and lowered the volume of her voice. "I guess." Her heart pounded and her head swam with the details.

"What did you see?"

She stopped moving and dropped her head. "His backside...his...his ass. I saw his ass as he was doing her. He was right in front of me, what the hell do you think I saw! And that's not why I'm calling you." She realized the volume of her voice had risen. An older couple was staring at her.

Jess shrilled and shrieked in her ear so loud Cassie held the phone out. A notification flashed across the screen sending her stomach deeper into the ground.

"Shit." Again, she drew the attention of the old couple. She gave them an apologetic look and put the phone back to her ear. "I think he just texted me. What do I do?"

"What does it say?"

"I don't know." She withdrew the phone from her ear and clicked on the message.

Lucas: Everything alright? Not like you to be late.

She returned the phone to her ear.

"He wants to know if everything is okay since I'm late." She nibbled her lip.

"Ask him if he wore a rubber so his friend isn't late—"

"JESSICA!" Cassie shrieked. Jess fell into fits of laughter. "Seriously, what am I going to say here?"

"Tell him the train was late or something. Make it up, Cass."

"You know I suck at lying."

Jess sighed into her ear. "Your history of hopeless honesty does make this a problem. Keep it simple. Where are you right now?"

Cassie glanced at the signs around her. "Between a pizza place and coffee shop."

"Tell him you got stuck in line at either one, but that you'll be there in a minute."

"That could work," she muttered. It wasn't a total lie if it was colored with shades of the truth.

"Now go to the meeting."

"Jess, how can I look him in the face after seeing"—she tried to find the appropriate word—"*that* side of him?"

"You can and will. And when you're done, you'll come to my house, have leftover meatloaf, and give me a detailed retelling of every single thing you saw."

"You're a mess, you know that?"

"I'm a stay-at-home mom clinging to my sanity. I'm living vicariously through you."

She smiled at the thought of Jess, standing in her house unshowered and covered in toddler gook. "I'll drop by—"

"And give me details."

She chuckled and promised to do just that before hanging up. She gritted her teeth and texted Lucas back.

Sorry, got caught in line at a pizza place down the block. It's late, so I'll just email you.

She hit send and prayed he took the bait. She didn't know what time his plane left, but she hoped it was too soon to meet. She watched the three dots appear and then:

Lucas: It's not too late. Come over.

Her stomach twisted and she plunged her hands deep into her coat pockets, dragging herself back to the scene of the crime.

Chapter Thirteen

Fueled by dread, Cassie's knees quaked. The lying was one thing she was bad at. But pretending she hadn't seen Lucas doing what he was doing took things to a whole other level. She wasn't confident she could pull any of it off.

She stood before the closed door a beat longer to settle the flapping in her stomach.

When the door sprung open, her eyes lurched up to meet Lucas's. His head angled as he regarded her with a raised left eyebrow while working the button of his left cuff.

"Everything okay?"

"I was just, uh." She tried to find something to complete the thought that didn't make her sound like a crazy person. "Trying to remember something."

Lucas peered at her through narrowed eyes and moved back inside the apartment. She followed, determined only to look at the back of his light gray shirt. But her eyes roved from the muscles moving between his shoulders down to the charcoal pants that accentuated his...

Stop this nonsense.

They continued into the kitchen. Cassie stopped at the counter and placed the binder on it to open it. Lucas still had his back to her, but she could see him working the black and champagne striped tie in the reflection of the stainless-steel refrigerator. The shirt wrinkled around his bicep and did little to shield the muscle beneath it.

"I need to ask you about the sitting area," she said and cleared the dust from her throat.

"The what area?" he said without turning. His hair looked wet like he'd just gotten out of the shower. That made sense since he likely needed it after—

"Cassie?"

Her gaze snapped into focus to meet his face.

"The sitting area." She picked up the binder and moved toward him. But the corner of it caught on the counter and began sliding out of her hands.

He snatched the hefty book before it completely fell away, probably saving her toes in the process. When he placed it on the counter, he planted an oversized hand on either side of it.

"What am I looking at? Besides a bunch of brown furniture."

"Not that." Cassie reached across him to turn the page. "These paintings."

"Where are these?" Lucas shifted his body and his shoulder grazed hers. It sent a pang down through her.

"Some of them are up for auction. Others are for sale from private collections."

He swiveled his head to look at her. The citrus shampoo from his damp hair and the musk from his skin invaded the narrow space separating them.

"Why were you late?"

The smell and the heat of his breath melted her from the inside out. Inhaling courage, she looked straight into those icy eyes and willed herself not to blink.

"I told you. I got stuck in line down the street. Now, what do you think of this color scheme? Lighter colored prints would add some contrast to a darker area." She tore her eyes away from his, though the weight of his gaze lingered. She pretended it wasn't crushing her and swallowed another boulder.

Why did Lucas cause her to come so undone? Never before had another human ever come close to rattling her insides like he did each time they met. Her body's involuntary reaction unnerved her. Something about him left her exposed. Vulnerable. Like he had the power to reach into her head and know everything there was to know about her.

"Where's the slice?" he asked.

Cassie tipped her chin up a bit higher this time before answering.

"I got out of line when I got your message." The lie flowed easily like it was perched there, ready and waiting. *Impressive.*

Lucas's gaze swept across her, narrowed and intent. She'd never met anyone so adept at conveying so much and revealing so little. He pushed away from the countertop and crossed his arms across his wide chest. "Why did you stop painting?"

"I told you. My hand—"

He shook his head. "Before that."

Her mind raced. When had she told him that?

"At the diner, you mentioned that you were an art restorer," he continued, obviously sensing her confusion.

"Yeah. That. I still consider that painting, just not my own." It's what she always told herself every time she brought a piece of art back to life: she was a part of something special. It wasn't the same as when she had sketched or painted her art, but it filled her creative heart halfway, which was better than not at all.

Lucas's intense glare filleted her open like a knife. "Why not paint your own stuff?"

"Because mine weren't making money." The bitterness dripped from her lips too easily. She clamped them shut before she could finish the thought. She put away her canvases because she had needed to make money. Though, if she was really honest, which Lucas made her want to be, she had stopped even before Jason's poor business sense got them into their first financial bind.

"Did you become an artist for the money?" He caught her again, peeled open her skull, and peered inside.

"Things got in the way."

"Things?"

She huffed. "Life, Lucas. Bills and—" She didn't trust herself to go further. "Stuff." There are things he could never understand, like worrying about the cost of medication or pinching pennies to pay bills.

"If I got you in with a specialist, would you go?"

"What are you talking about?"

Lucas dipped his head toward her. "Your hand."

It took a few seconds for the words to sink in. She willed herself to speak. She opened her mouth but lost the words somewhere inside.

He continued. "There's a surgeon who has some new procedure transplanting synthetic nerves. It's pretty successful. Dr. Anna Patella. Ever heard of her?"

"Yes." Her voice trembled. Dr. Patella was the surgeon who she'd been dying to see. The one with the clinical trial. The one her own doctor said was too long of a shot to even attempt.

"If I could get you an appointment, would you go?"

She shook her head.

Lucas stood a little taller, his eyes unrelenting as they searched her face for a reason.

"I can't get my hopes up," she said. "You don't get it. You can't possibly..." Her voice trailed off as the squeeze in her throat choked off the rest.

He stepped back and leaned against the counter. "Try me."

"Meeting her won't do anything if I can't pay for the surgery." The wave of frustration washed away the sadness that sat in her chest. "My insurance company denied my request for a consult. So she may tell me I'm an excellent candidate and one of the seventy-six percent the surgery helps."

Cassie swallowed the fire, though the flames licked at the mere idea that she might have a shot at getting better, but not the money to do it.

"And it'll be worse, knowing that the thing I want more than anything can't happen because some asshole behind a desk says I'm too high risk for an experimental procedure." The words shot out of her mouth fueled by the anger swelling her lungs. "Now, are these paintings acceptable? Yes or no. That's all I need from you."

Lucas's features remained unaltered by her words. The seconds crawled, forcing Cassie to remain in limbo.

"I think I understand."

She scoffed. How could he? Not only did he not have a part of him stolen, but even if he had, he could afford to fix it. He didn't need insurance and didn't depend on some no-face adjuster sitting in judgment.

"You don't think so," he continued.

"No, I don't." Her confidence felt like a flag draped across her shoulders.

He nodded curtly and gestured at the open binder. "I like what you did with this."

She looked from his face to the binder. "Thank you." She flipped it closed.

Lucas removed a business card from his shirt pocket. Setting it down in the vacant space, he slid it toward her.

The name and address of Dr. Anna Patella. A handwritten date and time along the bottom. She was sure it was Lucas's writing. The card scorched her fingertips as she picked it up.

"It's an appointment. For tomorrow," he said.

Her brain ran short on logic as she reread the card.

"How is this possible?" she quivered.

"I know someone who could get you in." He dipped his head slightly and looked back at her through long ashen lashes. "I didn't know you felt like this, which I do understand even if you don't think I do. So it's up to you. Go or don't. It doesn't affect me either way."

He pushed away from the counter and disappeared down the hall to his bedroom. She stared down at the card in her hand, the breath trapped inside her chest.

Tomorrow she could see Dr. Patella. She could find out if there was even a chance she might get back to painting—to *living*.

Did she deserve another chance? If she was a candidate, the outcome would determine her worthiness.

Lucas returned, suit coat in place, leather travel bag slung over his shoulder, attention glued to his phone.

"Anything else?" he asked without raising his head.

Silence took hold of her. She should thank him, but it all seemed so small in light of their conversation and what trembled in her hand. "No, that's it. Have a safe trip."

Chapter Fourteen

The second hand on the clock thudded as Cassie looked over the walls in Dr. Patella's office. Every certificate, photograph, and accolade were familiar. Cassie had spent an embarrassing amount of time researching the doctor after hearing about her surgical breakthroughs with nerve restoration. While others had done similar work, Dr. Patella's achievements had shot her to the top of the field.

Not every case was a success, and Cassie spent an equal amount of time reviewing the gory details of the failures. The reasons for these were unknown, much like those behind why some people were struck with the nerve condition in the first place.

Cassie's neuropathy was the sort of anomaly that necessitated the side-effect warnings on medication. The one in a million who experienced an adverse reaction to an anti-seizure drug they had given her in the ER. The doctor had used it to stop the seizure caused by all the estrogen flooding her body during another round of IVF, and the last shot she had given herself against medical advice.

The medication they had used in the ER was safe, only known to cause neuropathy in long-time users, like those with epilepsy.

But all it had taken for Cassie was one shot. Her body, for reasons unknown, proved the perfect host for its rare malfeasance. Now she sat, knee bouncing, heart thudding, waiting to hear if she had any chance of getting back the thing she most wanted.

She had spent the last twenty-four hours beating back possibility and despair as they took turns rising and falling. She had decided to shoulder the onslaught alone, not telling Jason, knowing he'd pepper the moment with a chorus of wait-and-sees. She'd also not told Jess; she couldn't have borne dashing the hope Jess would surely hold.

The only other person who knew she had this appointment was the one who had made it for her in the first place. Why Lucas did it remained a mystery, as did how she would pay for the surgery if the doctor gave her the green light. Her trust fund balance was sizeable, but surely not enough for this.

Lucas should never have gotten involved. She didn't understand why he took such an interest in her. She tried not to think about it too long because anytime her thoughts lingered on him, her stomach fluttered.

The office door opening startled Cassie back to the present. The nerves that had dulled sprang back to life in her stomach and pumped panic through her body. Dr. Patella swept in, tinging the fear-soaked air with hope.

"Mrs. Reynolds. Cassie. May I call you that?" Dr. Patella asked as she sat.

"Please do. Thank you for seeing me, Dr. Patella."

The doctor nodded and tapped the screen of her tablet, bringing it to life. The woman moved her head back and forth, up and down, as she alternated between swiping the screen and trailing a finger across her chin. Dr. Patella was short and stout, with apple round cheeks that lifted thick, black-rimmed glasses. Short raven hair threaded itself around her ears and complimented the olive complexion of her face.

Dr. Patella put aside the tablet and rested her elbows on the desk. Her dark gaze held Cassie's for a few seconds. She seemed to be waiting for the answer to a question that hadn't been asked.

"Your case is extremely unusual," Dr. Patella finally said.

Cassie cleared her throat. "Yes, it is."

"But not impossible." The doctor grinned. "So what did this condition take from you?"

Thrown by the question and directness, Cassie sat back against her chair. "Everything," she said down toward her lap. She remained fixated on her right hand as she moved the fingers bit by bit.

"You're an artist?"

"I was."

"You still are. And I have no doubt you'll get back to it in due time."

She shook her head. "If only." The pain of her loss, her lifetime of it, landed fully. Since birth, she had seemed predisposed to hardship. It had started mere minutes after she was pulled from her mother and continued through her lost pregnancies. How bittersweet was it that she had annihilated her art—the thing that gave her purpose and life—while trying to have a child of her own?

But the truth was, her hand had been an excuse. Yesterday, she had almost told Lucas something she'd never told anyone, not even Jess. The passion for art had been stripped from her heart years before the nerve damage made it permanent. Though she tried to recapture it, she couldn't. It never felt the same. Never moved her as it once did. Instead of filling her with magic, it pulled upon her like a hand reaching into her chest and removing her insides one by one. Because she couldn't work around that feeling no matter how hard she tried, it had been easier for Cassie to stop and let her art become the sacrifice for their financial stability. The day she lost her hand snuffed out any glimmer she could and would get back to painting.

If only she had gone to Paris after her dad died.

If only she hadn't taken that stupid restoration job.

If only she had listened to the doctor when he sa—

"What do you say we try and fix it?" Dr. Patella's voice intruded on Cassie's spiral.

"Really?" The whisper escaped without much breath behind it.

"Really. There's no guarantee, but from your medical records, I see no obvious reason that this surgery shouldn't work." Dr. Patella pulled the tablet back and tapped around. "I can get you on the schedule two weeks from today." The charcoal gaze waited.

She stared, paralyzed by thoughts and feelings and air. "Two weeks..." She didn't dare continue speaking, afraid the doctor would correct her misunderstanding.

She looked at her hand. Instead of seeing the curse she was certain she had done something to deserve, she saw possibility. Might she once again hold a brush, a piece of charcoal, a sky-blue pencil? She had a choice. She squared her shoulders. She wouldn't allow fear to yank away the lifeline Dr. Patella cast out to her.

"I'll do it." Resolution coursed through her body. Maybe now she would use the trust money and travel to France, go to the Louvre and meet the fabled Mona Lisa, her mom's favorite. Or sit in the Parc Monceau where Monet had painted and let his ghost whisper through her.

She shook away these thoughts, refusing to let herself get her hopes up this would fix her life. That it would fix her.

Even if it worked, there was always a price. Every dream she had chased, every choice she had made came with some kind of repercussion that damaged her further. Though she had endless examples of her poor choices, she refused at this moment to dampen the spark flickering in her chest.

The doctor was saying something about risks, side effects, and possible damage, but she couldn't hear any of it over the drumming of her heart and the whooshing of her breath. She inhaled the possibility of what might lie ahead. For the first time in a long time, she allowed herself to feel something she had long since locked away: hope.

***

"I'll have a lot of long days over the next three weeks." Jason scooped out another helping of scalloped potatoes.

"For what?" she asked. She'd been waiting for an opening to tell him about the surgery since he had settled at the table.

"Getting ready to pitch the chief of police that the prototype has limitless uses for everything from radios to batons. If he invests, we'll be set for life."

She bit back the sarcasm that begged to burst from her lips. This wasn't the first time Jason had claimed if one thing or the other happened, their financial woes would be fixed.

"It'll mean a lot of late nights and weekends still. But I'll come home for dinner at least once a week. I'll even cook," he said.

"I'll hold you to that," she said. He resumed eating and Cassie took the lull in conversation to deliver her news. "Do you remember that nerve specialist in the city? The one with the experimental surgery that could repair nerves and restore use?"

"No, but assume I do." He sat back and crossed his left ankle over his right knee.

"Getting an appointment with her was impossible."

"Okay."

She inhaled. This next part wouldn't land well. She'd had few run-ins with Lucas over the last couple months, but if and when she mentioned him to Jason, his disdain was clear. "As it turns out, Lucas knows som—"

"Lucas?" Jason bristled.

"Yes, Lucas. The man I work for. *Your* investor," she shot back with a little sour taste.

He winced and receded. "Sorry. Go ahead."

"He got me an appointment with the doctor. And I went today."

His brow folded. "Okay."

"Well..." Cassie tried to swallow the burn, but the tears tickled the corners of her eyes anyway. "She said I'm an excellent candidate. So, I'm in the trial."

The hardness of his face melted. "Really?" He rose and swept her from the chair into his arms. The crush of his body to hers was warm and welcome.

She closed her lids and burrowed her face into Jason's striped polo and the wood and leather scent forever embedded in him.

"This is the best news I've heard in a very long time," he whispered against her head.

Chapter Fifteen

MONTH THREE

N othing made time stand still quite like the promise of a second chance. Yet for Cassie, two weeks passed in what seemed like two days. Most of that she attributed to the onslaught of work at Lucas's apartment. Not only was the construction crew humming along, actually staying close to the timeline, but she and Jeffrey had finalized the new decor for half of the main living area.

They were flying high, believing themselves ahead of schedule. Then two days before her surgery, the train flew off the rails.

"We are so screwed," Jeffrey lamented in the cab. He collapsed back into the headrest and rubbed his temples.

"We'll be fine, Jeffrey. We just need to make some changes."

"Changes? We've already made shitty concessions with furniture and flooring and wallpaper because of the original deadline. Now he's cutting the project two months short and—wait—what were his exact words?"

Jeffrey clutched his phone in a dramatic reenactment, complete with whitened knuckles and wide eyes infused with lunacy.

"I don't expect this to change the quality of your work." Jeffrey stabbed a single finger in the air with every word he quoted from Lucas.

"It'll force us to get a little more creative is all." Her attempt at comfort failed miserably, evidenced by a groan eking out from between fingers that smothered his face.

She shifted about in her seat. Her mind hummed as it tried and failed to reach some sort of fantastical idea to stop Jeffrey's stress-induced spiral.

"And," he said, snapping his head up, "did you get his new travel schedule from Stephanie?"

"No."

"There isn't one. He's barely leaving the city the next two months."

This complicated things a bit. The construction took priority during working hours when Lucas was away. To meet the original deadline, Cassie and Jeffrey had concocted a plan to work on the stylistic details on the nights Lucas was out of town. They were slated to start in the weeks following her surgery, but Lucas's lack of travel would make that impossible.

"It's an unpredictable schedule, Jeffrey. It changes so often and even if it holds, we've got almost four months—

"Three full months, Cassie. THREE."

"I'm sure he'll give us whatever access we need." She peppered her tone with confidence.

Jeffrey shook his head and thudded back into the seat.

She let him have his moment and turned to the window, watching the city passing outside. The timing of her surgery was problematic under this accelerated time frame. It could be four weeks before she regained the full use of her hand at the very best. And if the worst happened...

She shook this away, staring outside at the wintery cityscape skirting past the window.

One millimeter a day. That's the standard growth rate for transplanted nerves. But Dr. Patella's procedure would accelerate that by utilizing lab-grown replacement fibers to connect the three damaged portions of her median nerve. The integration of her nerve with the implanted material would determine not only recovery but success.

"Are you nervous?" Jeffrey asked. He was looking at her now, his face the picture of calm.

Rubbing a familiar pattern in the webbing between her right thumb and index finger, Cassie said, "I'll be glad when it's over." Because then, she would know how to navigate the rest of her life. Her hand would either be unchanged, better or—

"Me, too. Because I need you, Cassie. And that's not me being dramatic. I can't do this without you." He covered her hand with his.

She smiled and did her best to squeeze his hand. Warmth filled her chest. It was nice to be needed. Meeting Jeffrey had altered the course of her life. He had taught her so much about design and exposed her to a whole other business that was art-adjacent. It filled her with relevancy and kept her excited about going to work each day. Whether this surgery worked or failed, she had zero intention of letting him down.

"Jeffrey, you are absolutely being dramatic, and I love you for it."

***

She left Jeffrey an hour later for her pre-op appointment. It was the final hurdle Cassie needed to clear before surgery at the end of the week. In the past two weeks, she had been prodded, had a thousand vials of blood drawn, and been scanned from head to toe—twice. Her medical history was laid bare for all to see, including the thing that had led to this moment in the first place.

The physician's assistant finished up the cursory physical exam and sat back on the squeaky stool swiping the tablet screen every few seconds.

"Sorry if this all seems like overkill," the PA said.

"It's no problem. I'd rather this than..." She hadn't needed to finish; the PA absently nodded.

Cassie let the silence settle back in. She nibbled her lip and considered how to broach the subject of payment again. She'd asked during her first appointment and had been told that the grant was processing and the final amount due, if any, would be discussed at a later date.

"You've had one major surgery before this?" the PA asked.

Cassie's stomach clenched at the mention. "Yes."

"Can you tell me about that?" The PA squeaked the stool to the wall and leaned back.

"It's in my chart, isn't it?" This is the last thing Cassie wanted to talk about. Almost.

"Sure. But medical charts are like phone books. No depth or under-standing about what's in it. Dr. Patella and I like context."

The PA folded her hands, laying in wait for the answer. The reflection in her glasses beamed back at Cassie, making exact eye contact difficult. It didn't matter. She didn't need to see the woman's clinical stare.

"It was an emergency thing." She cleared her throat and waited for the PA to do anything, but the woman remained attentive. "I had too much estrogen from the IVF. It's what caused the seizure that sent me to the hospital."

Her breath grated when she tried to fill her chest with courage, but the memories constricted the movement, killing it halfway through the cycle.

"My blood pressure skyrocketed and that's when they found a cyst on my ovary had burst. And then I started bleeding."

The heat of the thick tissue hitting her thighs was the first thing Cassie remembered from the emergency room. Then the lights. The scorching up her arm. The yelling. The voices all urgent, chaotic. Calling her name. Barking orders. Transfusions. Clots. Emergency surgery.

"They took me to the OR. The cyst was one thing. But it turned out I had fibroids in my uterus, too. So the swelling from the cyst, plus my blood pressure, caused those to rupture inside the muscle. They had to make a choice." Cassie forced the bile back down her throat. "Well, my husband had to."

It had aged Jason. Deciding what he did. Knowing she might die if he didn't. Knowing it would kill her if he did.

"They removed it all. The ovary." Cassie forced herself upright as tears threatened. "My uterus. They had to. The ruptures tore the lining and the bleeding was too much to stop."

She had woken up to a hammering away at her head in that sweltering hospital room. The doctor's voice a million miles away as he explained. The knowing then that it was over. Her journey to carry a baby, to be the kind of mother her own never had the chance to be.

"That's when this happened, too." She lifted her hand, regarding it again as the constant reminder that this, all of it, was her doing. Her fault.

If only she had stopped the next cycle. If only she had waited, given her body a break. But she couldn't. She had refused.

Cassie wanted. That was the problem. It was like the other times she wanted something and tried to get it. They all ended with her paying a bigger price.

The PA nodded. "Thank you for sharing those details. I'm sorry you had to go through that. In better news, you're medically cleared for this surgery."

The past released its hold on her as she exhaled. She couldn't get her uterus back, but she could, perhaps, have a chance to return to her first love and herself. It wasn't a want this time—it was a need.

"There's just one more thing," the PA said.

Tightness returned to Cassie's chest, the reprieve over. The money was the wild card in this whole thing, at least in her mind. "Is it my insurance company?" If this came down to money, she would open her trust and use whatever was in there, even if it was only a down payment.

"No, everything is all set on that end."

The air in the room ceased to move.

"Seriously?" she whispered.

The PA chuckled. "Yes. But I do need to know who is taking you home after the procedure on Friday. You need someone to take care of you for the first twelve to twenty-four hours after the surgery. Being alone is dangerous for you and a liability for us."

She nodded blankly while she searched for an answer. Jason's meeting with the police department had gotten moved up to this Friday, the same day as her surgery. He offered to change it, but she insisted he keep it. He didn't fight her on it.

Jess would definitely come if Cassie asked, but Greg was out of town, so she would need to bring the twins. Cassie didn't want to scare them if she came out of surgery looking like a zombie. So that was out. She could ask Jeffrey, but he would have to cancel two appointments with potential clients. She couldn't let him do that, even though he would.

She didn't want to disrupt anyone else's day.

Maybe the timing would work out, and Jason could come by after his meeting to pick her up. She would just call him when she was in recovery and he could come then.

She chewed lightly on her lip and looked up at the PA. The crinkles in the woman's brow spelled trouble. "My husband," she said, finally, and deepened her voice to bolster the words. "He'll meet me here to sign me out."

The PA nodded and tapped the screen. "Jason Reynolds?"

Cassie nodded.

What would she do if Jason didn't answer? If she could get downstairs unaccompanied, tell them Jason was waiting at the curb because he couldn't find parking. She could then hail a cab to take her home. That was her original plan. Did they really need him to come up to the office?

"Great, then we're all set. We'll see you bright and early Friday morning."

She smiled, though it was tight, her joy squelched by the tiny squeeze of logistical doubts her pride created.

Things would work out, and even if Jason didn't show, what's the worst that could happen?

Chapter Sixteen

S he was stuck, a heaviness draping her whole body. Was she in the ocean? Encased in cement? The plush fabric beneath her told her no, she was somewhere safe, though her body strained under a phantom weight. Cassie willed her limbs to move, but all she got in response was a dull pulsing from her head.

Her brain remained fogged, holding onto the remnants of the dream world. Tap. Tap. Tap. Like a finger poking into the folds of gray brain tissue. The intensity increased to a steady beat that reverberated around her skull.

Cassie winced and tried to peel apart her eyelids. They remained shut, unyielding even as she rattled her eyeballs around, hoping the movement would force the stickiness to come undone. Light seeped into tiny slits, only making the ache in her head worse.

Her stomach soured and thumped and burned. She moaned as the pounding in her head gave way to twirling. Saliva poured into her mouth and beads of moisture tickled her forehead. She needed to get to a bathroom, but the cement wouldn't loosen its grip. She swallowed against the vomit in her throat, washing it away along with every bit of moisture from her mouth.

A cool sensation washed over her face, whisking the sweat and heat and nausea away with it. The movement of the soaked fabric across her forehead was gentle. Fingers drew through the hair at her temples, unsticking strands from her cheeks. When the washcloth slid down her face to her lips, she opened her mouth, sucking at the moisture, willing it to quench the drought.

"Don't move." A voice rasped near her ear. Cedar and citrus came with it and comforted her, as did the fingers trickling through her hair. "You might get sick if you move too fast. Give yourself time."

Her lashes broke free from the gunk that plastered them and she fully opened her eyes. Light stabbed her eyeballs and she slammed them shut again. She tried to speak, but her tongue stuck to the inside of her lips.

"You had surgery."

Her lids flipped open again and she fought against the fog and blur. The hands were gone from her head and she blinked to bring the shapeless form into focus. He was close and the more she tried to make herself see, the more elusive the world seemed.

A plastic straw struck her bottom lip and she closed her mouth around it. The cool liquid flooded in, washing away the grit. But before it quenched her thirst, it was gone.

Raising her head from the pillow, she stared at him, trying to figure out why he insisted on depriving her of the thing she needed.

"Jaaa-sson." Why was he so quick to take things away?

"I'm putting some pills in your mouth."

She opened her mouth and the tablets clung to her tongue before she could get enough water to push them down. She swallowed them finally, letting the relief of each intake of water wash through her.

"You'll get sick if you drink too much." But he didn't fight hard to regain control.

After her mouth cooled, she released the straw. When it was gone, the bed shifted. Her sight blurred and sharpened, like a camera lens that couldn't decide where to focus. She fought to fix her gaze on the details in the wood-paneled ceiling.

The sound of one, two, three steps on hardwood to her left caught her attention. The slight crinkle and squeak of fabric sliding and settling on leather. She rolled her head a little too fast, and a bout of spinning sent everything topsy-turvy. She waited until things stopped moving and she could see him.

Lucas.

She blinked and widened her eyes.

"Why are you here?" she rasped. She darted her gaze about the room trying to gain some comprehension.

His hazy face bobbed.

"I live here." His features came into focus as he leaned closer. "Tell me, Cass, what was your plan for getting out of the surgical center? Because whatever it was, it didn't work."

A scene darted across her brain. Someone wearing green scrubs asking when her husband was going to get there. "I don't remember." She stared back at the ceiling of Lucas's bedroom.

"They called me."

Her head swirled around that faint memory.

"You told them that I could pick you up after Jason was a no-show," he continued.

"Why would I do that?" Cassie wasn't really speaking to him, just shooting out words into the air around her.

"Jason thinks you're recovering at the clinic, which I figured was better. There's a good chance you won't remember being here with the drugs you're on."

Cassie lifted her left hand and stared at the flesh-colored bandage crossed over the back.

"He doesn't like you," she said.

"Most people don't."

She dropped her hand back to the bed and lobbed her head toward him. She stared at him, unwilling and unable to look away. He was like that though, wasn't he? Magnetic. So many people were intimidated by him, scared of his power and presence, though she didn't count herself as one of them. He was a man, a mortal in the body of a Greek God. One that she would kill to see naked from every angle.

Lucas remained motionless. The light from the floor lamp rimmed his dark blond locks in a shimmering halo. His smooth skin glowed as the light rained down, softening the cut of his sharp jaw. And hard. Kind of like the muscles that stretched across his back all the way down to his heels.

"Red stilett-OO-s." The words jiggled her lips, carrying beads of spit with them.

"What?" the Lucas haze asked.

"I saw EVERYTHING," she whispered or yelled or cried. "Your butt is purr-ffect." A storm of giggles squeaked from her chest, and the world shook right along with them.

"The night you were late?"

"Yup."

The Lucas haze shifted.

She giggled having just told a huge secret. "Bet you didn't know."

"No, I did," he said.

"How?"

"You're a horrible liar. Plus, I can tell when you've been in my place because you always leave the blinds open."

She stared at him or at least in his direction. Her head was heavy, gravity pulling her further into the pillow. "Fine," she huffed into the air. "I didn't watch. But I wanted to." She exhaled like a horse through her vibrating lips. "Sex is soooo boring when it happens, which has been forever. Jason rolls on top of me for three minutes and then he's done and falls asleep. The end."

Her lids fell under her lashes like curtains weighed down to keep them from blowing away in the wind.

"Tell me about Frank. You were muttering his name just now."

Cassie sighed at the ceiling. "He's dead. I killed him."

The spit in her mouth choked her. "Frank was a thief. He stole from Jason. Then, he asked Jason to give him more," she sighed. "I said no. So Frank shot himself."

"That wasn't your fault," Lucas said. "It never is when someone chooses to die that way. Even though it can feel otherwise."

She blinked the space between them into focus. He seemed to understand and the way his head tilted ever so slightly to the right as he stared down at her seemed even empathetic.

"So you know what it's like?"

He shifted in his seat. "I might."

She wanted to ask more but her train of thought was derailed by all the fog.

"Why did you start restoring art instead of painting your own?" he asked.

Cassie squinted against the light behind him and let her head fall back to the pillow. "Ah. That. You see, here's the thing no one tells you. When you marry a guy who is really shitty with money, sometimes you have to give up something you love to do something to save him." A sigh heaved from her chest. It seemed ridiculous now that she gave it air to breathe. And that was only half of the story. "Can you keep a secret?"

"What do you think."

"I think," she said, floating in the air just above his bed. "I stopped painting because it got too hard. I never told anyone that my dad called me the day before he died. He wanted to have dinner with me. I said no because I didn't want to give up the studio time. I loved to sketch and paint before..."

The undercurrent of grief that always pulled at her when she thought about her dad gripped her hard. Losing him had severed some creative bond in her chest, one he had nurtured and stoked and encouraged her entire life. Without him and his love, art simply abandoned her.

As it should have. It was her choice, her selfishness, that robbed her of one more dinner with her dad. The minute she chose herself, regret ate away at the art in her heart.

"I'm so sorry, Cass," Lucas whispered. The cadence of his tone was gentle and soft, the complete opposite of every other part of him.

The fuzzy face. His eyes, a drop of argentate in a sea of cerulean blue, gazed back at her. If only she could put pencil to paper, brush to canvas, she would immortalize those eyes and the mysterious man behind them.

She fought to stay awake, clawing at the surface where light meets dark. So much had been taken from her.

She would never see her dad again.

She would never meet her mom.

She would never be a mom.

She would never create another thing.

She would never live the life she had dreamed about.

The weight of her grief crushed against her body, dragging her back underwater and Cassie was powerless to stop it. Even Lucas wasn't strong enough to save her. So she gave up and let the abyss take her.

Chapter Seventeen

MONTH FOUR

Jason

J ason paced the hall outside the police commissioner's conference room waiting to clear the next hurdle in the approval process. Now he needed the vote. Once it came, he could breathe again. He had given the commission everything they requested over the last month: patent details, updates, and samples of the material fashioned into belt clips, and other tools.

This whole thing had cost him all his time, and most of Dalton's money. He had a couple hundred thousand left in a reserve, but that would not stretch far.

He paid his mortgage and a few of the secret credit cards, but not the trust. If this money ran out, he worried he would be forced back into debt, leveraging all the same things he had just paid off. He needed this contract with the police department, or the other half of the money from Dalton.

He sat down in one of the chairs lining the wall outside the door. The empty hallway gave him plenty of space to think about the deal with Dalton.

Had Cassie already betrayed him?

Her romantic notion of marriage and love gave him comfort she hadn't, or wouldn't, stray. She wanted nothing more than to have an enduring love story, much like the one her parents had lived.

Jason also knew it wasn't possible to maintain the passion for life and each other that his wife believed her parents had. The fairytales her father tucked her into bed with each night always left out the hard stuff: sinking businesses, failed fertility treatments, suicidal best friends.

He and Cassie had endured plenty of the bad over the last decade. But things were on the way up. He could feel it. Their marriage wasn't perfect, but he wanted to start reconnecting with her after the difficult years they'd endured. These last few months, on the other hand, had done the opposite. They were spending less time together, drifting further apart. He was being carried out to sea and she remained parallel to the shore. Jason shook his head. The heat in the hallway did nothing to help his stress.

Cassie's work with that interior designer had breathed life back into her. Even though her pace slowed after the surgery, it hadn't kept her down long. Five days after the operation, she returned to the city—to Dalton's apartment. She worked late most nights doing whatever it was she did. The surgery had been successful, though Jason had yet to see her pick up a pencil or brush. He wondered when she might and whether she would go back to the restoration business or stay with this consulting gig.

The possibility of what their life could look like in a few months sent a thrill shooting through him. If the patent went through and then the police used him to source their plastic for manufacturing their parts, Jason could write his own ticket for the first time ever.

Then what would become of this dangerous game he and Dalton were playing? What effect would it have, if any, on Cassie? Jason had forced her into his money issues, all because he, like Frank, refused to give up on a good idea. He made Cassie an unwitting accomplice—or rather, collateral damage.

Whenever Jason allowed himself to ruminate on Dalton's reputation for getting what he wanted, a prickly heat welled in his gut. The outrage of his moral compass bubbled to the surface. But if Jason landed this contract, he would have no more need for Dalton or his money.

The perspiration gathered at his waistband made the discomfort grow exponentially. He unbuttoned the jacket of his newest Dolce & Gabbana suit. If he was going to wine and dine the upper echelon, he needed to look the part.

"Mr. Reynolds? Come on back in." A woman stood in the conference room doorway.

Jason smiled and jumped up. He buttoned his jacket and smoothed his hair as he took a few steps. He knowingly stood at the precipice. If everything went the way it should, he would call Dalton and tell him the game was over.

***

"How much longer did they say this time?" Bill asked Jason from across the desk. Bill had brought subs from Little Anthony's and even though Jason wasn't hungry, he accepted the gesture and forced down the food.

"Two, maybe three months. They want to do some private testing before committing." When Jason had heard that from the commissioner his stomach had turned inside out. While it wasn't a refusal, it was a setback. At the very least, another delay.

"I'll send an invoice for the material they want tested."

Jason shook his head and threw his napkin on the desk. "Don't. On one hand, I want to charge the assholes for every bit of it. But on the other, I think it might help if we give it to them." With every sample of material they gave away, though, they were bleeding money. Jason hoped the commissioner would appreciate all of his goodwill gestures.

The two men sat in silence and continued to eat. They had been here before, brainstorming ways to dig out of a financial deficit. Jason waited for Bill to finish his last few bites before asking the harder questions. "How bad?"

Bill looked up as he dabbed red sauce from the corners of his mouth. "Not like it was before the money from Dalton, if that's what you're asking."

"How long before it's gone?"

Bill stretched his neck and rubbed the base by his shoulder. "Two months. Maybe longer if you furlough people."

Jason shook his head. "No way. These people need their salary."

Bill leaned forward. "What about you? You're going to have to stop taking a paycheck again. Don't you need yours?"

Jason got up and strode to the window overlooking the factory floor. The men and women working here didn't have any inkling of how bad their financial situation was. Neither did Bill, not completely.

"Two months?" he asked over his shoulder.

"Yes. But you can't give any more product away."

He sighed and crossed his arms tight around his chest. "Stop paying me now. I've got enough to tide me over. Plus, Cassie gets a check every two weeks, so that'll pay our bills."

Bill cleared his throat and Jason waited for whatever the man was trying to work up the nerve to come out with.

"Maybe she could talk to Dalton on your behalf since she's working for him now. She's got a better shot with her access," Bill said.

If he only knew.

"She barely sees Dalton. He's always gone. She works with the designer."
Jason turned back to the desk and settled into his chair. Before he spun to
face Bill, he paused at the wedding picture and bitterness burned his gut.

Everyone, Frank included, told Jason how lucky he was to have landed
Cassie. It wasn't just her youth and beauty that had made him fall for her.
It was the passion with which she lived life. Even in the grief that had
shrouded her and consumed her through the years, something about her
spirit remained pure.

He remembered their wedding night. The satin gown coming apart in
his calloused hands, and the lace of her tiny white panties. Moving on top
of her, inside of her, laying claim to her. She was his. From that night on,
he believed she always would be.

What would Bill say if he knew it was the access *to* Cassie that prompted
Dalton's money? That if she allowed Dalton even more access in the next
couple months, they would get another influx of money?

"I'm not putting her in the middle of this," he said.

Bill put up his hands in surrender. "You're the boss." He stood, gathered
the trash, and left the office.

Jason plucked the wedding picture from his credenza, ran his fingers
over the image of his wife. Then he opened a drawer and shut the memory
inside.

Chapter Eighteen

MONTH FIVE

Cassie

"Jeffrey, I swear I'm changing my number," Cassie said into the phone. This was the fourth time he had called in a panic about something in the last twelve hours.

"Don't do that to me. Please. It'll push me over the edge." The man was a complete wreck. Construction was two weeks away from wrapping up, which meant the rest would be up to them. With the expedited deadline looming six weeks away, they had little room for error.

"What is it this time?" she asked. She sat in Lucas's kitchen, going over the last-minute details for the art auction that morning. It was a first for her and the construction crew was gone for the moment. She had needed the quiet time to prepare.

"Belinda pulled the Majorelle case from the auction," he said.

"Shit," she whispered. Immediately, she regretted speaking aloud.

"I know, Cassie. That's exactly what I said. SHIT."

She flipped the auction catalog to the Majorelle page. The piece was supposed to serve as an accent piece in Lucas's bedroom. The style, size, and wood fit perfectly with the rest of the decor, plus it functioned as a display case of sorts for some of the accolades he had earned throughout his career. Now, they'd have to go to Plan B.

"It's okay, Jeffrey. Just breathe."

"It isn't working, Cassie. My nerves are shot. If we don't finish this on time, my ass will be excommunicated. Remember Antoine and Hillarie? Their dismissal from this project killed their clientele. If we fail, I'm going to have to move somewhere like Montana or Kentucky." The last words came out barely audible; he'd stressed himself until he was hoarse.

"At least you'll get to wear a cowboy hat in either place. Total bonus." She pictured Jeffrey on the other end of the line going red-faced at that. His brilliant, talented brain was only ever undone by the dramatic way with which he handled unexpected deviations from plans.

A throaty noise hit her ear.

"Jeffrey?"

Then a definite gag.

"I'm getting sick."

When the call ended, she shook her head. Cassie understood how much this project meant to Jeffrey and his career. He had been on the rise when Lucas tapped him in on this, and since taking it on, his calendar was steadily filling. The stakes were now so high that, should the project flop, he would be just as much a non-entity as Antoine and Hillarie. Cassie, however, believed it wouldn't happen.

She returned to the photo of the étagère and traced the lines of the piece Louis Majorelle had crafted at the turn of the twentieth century when so much about his world had changed. Cassie could relate. She thought of the man running his hands across the chestnut-colored exotic wood grain and meticulously molding the flower detailing that danced along the top and dripped down the sides. Majorelle had been a master at infusing his pieces with details that brought the outside world inside.

"Damn." She closed the catalog and slid off the stool. She had a backup for the piece in Brooklyn, but it would mean an extra trip tomorrow that would set her back several hours. She considered the differences in cost and saw a small bright side. It may shave some money from the budget.

She walked around the nearly completed living area and mentally cataloged the differences between what it had looked like the first time she crossed the threshold and now. Instead of dark colors, hard lines, and cold surfaces, what greeted people now was warm and melding. The space remained masculine and powerful, an echo of the man who lived here. But unlike him, the space no longer intimidated—it invited.

Her phone chimed with a message.

Jeffrey: I'm going to lie down. Can you solve this newest cluster? Please?

She smiled and texted back.

I've got it, yes. I'll call you later.

She put down the phone and noted the time. She would have to start driving to the auction house to check in and settle down before the bidding started. One thing already wasn't going as planned; she couldn't stomach the possibility that more would go wrong today.

A bang at the door startled her, and she guessed it was the construction crew. She gathered her stuff, thinking nothing of it. Then the sharp footfalls stopped.

She turned. Lucas was surveying the space with his incisive gaze, travel bag still affixed to his shoulder.

Her stomach sunk. "You weren't supposed to be back until next week."

"I finished early. No need to stay." He started down the hall to his room, where construction chaos waited. She opened her mouth to caution him about the walls stripped down to the studs and missing floorboards.

"What the hell happened in there?" His voice rumbled as he returned.

"Look, I know it's probably startling, but—"

"That's a fucking understatement. It looks like a bomb went off." If Lucas could shoot lasers out of those icy eyes, Cassie would surely be dead.

"They found a leak behind the wall and had to open the whole side, and part of the floor. And there was mold." It had been an unfortunate development, but the construction foreman pointed out it was a miracle they had made it so far without encountering an issue.

Lucas's jaw pulsed as the stare-down continued.

She swallowed. "It should be fixed in the next two days."

"And no one thought I should know."

"W- well, no. You were gone, and we thought..."

A crimson haze splotched the skin around his collar.

"I'll get them to come back early and..." She realized the problem. "The noise restrictions will kick in before they can finish. They won't get it done before tomorrow." She bit her lip.

"That's great. I'm gone three nights and come home to this shit. Wonderful." He said the last bit down to his phone as he hit a button and held it to his ear.

"I'm sorry, Lu—"

He dismissed her with a wave. "Stephanie, get me the suite at the Ritz for the next few days. My place is torn to shreds."

Cassie exhaled. She needed to leave. Now. But the butterflies dive-bombing her stomach no longer had to do with the auction. Disappointing Lucas turned out bad for anyone who did it, as unintentional as it may be. If this came back on them—on Jeffrey—it would surely ruin the man she'd come to feel so close to. It wasn't fair, though since no one had done anything intentional to elicit Lucas's discontent.

She pressed her left thumb into her right palm, but what had once been a comforting, or at least calming move, backfired as pain shot back at her. The physical therapist continually cautioned the nerves were hypersensitive now, every sensation amplified as her brain worked to get the impulses back in line. Cassie shook her hand as sharp jagged tics crackled and ricocheted through her palm and into her fingertips.

She had to get out of here.

"Where are you going?" Lucas's voice shot her between the shoulder blades.

She only halfway turned, intent on finishing her exit. "I have to get to the auction."

His presence pressed down on her. "Where is it?"

"Global House on York."

Lucas looked between her face and something behind her. The crimson wave along his neck rippled up to swallow the freckles at his jawline.

"Let's go." When he moved past her to the door, his motion teetered her out after him. She continued to the elevator while he locked up.

Was this it? Was he kicking her out? Would he tell Ronnie to bar her and Jeffrey from the building? She now regretted the cowboy hat remark as Lucas remained at her side the whole way out.

"Mr. Dalton, sir," Ronnie started. "Your driver left a momen—"

"Get him back now or we'll be late." Lucas pushed out the doors to stand at the curb where the car would arrive. The sun rained over him, glistening the black threads woven through his slate suit. Ronnie barked into the phone, and Cassie's legs propelled her outside to join Lucas.

The car screeched to a halt less than a minute later, and they were hustled into the back.

"Where to, Mr. Dalton?"

"Global House on York. And make it fast." Lucas turned his attention to his phone, his long fingers working the screen.

The knot tightened in Cassie's gut. Something wasn't right. Nothing about the last few minutes was. The air since he had walked into the apartment became toxic, soaked with disdain. His discontent morphed from mere annoyance to seething indignation.

"Am I missing something?" she finally asked.

He wrinkled his brow at the screen but never looked away from it. "I don't know, Cassie. Are you?"

"Are you coming to the auction?"

He finished with the phone, slipping it inside his jacket. The act of straightening his plum tie lasted far longer than it should have.

"Does it bother you if I say I am?"

"Yeah, it does." Irritation teasing her chest seeped through her words.

"I want to see what I'm getting for my money."

"You don't trust me all of a sudden?"

"I have a right to be concerned. Especially given the shit storm I just walked into." His voice deepened and a tinge of grit came out with every word.

"Is there something we've done so far that you don't like?" She didn't hide the challenge. Contempt at his sudden mistrust tumbled out along with her words.

"You don't like me being here."

"What I don't like," she snapped, "is the way you're talking to me. It isn't my fault that you came home unannounced four days early. Had I known, I would have made damn sure that you were either alerted to the delay in construction or that your room was put back together. Absent a heads-up, it's impossible to have known about your arrival. I'm not a mind reader."

Frustration pounded her chest and accompanied every syllable. She didn't flinch or look away. Never breaking eye contact, Lucas withdrew the ringing phone back out of his jacket.

He lifted it to his ear, his piercing gaze continuing to hold hers. Cassie would not back down. He was in the wrong. Full stop.

"Call me when it's done," he said finally to the faceless voice on the phone. He pulled his attention away to look down at the screen.

Somewhere in her brain, a little voice expanded, overtaking the dominant one that had brushed off every instance of toxic behavior by anyone ever. Bullies were no longer something she would tolerate. She had plenty of experience with those who mocked her, first for not having a mother—*that's the girl whose mom died*—followed quickly by those who excluded her for simply not conforming to the norm—*that's the weirdo who would rather paint than go to the party*.

Then, too, there had been the *concerned* voices who course-corrected her under the guise of doing what was best for her. Like her husband.

After decades of putting up with harsh tones and biting words, that little voice took center stage and refused to let things go.

Chapter Nineteen

"Welcome, Ms. Reynolds." Belinda Gideon welcomed Cassie with a firm handshake and an auction paddle numbered 131.

"It's nice to finally meet you, Ms. Gideon." Cassie attempted to maintain a modicum of calm and smiled at the auction house manager. She resolutely left the anger at Lucas behind her.

"I'm excited you could make it. You've sent me so many excellent inquiries these past few months. I've enjoyed our exchanges." The older woman smiled, forcing the tight skin on her face even tauter. It was clear Belinda had undergone some enhancement, but Cassie didn't blame her. The woman's role as the manager of one of the most famous auction houses surely came at a price.

"I'm sorry to hear the Majorelle piece is no longer available."

"The collector changed their mind. It happens." Belinda was very diplomatic and maintained the privacy of her clients. With millions of dollars on the line, discretion was paramount. Cassie often wondered if that was partly due to the questionable ownership and lineage of some of the older pieces that passed through. While Global House and every other reputable auction house vetted every piece, news stories about forgeries and stolen pieces still cropped up every now and then.

"I was so looking forward to it."

"I know, but I bet the new item we've put in at Lot Ten will pique your interest." The woman punctuated her words with a wink.

Cassie nodded and set off to find her seat. The gallery was packed with well-dressed society representatives who, like her, were here at the behest of a hoped-to-remain anonymous third party. So much wealth represented in one room set her stomach fluttering.

Her assigned row was to the rear of the gallery, and her seat in the dead center. She nodded to the older gentleman on her left, who tracked her progress all the way from the aisle to the seat.

Chimes signaled the imminent start of the bidding, and those mulling about moved to their seats. Cassie sat back and flipped through the catalog, curious to see the mysterious addition. She fanned the pages and stopped dead. A multi-color splashed canvas jumped off the page and knocked her square in the face. She didn't need to see the number to know it was the new piece. She'd seen it in person for the last time in December when she and Jeffrey supervised it being packed away by an art storage and conservation expert.

It was Lucas's Jackson Pollock.

She blinked at the page, unable to do much more. The seller was listed as anonymous, striking Cassie as odd. Why wouldn't Lucas want people to know it was his painting? For him, image and reputation bled into one.

"You're a fan of Pollock," the older gent to her left said.

"I-I'm just surprised to see it."

"It was last minute apparently. I'm sure someone in here will steal it." He smiled and then turned to the front. Applause rang out as the auctioneer came into view.

"See anything interesting?" Lucas said, settling in beside her, bathing her space with cedar and citrus.

"It appears so."

She did her best Lucas Dalton Death Stare hoping it worked in reverse. It did not. It did succeed in eliciting a Lucas Dalton Single Eyebrow Raise.

Cassie huffed and turned to the stage.

The excitement quickly absorbed her. The first three lots went fast, but then the auction stalled at the fourth, a painting by Piero Manzoni, the Italian artist known for showcasing materials instead of scenes on canvas. This particular one was clay on canvas and colorless, much like other Manzoni pieces. Cassie internally cringed as the bidding got heated and ended well above three million dollars. While she appreciated abstract notions of creativity, she could not see them all equally as art.

Things proceeded again and then the fifth item, a Rodin sculpture, came up. It was the first of three pieces Cassie was here to procure. The headless and limbless female bust stood thirty-three inches tall and would fit Jeffrey's custom-designed office nook. The dull jade green of the statue would stand in stark contrast to the deep gray and navy color scheme around it.

The auctioneer's call awoke a clamor of rustling in Cassie's belly. She was about to enter a live art auction. At Global House. The bidding started, and faceless beings raised paddles like battle flags.

Maybe this was a bad idea.

Then, as hands started dropping with each count by the auctioneer, she forced down the doubt and thrust up her hand.

"That's three-eighty to one-three-one. Do I hear three-ninety? Three-ninety?"

She did it. She got a bid in.

"Three-ninety to one-eight-nine. Four? Do I hear four?"

Just like that, she was outbid. This dance continued in earnest as each wave of a paddle raised the stakes ten thousand dollars until the price stood just fifty thousand below her threshold. Her research told her not to go above that mark. So when the auctioneer began the final call, she raised her paddle one more time.

"We've got four-fifty. Going once. Four-fifty going twice. Last call for four-fifty."

Lucas could get at least a hundred thousand more for it in a few years.

"Sold to one-three-one," the auctioneer declared, and the crowd shifted its attention toward her. She dipped her head in gratitude and settled back into her chair. Her spine hadn't relaxed since the bidding had begun.

Renewed energy surged when her older seatmate leaned her way.

"Well done."

Armed with this new boldness, she went for the remaining two items on her list. She kept the same rhythm of quiet reserve and inward trepidation to enter the bidding. Then, she swooped in toward the end to claim both.

Through it all, she remained unmoved by Lucas to her right. She never acknowledged him. He could have left; she wouldn't have noticed or cared.

"Our final item of the day, Lot Ten is a late addition. It is an original painting by the brilliant abstract impressionist Jackson Pollock simply entitled Number 16. The authenticity and lineage of the painting have been verified and certified." The auctioneer stood silent for a moment allowing the gallery to get a good look at the painting. Whispers pierced the room, and Cassie watched the ripples as people prepared to pounce. She rolled her eyes and set down her paddle.

"Bid on it," Lucas rasped against her right ear. Her neck tingled where his warm breath hit the skin, raising goose bumps.

"Excuse me?"

"You heard me. I need you to make sure someone here pays at least what I did."

She scoffed, and the man to her left tilted his head in her direction. She covered her mouth as if stifling a cough.

"You're crazy, you know that?" she whispered back to Lucas without turning her head.

Was this even legal? Or ethical?

Lucas had paid fifteen million. Cassie hadn't researched the piece, so she didn't have any concept about the demand for it. Pollock was ultra-popular, especially in sophisticated city society. But at that price point, it would only appeal to a very select group.

She nibbled her cheek and formulated a new strategy. Instead of pacing herself, she joined the sea of paddles at the eight-million-dollar starting bid. The older man next to her leaned forward, but he didn't engage. She suspected he was only here for the Pollock since he hadn't shown interest in anything else.

Eight rounds in, and the price had risen to twelve million. The man to her left still had yet to go in. She sat back with the paddle idle in her lap. She spent the next few minutes tracking the active bidders. At least four original players were in the hunt.

"Do I hear twelve and a half?"

The room remained bewitched. The auctioneer waited, allowing people in the space to consider the weight of the price. If there was a shot to get the fifteen, Cassie needed to act.

"Twelve point five. Yes, thank you one-three-one."

The people in front turned back. Cassie worked to remain fixed on the auction stage, letting everything else blur around the edges.

Come on.

"Do I hear thirteen?"

Come on.

"Thirteen," the man to her left called.

Gotcha.

"Thirteen, to seven-zero-four. Do I he—"

"Fourteen," Cassie chimed.

"Fifteen." The reply came on the heels of her own. As he lowered the paddle, he looked at her. "You're going to lose this one, sweetie."

She raised her paddle while still looking at the gentleman.

"Sixteen." A wave of whispers surged through the room. It was just the two of them now enemies in an open battlefield.

"Do I hear sixteen point five?" the auctioneer beckoned, looking straight at her seatmate.

She fixated on the auctioneer, forcing a look of stoicism about her. Inside, she was a mess but she didn't dare show it. If she was wrong, Lucas would be stuck paying for his own painting again. Maybe it served him right at this point. But the more unfortunate consequence would be she'd have to check Jeffrey into a mental hospital for the breakdown he would have.

"Seventeen million," her neighbor belted out.

"Eighteen," she responded without missing a beat. The room fell dead silent. Her heart punched her ribs. But she fought with every bit of her will to exude nothing but a calm and confident front.

"Going once," the auctioneer called out. The silence deepened. Cassie remained steadfast.

"Eighteen going twice."

She tightened her grip on the paddle in her right hand, squeezing the handle. She didn't want the shake to betray the horror coursing through her body. The moisture from her palm seeped onto the handle, and in that moment, where time stood still, she realized it had been over three years since she held something so tight in that hand.

The joy inside erupted in a smile.

"Twenty million!" the man cried.

The room inhaled a collective breath. And Cassie exhaled for the first time in minutes.

She regarded her seatmate, making a show of it. He sat ramrod straight, his face flushed and punctuated by beads of sweat trickling down his sideburns. His left hand curled around the edge of his seat as he waited for the gavel to drop.

Her smile. He had interpreted it as a sign of hope or pride or confidence. He wasn't wrong, not entirely. It was all of those things and so much more, but not for what he had assumed.

"Twenty million going once," the auctioneer called. "Going twice."

She shook her head and sank back. The battle won. "Congratulations," she said, and the man's shoulders fell several inches.

"Sold! To the gentleman with paddle number seven-zero-four!"

Applause erupted, every person gazed at the older gent with awe as he stood and bowed. Cheeks stretched wide with triumph, Cassie turned to share the celebration with Lucas, only to find his seat empty.

"I hope you aren't too cross with me." The victor offered a hand to Cassie as the gallery emptied around them.

"Of course not."

"My boss will be over the moon." The skin about his eyes and lips crinkled as he bent closer. "Don't worry. If your boss wants to see the piece, it's going on display next year."

"Really? Where?"

He smiled and put a finger up to his lips. "The Met," he whispered.

The Metropolitan Museum of Art had always been and still remained a sacred place for Cassie. Jess had once called it Cassie's Church, and the sentiment stuck. It was, for her, a quiet and reverent place full of every whisper of every dream she ever had. It also held space for her worst nightmare.

The morning after her dad's accident, she had wobbled out of the police station, broken by grief. Somehow, she had walked to The Met, while the words drunk, blindsided, and instantaneous looped mercilessly through her brain. She sat in the Impressionism room, trying to make sense of something that would never make sense. She spent all day lost in Claude Monet's *The Parc Monceau*, committing every hue and brush stroke of every leaf and flower and blade of grass to memory. She had planned on spending many hours in that same park when she moved to—

"Promise you won't tell?" The older man's rasp shook her from the grief that often skirted her thoughts, hijacking them if she lingered too long. "It'll be announced next month after the Paris auction."

—*Paris*

She reassured the man with a nod. "My lips are sealed."

Chapter Twenty

T he house seemed eerily silent when Cassie returned home that night. The door shutting behind her echoed down the hallway.

"Nothing new here," she said to her empty kitchen. While it wasn't surprising Jason wasn't home, it was disappointing. He had known how big today's auction was for her, yet he had remained locked in his usual work world. Sure, she understood he was still building some sort of legacy for Frank and for himself, but today of all days, she had yearned for a sign he had been listening to her.

Her stomach rumbled, reminding her she hadn't eaten anything since morning. She pulled out the piece of lasagna leftover from dinner at Jess's earlier in the week and warmed it up. Her phone pinged.

Jeffrey: You need to work for me.

Jeffrey's response to her auction retelling tickled her lips. Over the last few months, she had gained confidence in herself, bolstered by Jeffrey's encouragement of her work, her eye, and most importantly, her intuition. She hoped he would keep her in mind as a consultant on future projects.

Cassie: We'll see. Let's get through the next month first.

His response of smiley faces and hearts flashed across the screen.

She put down her phone and fished out a bottle of wine from the pantry. Her day deserved a bit of celebrating even if she was alone. She lit candles and set the table, wanting to make the night special for herself. Satisfied with setting the mood, she picked her phone back up and sent a message to Jess.

Call when you can.

She wanted to share the thrill of her day with someone besides her work partner. The auction, even now, fueled the thump of her heart and the surge of blood lighting up its path to her brain. The battle with the old gent and her victory had invigorated her.

Then there was the other thing the man shared. Not just about the Pollock's final resting place at The Met, but about the timing. It would be announced after the big auction in Paris.

That city was her white whale, the thing she chased and wanted and did everything humanly possible *not* to get.

Her dad had filled her head with Paris. The way it smelled (sweet and musky), tasted (bitter and rich), sounded (alive and throaty), and looked (ancient and modern). The lights, the music, the people, the food, the actual air—her dad had indulged every question she posed. At the end of any conversation, when he couldn't come up with another word to describe it, he would simply tell her it was magical.

"What makes it magical?" she had asked as they stood outside the ice cream shop. Her nine-year-old self had been fighting with untamed strands from her pigtails catching in the stickiness around her mouth.

Dad got a faraway look, the one that meant the recollection of whatever tumbled through his head centered around her mother.

"For one, your mom." When he tilted his head, the summer sun high-lighted the silver springing up in his chestnut beard.

"But what else?"

He dropped his tall and sturdy frame down to meet her teeny waif one.

"Well, you." He caught a drip of chocolate oozing from her chin and wiped it away.

"I've never been to Paris."

"What if I said you have."

Cassie sunk her teeth into the crinkly cone, causing pieces to splinter and fall apart on contact. She shook her head at her dad's there's-something-you-don't-know face.

"What if I told you that once upon a time, the most beautiful woman in the world and her much less handsome husband spent four glorious days in the City of Light, eating all the best food, drinking all the best wine." He leaned closer to ensure Cassie heard this next part. "Looking at all the best art..."

Cassie's lungs expanded, "The Louvre!" Her invocation of the name had the same effect as almost anything else she said, which was to cause a smile to widen his face.

"Yes, the Louvre. And the beautiful woman and the ogre man—"

"Dad! I know it was you and Mom."

"For the purpose of this story, it's beautiful woman and ogre man."

"Dad!"

He snickered and the smile widened. "The two walked through the halls of the Louvre, the beautiful woman much more enthralled than the ogre, who only wanted to go get a croissant. But he went and held her hand and listened to her regale him with so many thoughts and feelings and wonderings at each and every single thing, especially the Mona Lisa." Dad paused and produced a napkin from his pocket on cue as Cassie popped the last of the cone into her mouth.

"But how was I there? I wasn't born."

Dad wiped at her face, her hands, her nose.

"You kind of were. You were a whisper in that beautiful woman's heart and spirit. And little did the ogre know but later that night, after he got his croissant..."

His face fell, his eyes moving to some faraway place.

"Dad. I wasn't born yet."

The life came back as he wiped a piece of her chocolate-soaked pigtail from her cheek.

"No, baby girl, you weren't born. But that night after walking those hallowed halls surrounded by all that beauty, we made you."

The oven timer pulled Cassie away from her reminiscent wandering. She grabbed her food, the bittersweet past rising to douse the hunger pangs.

Her nine-year-old brain had no idea what he meant then. Now her thirty-six-year-old heart broke thinking about it.

Cassie sat down to her romantic meal for one, her mind meandering a few moments longer through the past, her dad, and her dreams of Paris until the phone pinged.

Hoping it was Jess, she jumped to check it.

When Lucas's name flashed across the lock screen, Cassie's eagerness stalled. She considered leaving it unread, but then a second one came in.

"What the hell," she said to no one.

Lucas: Meet me at Waffles and Wags at 8:30 tomorrow.

And then.

Lucas: Please. I would appreciate it.

She gnawed at her cheek and calculated the odds he might be firing her. On the plus side, she just made him a couple million dollars. But the whole telling-him-off-in-the-car bit made the likelihood of her continued employment on the project doubtful.

She typed out a denial explaining she had an appointment in Brooklyn with a collector. About ten words into the well-crafted, thoughtful, but bitchy rejection, she realized if she got fired, she had no reason to go to Brooklyn.

She shook her head as she deleted her response for a one-word affirmation:

Fine.

Returning to the table, she lifted her wine glass in a solo toast.

"To crossing bridges and burning them down."

Chapter
Twenty-One

Waffles and Wags was a popular Upper East Side staple, and Cassie worked her way past the line extending halfway down the block. The quirky decor and premise of allowing dogs and owners to dine at tables together made the café quite popular.

Bacon and maple-infused air triggered her mouth to water and her tummy grumbled its displeasure at making it wait. Cassie shifted her weight waiting for the hostess to return to the podium. She didn't see Lucas among the half-human, half-canine crowd. Pets didn't seem like his scene, but according to Jess the Waffles and Wags eggs benedict was the best in the Upper East Side.

During last night's telephone debrief, Jess had squealed over each and every detail about the auction Cassie recounted.

"You're a total art badass." Jess crunched over the phone; a sign she was trying to stay awake by eating salty snacks.

"That's not exactly true." She had kicked back another glass of wine; a sign she was trying to knock herself out.

"And I bet your sexy boss thought so, too."

"Yeah, well, I'm fairly sure he's firing me at breakfast."

While the Pollock sale was ultra-successful, Cassie still assumed Lucas wouldn't forgive her outburst. She wondered if the cafe provided emotional support dogs to patrons who lost their jobs over chicken and waffles.

"Why?" Jess had asked.

That's when the conversation continued for far longer than it should have as Cassie filled Jess in on the drama leading up to the auction.

"What if he sends the waiter over with a note firing you while you're chowing down on your overpriced eggs benedict?"

Cassie giggled as her cheeks tingled with the wine. "Nah, he'll do it himself. I think he probably gets off on conflict."

"We also know he gets off on—"

"JESSICA!"

After an alcohol-infused fit of giggles, Cassie settled back into the couch while Jess filled her in on her day with the twins and Greg. Nothing made Cassie's heart ache like listening to what Jess called the boring and mundane and gross details of her day because children were part of the kind of life Cassie once longed for.

The Waffles and Wags hostess returned, but before she could launch into her excuse about the wait time, Cassie asked if Lucas was there. The hostess nodded and led Cassie to the furthest table in the back corner. Lucas sat with his head already hidden behind the Wall Street Journal. A cup of coffee wafting steam at his elbow. The sleeve of his jacket was a rich blue, akin to the swirling sky in Van Gogh's, *Starry Night*.

Cassie sat without a word and started perusing the menu, willing her leg to cease bouncing under the table.

"I recommend the eggs benedict," Lucas said from behind his barricade. "If you're wondering."

She nodded, though he couldn't see, and forced her eyes in any other direction but him, especially when the paper rustling signaled his relinquishment of the wall between them.

A waiter approached with a carafe, poured a cup full of coffee for her, and set down a bowl of creamer buckets.

"What can I get you today?" he asked.

She ordered the eggs benedict because she was going to anyway, though she hated that Lucas would believe she did at his suggestion. While she wrestled with the optics, in the end, she decided not to care what he thought. She gruffly opened the creamer buckets and bit back on her sourness.

"That was quite a show yesterday," Lucas said after the waiter retreated.

She kept her attention locked on the spoon's handle, watching the dark roast brighten with the flood of cream she tipped in. She kept her nose attuned to its rich aroma to diffuse the hint of cedar and citrus emanating from Lucas's skin and hair.

"You made me back my money and then some. I wasn't expecting that."

She swallowed the retort rising in her throat. All the things she wanted to say bubbled up. She had become accustomed to people underestimating her through the years, including Jason. He had encouraged her art aspirations at first, but after a few years of his own business failures, he started discouraging her from the artistic path she wanted. Only her dad and Jess had always believed her capable of any dream she chose to chase. Yet, like a dog wrenched by the violent jerk of a leash, Cassie's dreams always remained just out of reach.

She had come here prepared for the worst. Yet, Lucas had showered her with praise. She'd become so used to Jason's indifference to her successes her default reaction was negativity. She had no shame over her behavior before the auction yesterday. She needed to stop dipping her head and avoiding whatever consequences Lucas wanted to dole out.

She lifted her gaze to his and tried like hell not to let the sight of them jostle her. The blue in the Starry Night suit, coupled with the deep sangria shirt and mustard tie, made him look like a masterpiece.

"Look, if you're firing me, just get on with it. No need to break it to me gently." Her own voice surprised her.

A flicker of doubt skimmed across the folds in his face. Lucas's every move seemed so calculated, so *precise*. In those moments where the mask slipped ever so slightly, the effect tugged at her core and fanned the spark he'd struck the first moment they stood together in front of that Pollock.

"First of all," he said, reaching across the table for the carafe, the single motion showcasing the length of his arms. "I never do anything gently." He looked up at her from under long ashen lashes.

Dear God.

The vision of his muscled backside thrust into her brain. She had a very good idea of how hard he could be.

The breath caught in her throat, and she doused it with coffee to keep it from choking her.

"And second, why would I fire you?" He retreated into his space.

"What else could it be?"

"Maybe it's just breakfast. In appreciation of the work you do."

"I don't buy it," she said.

"Why not?"

"Because I yelled at you, and I know you don't tolerate that sort of thing."

Lucas tilted his head slightly and appeared to ponder her words. An inexplicable force throbbed in the air between them, causing Cassie to push harder into the chair back to widen the space. The pull he had over was unsettling, and attractive as he was, she was not only married but certain he didn't have this same reaction to her. She needed to stop interpreting everything as some kind of attraction between them. If anything, it ran one way, not the other.

"I was wrong to speak to you that way. You had every right to stand up for yourself." His words came out softer, not in volume but in tone.

Of all the things Lucas could have done, this was the one Cassie least expected. The powerful man across the table seemed humbled, gentle even. The reaction was so far from his norm and sent a ripple of nerves through her chest.

Except this wasn't the first time his harsh edges had softened. She had witnessed several instances that cast him in a very different light than the image he cultivated. Even Jeffrey's recounting of the way Lucas had behaved after her surgery left an indelible mark. According to Jeffrey, when he had arrived at Lucas's apartment to take her home, Lucas carried her down to the car and rattled off instructions to Jeffrey on medication and wound care.

"I shouldn't have snapped at you like that," Lucas continued. "I was angry at a lot of things, none of which had anything to do with you. I took it out on you, and for that, I'm sorry."

His words crumbled the wall of trepidation and mistrust Cassie erected in times of uncertainty. While her gut screamed he was sincere in this apology, something else annoyed her.

"And that stunt at the auction?" she asked.

"What about it."

She crossed her arms. "You should have told me about the Pollock."

"Maybe," he said. After a moment of silence, he asked, "Would you have gone along with it if I had?"

"Absolutely not! I don't think it was..." She didn't need to complete the thought because she had just proved his point. The smug expression diffused her annoyance. This man with his games and his mask that blocked her from his ulterior motives. She rarely walked away from him feeling confident in her interpretation of what had transpired because he somehow always threw her for a loop.

"What are you thinking?" His voice cut into her thoughts.

"You don't want to know."

"I hired you for your honesty, remember?"

"Fine." She sat up straight and drew in a breath of courage—or stupidity. "I think you're an asshole."

Lucas winced. A pang of guilt bounced against her ribs. For a moment, Cassie wished she could take back her words. She had crossed a line and gotten too harsh, all because she was hurt he didn't let her in on the plan to sell the Pollock—a painting *she* recommended he unload. Now she was the asshole and needed to make it right. But before an apology could cross her lips, the waiter approached, and Lucas shifted to allow the man to place their food.

When they were left alone again, Lucas lifted his icy gaze to hers and nodded. "At least you always let me know where I stand."

***

Emerging from the warmth of the cafe into the chilly spring air invigorated Cassie. Unlike the bone-cutting bitterness of winter a few weeks ago, now it was almost warm enough to go without a jacket. Then, as if on cue, the wind roared down the block and liberated a chunk of hair from her ponytail. She tugged her jacket closer even as she pulled out her phone.

Lucas finished a call while Cassie calculated how long the trip to Prospect Park in Brooklyn should take.

"What does your day look like?" He slid his aviators over his eyes, denying her access to them, returning to the enigma behind mirrors. He pushed his hands into the pockets of his black cashmere coat. Their meal had been comfortable, with bits of small talk (her) followed by plenty of contemplative silence (him).

"Since I'm not fired, I'm heading to an appointment in Brooklyn." She grinned when Lucas's grimace wrinkled his nose. "Not a fan?"

"Not particularly. A kid I played hockey with lived there. He was such a crybaby."

"So all the people in Brooklyn are crybabies? Because of a kid from twenty years ago?"

"More like twenty-five years ago, and yeah." He tilted his head to look up at the sun as it showered its rays upon him. It highlighted a patch of ashen stubble at his jawline that his razor had missed.

"Good thing you're not going. I would hate for Mrs. Martocci to bear the weight of redeeming an entire borough for you."

When Lucas chuckled, the slight upturn in his lips shifted his entire presence, stripping away some of the projected elusiveness. Another slip of the mask. "Maybe Mrs. Martocci is just who I need to change my mind. Kind of like you did about Queens."

Cassie chuckled. "Oh, come on, you called it a shithole to my face."

"Yeah, but that's better than what I said before I met you."

"You're ridiculous, you know that?"

"Which is a step up from asshole. See? It's all about perspective."

Cassie grimaced. "About that."

He stopped her with a wave, and his brows arched high above the aviators.

"Look, let's get something straight. Don't start pulling punches with me."

"Okay." She swallowed hard and couldn't think of anything else to say that he wouldn't shoot down for being apologetic.

He cast his mirrored gaze toward the street. She sensed he was lingering and, much like that day in the car on the way to the auction, her stomach dipped.

She cleared her throat. "I've got to get going so I can make the train." She peeled another strand of errant hair adhered to her cheek. "Thanks again for breakfast, and for not firing me."

He didn't move except for an intake of breath she watched expand his chest under the unbuttoned coat. "Does it have to be the train?" he asked. "Can't we take the car?"

We.

Lucas was inviting himself *again*. The reasons behind this eluded her. Reading him was an impossible task Cassie consistently failed to do.

"You want to come with me to Brooklyn?"

He nodded.

"This isn't some kind of joke, is it? Like you and Mrs. Martocci are also in business together, and this is a trick to get me to work some kind of deal?"

His lips widened into a genuine smile, revealing perfect teeth. "I swear. No trick." He cleared his throat. "I don't have anything else this morning, and I don't know exactly how to spend it. I'm not used to free time."

This was not the first time she sensed an odd or out-of-place vibe with Lucas. It wasn't bad or off-putting exactly. It seemed natural. He welcomed her like he wanted her as a companion or confidante, or something. But the notion that a man like Lucas Dalton needed or wanted a friendship with her seemed downright outrageous. She couldn't shake the growing suspicion something else lurked underneath all of his pleasantries.

She shrugged it off. His motives didn't matter. What did was Lucas wasn't going to take no for an answer, and she really had no good reason to resist. Plus, if she was being honest, she was intrigued and wanted to see more of the Lucas she believed lived underneath the mask.

"Okay, but it probably won't be too exciting. I'm just looking at furniture."

He shrugged. "My car then?"

"The train. There's no chance we'll get stuck in traffic."

He jammed his hands back into his coat pocket and dipped his head. She was sure he was about to refuse on principle. Is that why she was adamant about taking the train? On principle?

There was more to her aversion. Her nerves shot around at the possibility she liked being around him. She was married and though her relationship with Jason seemed to be skating on thin ice, she didn't want to cause any more cracks.

Still, the fact remained she *wanted* to get to know an elusive, incorrigible, rich, single, extremely handsome man who smelled good and made her insides quiver. That, in and of itself, was cause for her to exercise caution.

A small huff drew her back.

"We'll do things your way," Lucas said. "This time."

Chapter Twenty-Two

C assie and Lucas swam against the tide of pedestrians to the 96th Street station. The waves of people washing past forced Cassie to dodge and weave making it nearly impossible to maintain a steady pace.

Lucas, on the other hand, walked ahead without difficulty. He took up space and moved like the powerful force he was—a tall and confident man who displaced anyone and everyone in his path.

"How do you do that?" she asked from his left elbow.

"Do what?"

"Walk like you own the world."

He turned his head to her without stopping his forward motion. "I don't know what you mean." As the words left his mouth, a throng of people surged toward them. He didn't pause or sidestep as she did. Instead, he forged ahead, splitting the group around him.

"That's what I mean." She chuckled when they met back up. He shrugged, without pride. Others held themselves in the same way to give the world an illusion of their power. However, this was just who Lucas was—his essence. Cassie's intuition tingled that more lurked beneath his persona. Lucas was complex in ways she had yet to uncover and doubted she ever would.

They approached the glass canopy of the station entrance. Cassie bypassed the escalators and descended the stairs, trotting at a fair pace. Lucas dropped back to follow her down between the dark blue tiled walls etched with white architectural sketches. Below, the entry opened to a wide mezzanine level with soaring ceilings and bright lights, deceiving the eye into forgetting they had descended below the city streets.

"I need a ticket," he said.

"Sorry. I forgot. You can grab it at a kiosk." She altered course to the closest vacant station and tapped the display, something she'd done a million times. Seconds later, the machine ejected a new card.

He stared at it when she proffered it to him and the skin along his jaw pulsed.

Once through, they proceeded to the platform. Lucas stood rigid beside her, his stare fixed ahead at the dark blue tunnel wall. This particular part of the larger art installation depicted white sheets of paper scattered along the tunnel as if disturbed by a passing train.

"Isn't it cool?" she asked.

"What is it exactly?"

"Art." She turned. "There are pieces like this in a bunch of stations."

Lucas tilted his head, although he remained shrouded in a cloak of skepticism. "It's paper," he finally grumbled.

"It's life in motion depicted in a relatable image. This whole station was inspired by the simple ways people transition throughout the day. All art strives to make something beautiful and interesting, even out of the mundane."

"And how is this better than my Pollock?" His left eyebrow lifted.

"Oh, come on. At least we understand this. We can see what it is." She gestured to the tunnel wall. "How many times have you seen a train leave a swirl of paper as it passes?"

Lucas scoffed. "Actually never." He squinted against her wrinkled brow. "I've never taken the train."

"You've lived in the city your whole life and never rode the subway?"

"I only travel by car."

She shook her head. "You're missing out on a whole other part of the city."

"Yeah, the part that's dirty and smelly, and full of homeless people." He rattled off like a shopping list.

She scrunched her brows at him. A car ride was nice, a treat really, and it did avoid some of the unsavory aspects of mass transit. But a train ride gave her time and space to think in a bubble of her own making, though Lucas would likely argue sitting in the back of his car did the same for him.

"Did someone scare you out of riding the train?"

"My grandfather. And he didn't scare me. He educated me." He returned to staring out at the wall.

She decided not to push a man she had unwittingly forced outside his comfort zone. It was strange she had the power to do that. It again brought back unanswered questions and confusion when it came to unraveling Lucas. But she had a husband, and it wasn't her place to figure out another man's motives. Especially this one.

"I take the train all the time, and except for the summer, I'm rarely dirty. Or smelly." The reward for her attempt to lighten the mood was an elusive Lucas Dalton Smile.

He chuckled just as the platform filled with the roaring of the incoming train. Within seconds, it screamed into the station and squealed to a stop. The doors slid open, releasing the contained hoard. They poured and pushed their way out.

Cassie realized Lucas might get left behind if he didn't follow closely. She took his hand, pushed her way into the car, and pulled him halfway down the aisle. With a longer ride, she wanted to stay far away from the door to avoid the constant in-and-out of passengers. The train remained packed despite disgorging so many passengers. Finally, she came to an empty spot near the overhead rail though the pressure of those still entering pushed on them.

She realized she still had a hold of Lucas's hand and released it. "Doing okay?"

As the warning tone rang out, he loosened his tie. A tour group in matching branded shirts chose their car to invade, and she stepped closer to Lucas as bodies filled up every empty space.

"Yeah, I'm good. This is just..." He looked around at the crowd of people. "...different."

The doors swooshed closed, forcing everyone to heave themselves in tighter.

"You should hold on," Cassie said.

Lucas grabbed the overhead pole, which was more shoulder height for him. She gripped the bar next to him. The electricity of their skin brushing for a brief moment coursed down her arm. She shook it off. This teenage crush behavior needed to stop.

The train lurched forward, and the man behind her stumbled into her, knocking her off balance. She fell with the man until Lucas reached out and snatched her around the waist.

"You should take your own advice." He peered down at her.

Heat suffused her face. Stepping back, she reclaimed a small slice of the pole and focused anywhere but on him.

***

The train remained packed at each subsequent stop. Cassie again got bumped from behind, and before she could reposition herself, where, she didn't know, Lucas had pulled her to him again.

"Aren't you glad we didn't take the car?" he growled into her ear. Goosebumps popped over her skin as she gulped away the heat yet again. She looked at him, mere inches from her face, melting her from the inside out.

"I swear I do this all the time," she managed to eke out. His left eyebrow popped up again, forcing her to realize her mistake. "Oh, God, I don't do this—like stand with a ma—" But her words were swallowed by the screech and sounds of the next stop.

"It might be easier if you just hold onto me, Cass."

She saw no other way to do this unless she aggressively clawed an old woman's hand from the bar.

She bit her lip and threaded her arms through Lucas's coat and around his waist. Her eyes were even with his Adam's apple and the freckles that dotted it. She inhaled his citrus and cedar musk that made her head airy.

A man pushed past from behind her, and Lucas encircled her waist in a giant hand, crushing her into him, fusing their bodies from the chest down. Her heart pounded, and if not for the cage of her ribs, she was certain it would tear through her skin.

She slipped into her head for the better part of the ride. She needed to think of anything but *this*. She needed her body to stop reacting under the weight of him in any way but *this*. Firmly she pushed away the thoughts of Jason and what he would do if he happened to get on at one of these stops. While she would like to believe he might react in some adverse way, the reality was, he probably wouldn't even notice. Her heart sunk a bit at the truthfulness of this bitter pill.

When the announcement of their station blared through the car, Cassie lurched out of melancholy. She looked up at Lucas, startled to find him staring at her. A spark eradicated the darkness taking up space in her chest.

The 7th Avenue station was a far cry from the spotless one they had left. This place was old and worn; the air permeated with urine and must. They made their way to the surface, and Lucas's exaggerated inhale filled her ears when they broke the surface. He shaded his eyes with his glasses against the blaring sun.

"So, what did you think?" Cassie made a point to leave a considerable distance between them.

"Just as horrible as I imagined."

She rolled her eyes. "You would say that no matter what."

A faint trace of offense crossed his face. "Where are we headed?" he asked.

"The next block. Mrs. Martocci has a storeroom of furniture."

He nodded and pulled out his phone. "What's the address?" He put it to his ear.

She stopped. "Are you calling for help? It wasn't that bad."

"No, it was. I did it your way here, but I'll take the car back."

She peered down the street to the park as they walked toward it. Near Mrs. Martocci's building, the scent of fresh bread drifted through the air. Visions of her easel, a box of new pencils, and dad flitted through her head.

Those were sacred memories of afternoons spent with him at the Brooklyn Museum. Here she had spied her first gold-encrusted ancient sarcophagus and the shriveled and eternally screaming mummy lurching out from the top.

"There's a pretzel cart around here somewhere," she said.

"I don't eat pretzels. It goes against the rules."

"What rules?" She stopped at the stoop of Mrs. Martocci's building. Lucas's tie still hung loose and without a thought, she slid the knot back to its proper place.

"Mine."

"You have a rule against eating a pretzel?"

"I don't eat anything out of a cart." His tone didn't invite further questions.

She stepped back, crossing her arms against his stoicism. "This explains a lot about you, Lucas."

"How so?"

"It's not surprising. You come from another world than I do." If the man never took the subway because his grandfather had made it seem big and scary, avoiding food with unknown origins or sanitary conditions made sense to her.

Lucas again tilted his head, but his ringing phone stopped any further exchange. "I have to take this. Go in without me."

She started her ascent up the stoop, then stopped. "Are you going to be here when I'm done?"

"I'm not sure."

He took the phone call. By the time she got to the top step, a big part of her hoped he was gone.

Chapter
Twenty-Three

Mrs. Martocci's welcome came with hot tea and homemade short-bread. After the refreshments, Cassie picked through the store-house brimming with the furniture and art Greta had collected over five decades. Cassie chose two nightstands and an armoire. The prices were right, and with a little work, she could freshen up the aged wood in a few days. She wrote the check and arranged for pickup.

After the purchase, Greta kept up a voracious banter with Cassie that lasted well past ninety minutes. The two chatted at length about artistic styles, the monolithic period, the scandal in the Catholic church after *The DaVinci Code*, and then the current exhibit at the Brooklyn Museum.

This last tidbit made Cassie's skin tingle. The museum's Impressionism installation included some never-before-seen-in-America Monet paintings. He was her favorite painter, the one by whom she judged every other. The news invigorated her, a welcome change from all the messy morning feelings thus far.

As the two women stepped out onto the stoop, Greta gave Cassie's arm a little tap.

"That handsome man has been wearing a track in the sidewalk," she said into Cassie's ear.

Lucas, coat slung over his forearm and ear pressed to his phone, paced back and forth between the same four patches of concrete.

"I think he may be waiting for someone," Greta continued as the two women said goodbye.

Cassie tucked her hair behind her ear before venturing down the steps. To say she was surprised to see him was an understatement.

"I figured you'd have been long gone by now," she said as he ended the call.

His head craned back a pinch. "I thought you might like a ride back."

"I'm not going back to the city today. I'm babysitting in Queens a little later, but first I'm going to pop into the museum for a bit."

It had been a long time since she stepped foot into the Brooklyn Museum or any other. Since her dad died, Cassie didn't have the same connection to them or the art within their walls. Not even The Met had called to her after the night he died.

"I can join you if you want company," Lucas said.

"You want to walk around a museum with me?"

"Why not. I've never listened to a real artist talk about art before. Well, except to disparage a Pollock once."

Cassie's head tipped to the ground along with her sigh. "I'm not a real artist, Lucas."

"Sure you are."

She shook him off. "I stopped sketching and painting a long time ago."

His left eyebrow arched over his glasses. "But you've started again since the surgery."

"No," she whispered, rubbing a circle into her right palm the way she used to. "I haven't. Not once."

She stepped toward the museum. It didn't make sense she hadn't done more than think about painting and sketching since Dr. Patella had her grip a pencil in her office a few weeks ago. Cassie had skipped into the art supply store that afternoon, but two steps inside, an awful feeling gripped her. She couldn't shake it, so she walked away.

"Look, I'm really not up to talking, or company right now," she said, knowing Lucas was drifting alongside her.

When she stopped, his mirrored gaze remained fixed on her, much like that first day in Queens.

"That's the politest rejection I've ever heard." The folds of his forehead ground together, then went slack as the corners of his mouth raised. "I'm not used to it."

"Manners?"

"Rejection."

She bit her lip to refrain from spilling the thoughts that darted into her mind. What must it be like to go through life always getting what you wanted? Granted, she had never wanted for much growing up; her dad had provided everything and more. But as an adult, she seemed to face nothing but rejection and disappointment.

"Why are you still here?"

He slowly shook his head. "I've been asking myself that since we descended into that sewer. I guess you're good at convincing me to do things I don't want to do. Ever considered a job in sales?"

She guffawed. "No way! I'm horrible at pushing people. I can't even get Jason to pick up his dirty clothes and put them in the hamper three feet to the left."

They resumed walking toward the museum.

"I've never lived with anyone," Lucas said unexpectedly. "Besides my grandfather."

The admission shocked her because, once again, he opened up so freely around her. Perhaps he did this with everyone he got to know and it wasn't as big of a deal as she was making it.

"No one special enough to live with?"

"I never let anyone stay more than a couple hours."

She nodded dumbly while she processed this insight, another piece of the Lucas puzzle. Her head swam with musings she felt compelled to ask until she spotted the pretzel vendor on the path ahead. All other thoughts left her as she made a beeline for it.

She called back to him. "Sure you don't want one?"

He declined with a solid shake of his head.

Moments later, Cassie returned to his side holding her prize wrapped in wax paper. The pretzel's warmth seeped into her hand. She tore off a piece and popped it in her mouth, savoring the way the stiff outside and soft inside melded with the salt.

"The car should be here in a few minutes." As he studied her, a flicker of amusement passed over his face. She didn't care. She ate it the way Dad taught her to, from the outside in, saving the extra squishy middle twists for last. Every piece brought with it another memory from her childhood, ushering in joy and sadness with each bite of dough and salt.

After a few moments of bliss, she returned to the present.

"So, when you say you only let someone stay a couple of hours, you mean as long as it takes to have sex? And then what? Kick her to the curb until the next time."

It was bold to ask she realized. Maybe it was the delight from the pretzel flooding her insides. Or maybe Jess's lack of filter was finally rubbing off. Cassie didn't have many fact-finding opportunities to report back to her friend, though Jess asked all the time. Most of those queries ended with Jess's disappointed pout. But now, Cassie not only had the chance but also the lead-in since Lucas had volunteered the insight.

"I make it clear from the start that it's a one-time thing. And when it's over, whether we go to my apartment or a hotel I extricate myself."

She choked. "You extricate yourself? That sounds so clinical." She swallowed the pretzel piece and decided to lay off the rest until Lucas was done confessing. "So you've never been with someone more than once?"

He shook his head. "Never."

Her mind returned to the media coverage of him. For some reason, his high profile and wealth invited a whole level of scrutiny with implications Cassie couldn't begin to understand. That Lucas had to live in such a closed-off way fell heavy on her heart.

She shrugged. "I guess you have to be careful when it comes to letting people in."

"That, and I find it works best for me."

The sounds of the park filled the space between them. On the grass, a group of children played tag while their moms clustered in conversation. Cassie's heart lurched at what might have been.

"Still," she said. "Don't you ever get lonely?"

Again he shook his head, repeating his earlier assertion. "Never."

She couldn't comprehend that level of isolation, but Lucas wasn't like her. Her chest ached with empathy for a man who never knew a life outside of the one that was built around him. He had lived so closed off. Then again, hadn't she shut herself away from the world over the last few years?

Lucas's familiar black car slid to a halt at the curb, signaling the end of their morning.

"You can't leave without trying this." She offered Lucas a piece of the pretzel, and he bucked his head back like it would kill him. "I'll let you off the hook once you do. Promise."

He hesitated but then popped the piece into his mouth. He chewed slowly, then stopped. His cheek raised in one corner.

"It's good, right?" she asked.

"Much better than the train ride." Lucas grinned, his face lit. "Sure I can't give you a ride? I can take you wherever you want to go. I can even wait until you're through in the museum." He lifted his right arm like an oath. "I promise to give you space."

"I'm sure. Thanks."

"Have a good day, Cassie." He paused at the open door. "I almost forgot. Apparently, there's a big auction in Paris next month that coincides with a business trip I'm taking. Maybe you'd want to go."

The world around her seemed to stop. The noise of children playing, brakes squealing, trucks thundering past... All ceased to exist. In its place was a void of reality where Lucas had just invited her to go to...

Paris.

A hum bounced around inside her ears, clouding her head. She opened her mouth to speak, but no words came out.

"I-, uh, I'm..." The world was devoid of sense.

Paris.

"Is that a yes?" His voice came from miles away.

"I'm...not sure. Can I get back to you?" She gulped the knot rising from her stomach into her throat. "I have to check with Jeffrey and Jason and..."

Lucas put up his hand to stop her.

"Of course," he said. "Jason can come, too. If it makes it easier."

She slipped further into the void, standing here in a park she had visited with her dad lifetimes ago, dreaming about Egypt and art and Paris.

"I'll let you know." The words crumbled from her mouth as the reality crashed in.

Lucas retreated into the shelter of the car and it pulled away, leaving her alone on the sidewalk.

The last time she was a few weeks away from going to Paris, her dad had died.

After that, the fellowship and everything it stood for hadn't made sense anymore. She buried her heart and dreams alongside her dad. Her faculty adviser at NYU had implored her to reconsider. Even pushed the fellowship out to give her more time to grieve. He was disappointed six months later when she relinquished the opportunity and reenrolled at the university to get her master's. She took the safe route, her advisor had said on more than one occasion.

No one could understand the level of pain ravaging her body and spirit. Paris would not, *could not*, fix it. That day all those years ago when she had walked out of the hall and away from Paris, numb and depleted by six months of grief, she didn't realize she'd dropped her bus pass until she felt a light tap on her shoulder. Cassie had turned and met a handsome man with a kind, easy smile who picked up the pass and extended it to her. A construction contractor, he was doing work on campus. Would she like to grab a drink later?

That day her path had veered from that of an artist to a wife. And as Cassie made her way to the museum steps, she worried what this change in course might mean for her.

Chapter Twenty-Four

"Paris? Out of thin air?" Jess slumped into the kitchen chair.

"Yeah, it was weird."

Cassie arrived at Jess's fresh from the sanctity of the museum and filled her friend in on the turn of events. The Monet paintings did little to quell the bubble of energy sitting in her chest as her head whirled around Lucas's invitation. She left the museum less than an hour after arriving, too caught up in her own drama to lose herself in anything else.

"And you didn't say yes?" Jess asked.

Cassie shook her head while contemplating her friend. She hadn't been around as much to help with the twins, and while Jess was more than capable of handling her children, the exhaustion tugged at Jess's pale face.

"He's offering you a free trip to Paris. Wait, not free." Jess leaned forward, punctuating the words with an animated hand. "He's going to *pay* for your trip and then *pay you* to buy him art." Jess raised her eyebrows and searched the otherwise empty room. "What am I missing?"

Cassie's coffee cup handle had a well-worn chip that chuffed her thumb as she ran it back and forth.

"I told him I had to think about it. And, you know, talk to Jason."

She had picked up her phone a dozen times before she got here to call Jason, but every time put it away.

"Lucas actually said Jason could come."

This landed about as well as she had expected. Jess stopped mid-sip and gingerly put her cup back down on the table. After reading it like tea leaves for far too long, Jess's shoulders rose with a deep inhale.

"And you still didn't say yes." Her best friend scoffed and sunk back. "What's going on?"

Cassie shrugged. What was holding her back? She had put off going to Paris for too long. Now that she was far removed from a life as an artist, did she have any right lusting after the city? She had sworn if her surgery was a success, she would change. She would stop being scared and timid Cassie, too afraid of outcomes to take risks. She had promised to renew her wanderlust and strike out to explore the world beyond the confines of the boroughs.

She hadn't done anything about it. Yet. Granted it had only been a couple of months, and she was in the midst of this work project. And there was Jason. He remained so enmeshed with the factory it was unlikely he would go with her, not while there were still so many questions about whether the business could become a money maker instead of a money pit.

From across the table, Jess took Cassie's hand in both of hers.

"Go. For more than one reason."

Slowly, she nodded, the taste of bitter and sweet tickling her taste buds. Something about the glint in her friend's eyes gave her pause.

"What reasons?"

Jess withdrew her hand, dragging it back across the table to her coffee cup. She raised an eyebrow cocking her lips to one side.

"You've always wanted to go," Jess said with feigned innocence.

"And?"

Jess started flirting with her coffee, trickling her fingers along the rim and down the handle. "Him." Jess took a long sip from the hot cup and flicked her eyes up to Cassie.

Cassie wasn't sure what she meant until Jess relinquished her mug and smiled the way she did when they had spied a good-looking boy across the bar in college.

"You're crazy, you know that." Heat rushing up through her neck, Cassie stood. She went to the sink and ran the water, dunking dirty dishes beneath it. Her jaw tightened and chest heaved as she fought against the urge to acknowledge the snickers and giggles hitting her in the back.

Then she lost the battle and turned to find Jess in an all-out fit of laughter.

"I'm so glad I amuse you," she huffed.

Jess hiccupped and snorted. "You get so red, Cass. Every single time."

She loaded the dishwasher to keep her crimson face from providing any more ammo.

"Oh come on, Cass! Live a little. Go to Paris with a super-rich and insanely hot man. Spend his money. It sounds like a Hallmark movie, well except—"

"For the fact that I'm married? Yeah. About that." She spun again to face her friend and shook her head.

Jess shrugged off the comment and stood, batting at the air. "It's an adventure." She nudged Cassie with a gentle elbow in her side. "And who knows. Maybe it'll be the exact thing you need to start painting again."

Wiping her hands on a towel, she let these words sink in. Before today, only Jess knew she hadn't picked up a pencil or a brush since the surgery. That heat pulsing in Cassie's neck now licked her ears. She had shared this with Lucas before Jason. Then again, her husband hadn't asked. Lucas had.

Jess's wide blue eyes were encouraging her to do something Cassie had been dreaming about her whole life. But Jess was also sending another clear message.

"You don't think I should ask Jason to go with me," she whispered.

Jess pursed her lips and didn't attempt to mask her feelings.

"I think you've earned the right to have fun, Cass. Can you do that with Jason? Can you let loose? Follow your own path? Or will you be too worried about him? Will you stand up to his opinions and do what you want, or will you bend to his wants like every other time?"

Cassie bit her bottom lip and willed the burning in her throat to go away. All the years of diversion, of moving away from what she wanted and toward what Jason thought was best. In the end, Cassie couldn't blame Jason because she made those choices, not him. He didn't force her to abandon her painting to earn a steady paycheck doing restorations, he only suggested it. He didn't push her to do an extra round of IVF, but he did say so many times he wanted children with her, and he had never liked the idea of adoption.

What about Frank? Cassie had refused to co-sign the loan for that factory. She told Jason she was done bailing Frank out of whatever mess he was in. Again.

It was her number Frank called that night. Her phone held his immortalized voice. Frank's death was the moment everything between her and Jason had turned even further south. Their relationship hadn't been perfect, or even really great, before that, but Frank's death ripped their already stressed seams apart. Though there had been moments of togetherness between them since they were so short and insignificant that she found it hard to hold them. Their grief over all the things they'd never have as a couple ate at both of them.

"Cassie?" Jess said. Her hand settled on Cassie's shoulder.

She moved her cloudy gaze to her best friend. "You're right. I won't ask him to go."

Chapter
Twenty-Five

MONTH SIX

L ucas: Have you decided yet?

The text came through two weeks after he dangled the Paris carrot. Cassie poised her fingers over the screen. Jason's mood had plummeted from moderate to awful, so she still hadn't talked to him. The police department continued to drag its feet on the contract. On more than one morning, after she heard him pacing all night, he was passed out on the couch, cradling a half-empty bottle of whiskey.

Between Jason's long hours and now hers, they didn't have an opportunity to talk. Lucas's renovation was wrapping up, but they still had to finish the walls and decorate. Lucas had agreed to stay out of the space, which gave them nighttime access to the apartment. They used this time to paint, wallpaper, and stage it, without violating the nighttime noise ordinance.

The long days and nights gave Jeffrey plenty of chances to beg Cassie to work for him. Her continued employment would alleviate the financial burden on Jason and allow her to keep one foot in the art world she loved. Not as an artist, at least not yet. Though she walked through art supply stores on a couple of occasions again, running her fingers over sketchbooks and canvases, she still hadn't been able to buy anything.

But the idea of Paris had reignited her creative spark, and the longing to dive back into her own work pulled at her chest. Deep in the recesses of her heart, possibility sprung back to life. This trip could put her back on the road as a reemerging artist.

Her art was the driving force behind taking the risk to restore her hand. But now that she had it back, she was terrified she no longer had anything creative left inside. Maybe the events of her life had depleted every morsel of her soul, leaving her with nothing to pour onto paper or canvas. The thought of picking up a pencil and failing terrified her.

All of this ran through her mind as she hovered by the counter, filling another glass of wine, and contemplating the newest message.

Lucas: If I don't hear from you by morning, I'll assume you aren't going.

A new rattle of irritation grated against her ribs. Granted, she'd had plenty of time to get herself together and give the man an answer. He was doing her a favor, but his motivation remained murky. First the job, then the referral to Dr. Patella, and now, Paris. Cassie couldn't quite land on any discernible motive for his continued generosity, and it tugged at her gut.

"Can you grab me another whiskey before you come in?" Jason called from his chair, jolting her back to the task at hand. Tonight was it. She would end this one way or another.

She poured Jason a glass and brought it to him, working up the nerve to say what she needed.

"You okay?" he asked, his eyes moving over her face for a hint of what might be wrong.

"Actually, yes." She sat down on the couch cushion closest to his chair. "Something came up that we need to talk about."

"Okay." He leaned back and trained his gaze on her.

"I have a chance to go to Paris. To an auction." She inhaled.

His eyes widened in genuine interest. "That's big. How did that happen?"

Her chest stretched with tension. "There are some pieces for Lucas's renovation that I want to nab. Plus, there are items Jeffrey wants me to grab for other clients."

His gaze flicked to her lip, and she released it from her teeth. "Sounds great. So, what's the catch?" His forehead folded along with his eyebrows.

"Lucas is going for a meeting at the same time so we would be traveling together."

A good five seconds passed before Jason blinked. He grabbed his glass from the side table and peered into it, swirling the amber liquid. His eyes followed the glass all the way up to his lips where he drained it in a single swallow.

"How long have you been working for him?" Jason asked, knocking Cassie a bit sideways.

"About six months, I think."

She studied every pore of her husband's face, every line for a hint of what he was thinking. The creases along his forehead peeled apart as he put the glass down. He kept his eyes down, inspecting his hands from back to palm.

"So you're going to Paris with Dalton." His voice was unnaturally neutral. Especially given the implication of his statement.

"No, I wouldn't be with him. I'm sure we aren't even staying at the same hotel. It just made sense that his office coordinates the trip since they overlap, especially since I'm there first and foremost to get items for him." Cassie's mouth scorched, and the words clung to her tongue. "I haven't given him an answer. I wanted to talk to you." She cleared her throat to try very hard to not have this end in a fight.

He rocked forward, his head bobbing in time with some conversation she couldn't hear. After a few beats, he scoffed at whatever the imaginary voice said and swiped a hand over his face, shaking his head.

She bit her lip to keep her internal commentary from spilling out. Now that she was here at this moment, she didn't want to ask for permission.

"If you don't want me to travel with him, I won't. But I'm still going." Her bravado forced his head back up. "I'll open my trust fund and use it to pay my way." She felt, right or wrong, this was a line in the sand.

She hadn't picked up a pencil or a brush since her surgery, but damn it, if going to Paris brought the art back into her heart, it would be worth it. Even if that didn't happen, she would get to close the chapter without the persistent regret of missed opportunities and poor choices.

He shifted. The weight of whether he would bless this venture or fight it hung around him. She knew he didn't like Lucas, even if she didn't understand why. His disdain for the man had been clear from the start, but that never made sense. Lucas was an investor in his business, helping Jason out of a jam. Maybe the fact Jason needed help from a younger, more successful businessman ate at his pride.

But this wasn't about Jason and Lucas and whatever hung between them. It was about her and what she wanted.

The longer the silence went on, the more her head whirred with arguments and counterarguments. Jason didn't need to like Lucas for her to go to Paris. She was capable of choosing how to spend her time and with whom. And she was making money, unlike Jason. His paycheck stopped a few weeks ago. Hers was steady, and it kept them afloat. How dare he continue to try and control her and make her fe—

"It sounds like you're going whether I agree or not." He huffed and moved his attention back to her.

"Yes," she said, crossing her arms. "Though I prefer your support."

He lowered his head, drawing a ragged breath. "You should go. With him."

His voice jolted her heart like a lightning bolt. "Really?" She'd prepared herself for battle, but now that it wasn't necessary, that nervous energy surged toward excitement.

"I don't want to stop you when you've always wanted to go. And why pay when you can go for free." The tone of his voice was fringed with resignation and reluctance.

He rose with a grimace painted across his face and a hand planted on his lower back. "I'm going to bed." He moved away one stiff step at a time.

"Thank you," she called, left with the nagging feeling that something was off. It was more than his steps that seemed pained; so were his words.

***

Cassie sat in Lucas's private plane and aside from the crew, it carried only her, Lucas, and Arthur. She had flown twice. Both trips had been on large planes carrying hundreds of passengers. Once as a child to visit her maternal grandparents in South Dakota. She remembered little about the trip itself except her grandmother cried and her grandfather avoided her at all costs.

She didn't understand why they weren't like other grandparents who brought treats and read books using different voices for each character. When she was older, Dad explained the two never got over her mother's death. Seeing Cassie tore the scab off the grief, opening a painful wound. She never did see or hear from them again.

The second flight was to Jess and Greg's wedding on the Outer Banks of North Carolina, where Greg grew up. The wedding party spent the week leading up to the nuptials traversing the sandy shore and small towns dotting the landscape. Through a vodka haze, Cassie had promised to relocate there when Jess and Greg did.

Now, she tried not to freak out as she stared into the black void as the plane hurtled over the open sea. They had taken off at midnight so the passengers could sleep to reduce the jet lag. The trip would transport them six hours ahead of New York, and in just enough time to get to Global House Paris by the one o'clock auction.

"Can I get you anything, Ms. Reynolds?" The stewardess was very sweet and diligent in attending to her three passengers.

"Not yet. Thank you," Cassie said. The young woman moved on to Lucas and Arthur. Both hunched over a table still working like it was noon and not the middle of the night. Lucas didn't make eye contact with the stewardess, merely shook his head. Arthur at least had the decency to smile at her while declining.

The last few days were a blur. Her body remained ravaged by exhaustion, between work and the shopping trips Jess insisted they take. Cassie never wore sexy clothes, and Jess felt it her duty to spice Cassie's wardrobe up for certain occasions. Like the slip dress Jess insisted Cassie wear in her wedding. It had been simple, but its low cut and tight fit hugged her body far more than Cassie liked. She was modest, perhaps a result of being raised by a single dad. Her friend didn't care that Cassie was uncomfortable showing off her body. It was Jess's attempt at giving Cassie a confidence boost. Jason loved how Cassie looked in that dress, but not how others looked at her.

He would surely harbor that same love-hate for the little red dress Jess had insisted Cassie bring to Paris if he had been around to see it. When she resisted, Jess said if there was ever a chance to wear something like that, it was thousands of miles away in Paris, where she would never see any of those people again.

A sigh sunk Cassie deeper into the cushy leather seat back. Things with Jason were so hard. Navigating his moods added to her exhaustion and stress.

Something wasn't right with him, and she hoped it didn't mean she'd face another surprise like the foreclosure notice when she returned. He hadn't even made it home to drive her to the airport, sending some last-minute bullshit text she should grab a cab or risk being late.

Staring out the plane windows into the black void, something inside Cassie's chest snapped. The last thread of hope Jason would make a genuine change was now gone.

What was it Dad used to say?

The straw that breaks the camel's back often falls the lightest.

Cassie turned off the overhead light and leaned the seat back. Sleep hadn't come easy over the last couple of nights, no doubt fueled by anticipation and worry. But now her lids grew heavy as she nestled into the soft seat.

"We're landing soon," Lucas said.

She startled upright to find him sitting in the seat opposite her.

"Where did you come from?" She squinted against the illuminated cabin.

"It is my plane." A smirk twitched beneath his all-business expression.

She shifted and realized the light was coming from outside. The darkness of a few seconds ago had been replaced by blue skies and puffy white clouds. She craned her neck at the land sprawling beneath them.

"How long have I been sleeping?" she asked, smoothing her hair and trying to rouse herself.

"A while," Lucas replied. "Don't worry, I didn't take pictures of you drooling."

Her face heated and she swiped her mouth with the back of her hand.

"I wasn't drooling." Her skin felt dry, and now she watched as his smirk spread into a full-blown smile. No one was more transformed by a smile than Lucas. It softened his entire demeanor and made him more human.

"You weren't drooling," he said. "Just snoring."

"Don't you have a rule about offending people on your plane or something?" The embarrassment gripping her threatened to melt her into the seat.

"The only rule I have is I get to do whatever I want on my plane." He returned to his normal straight face, but his gaze flickered up over Cassie's right shoulder. The stewardess sauntered past, and Lucas glanced back at the woman's backside.

Cassie rolled her eyes. "You are such a cliché."

Lucas looked back to her, his left eyebrow propped by a smoldering grin. "I've been called worse."

Chapter Twenty-Six

The auction lasted seven long hours, but Cassie wasn't sure she blinked the entire time. The pieces up for grabs ranged from ancient Egyptian pottery to a Renoir. She caught her mouth hanging open more than once at the elaborate affair between the available pieces and the way the audience had tossed around figures in the millions like mere play money. She couldn't wait to come back again tomorrow.

She sank into the car on the way to the hotel and readied herself for the ride. The trip that morning to the auction house had pushed her nerves as the driver whipped around packed traffic circles and weaved in and out of cars. When she had spied the Eiffel Tower, she fought to strangle the burn at the back of her throat. Now on her way back to the hotel, Cassie's body succumbed to the grief she had kept a tight lid on for so long. Alone, with nothing but the shadows of her parents looming, she allowed the sadness to slip from her eyes.

She managed to pull herself together by the time the car reached the hotel. The facade, a grandiose Louis XIV white mason stone, was beautiful, but Cassie hadn't envisioned Lucas choosing such a spot. Then again, it was quite possible he was staying elsewhere.

Her perception of the hotel changed the minute she walked through the door. Over-sized chandeliers dripped with crystal inlaid with gold. The sculptured molding lining the marbled ceiling complemented the tiles beneath her feet. In a matter of seconds, she had stepped back in time into the greeting area of a French aristocrat's long-abandoned domain.

She gave her name to the lone attendant behind a large wooden desk, and the woman nodded while barking out orders in French to a porter who darted forward.

"Mademoiselle Reynolds, your bags are in your room." The hotelier spoke careful English through a thick accent. "Reginald will escort you." She nodded and handed the man the key.

The grandeur of the converted manor enchanted her as she trailed behind Reginald to her assigned room, which was quite a bit larger than Cassie expected. Its interior was modern, filled with a mix of contemporary luxuries with highlights of old charm. The centerpiece was an inviting king-sized bed, the ornately carved headboard inlaid with ebony and copper elaborations. The duvet and sheets looked so plush, beckoning her to fall in and forget about everything else for the night. She moved past it to the window and looked out over the street a few floors below. Cassie didn't mind the view or lack thereof. She knew the magic that waited; she didn't need to see it.

But some of that magic seemed out of reach. The auction house had buzzed with the latest strike by Parisian public works employees. The details of their demands centered around poor working conditions and subpar pay, but it meant there would be no bus service, and the popular tourist stops would be closed. While strikes of this nature and size happened frequently in Paris, they could last a week or more, ensuring the monuments and museums would remain shuttered.

Cassie fell into the chaise under the windows and checked her messages. Though it was after two in the afternoon New York time, Jason hadn't responded to any of her texts, but she did note that he had read them. A fresh batch of irritation burned her chest.

A knock at the door startled her. She hadn't ordered room service yet, although the grumbling from her belly told her it was a good idea.

Opening the door, she came face-to-face with Lucas. He looked like he had that morning, rested and ready to go. Was he human?

"Is something wrong?" she asked.

"No. Just wondering how things went."

"It was good. We didn't get everything today, mostly because there were at least three sheiks from Dubai driving up the prices. But I got a nice painting for your foyer."

He nodded his head and remained otherwise unmoved.

It was awkward, or maybe that was Cassie's groggy brain.

"Do you want to come in?" she asked.

"I actually want you to come out."

"Like into the hallway?"

Lucas chuckled and shook his head. "No, like out of the hotel. I'm going to one of my favorite clubs, and I want you to come."

She stepped back into her room. This was an easy pass. Her body screamed for food, a hot shower, and sleep.

"I'm exhausted. Plus, that's not really my scene."

Lucas's cool stare never left hers. Cassie wasn't sure what to say or do, so she remained silent to wait him out.

"Remember that time I told you I didn't ride the subway or eat food out of carts?"

Her gut dropped.

She gulped. "Yes."

"And yet, I rode the subway and ate a pretzel that came from a cart." He clasped his hands behind his back, pulling the buttons of the pewter button-down tighter against his chest.

She raised her hand in objection. "But you fought me and technically, you finished *my* pretzel."

"I did them. Even though I didn't want to. That's my point." He tilted his chin back.

"This is different. I'm jet-lagged and I haven't eaten dinner yet. I've bar—"

"Meet me downstairs in half an hour." His gaze swept over her, leaving behind a disconcerting trail of heat. "And you may want to change."

He turned away without another word and walked toward the elevators.

She couldn't protest, mostly because words escaped her. Cassie's defenses were at an all-time low. While she didn't mind being labeled a hypocrite for refusing, she did mind Lucas thinking her ungrateful.

But the last thing she wanted to do was get dressed up and leave this warm and cozy room.

Shit.

She called Jess, panic rising as she opened the suitcase at the foot of the bed. After four unanswered rings, Cassie gave up and threw the phone down on the silk comforter. Before she stepped away, it rang.

"Hey," Cassie said.

"Everything okay?" Jess asked. A lilt of sleep drifted through the phone and Cassie guessed Jess had snuck in a nap alongside the twins. She would give anything to play the sleeping game with them right now.

"Yeah, it's fine. I didn't mean to call. Sorry." She sifted through her suitcase, looking for an outfit worthy of a night out in Paris with Lucas.

"God, you can't even lie over the phone. What's wrong?" Jess huffed.

"Fine." She gave Jess the quick version of her current dilemma.

"I don't know why you're worked up. You're in Paris to have a good time."

"What am I going to do at a club?"

"I don't know, Cass. Dance? Drink? Flirt? Have..." Jess rasped dramatically. "Fun?"

Cassie paused her search when her hands hit soft fabric.

"And wear the red dress," Jess continued as if she had sensed exactly what Cassie's hands had found.

"I can't." She pulled out the dress by the teeny-tiny spaghetti straps that crisscrossed the very low back.

"Yes, you can. Do you want to embarrass your boss? Go looking like you do right now."

"It's not that ba—"

"Wear the damn dress, Cassie. Go to a nightclub. Meet a hot French man or two and live like you're 36, not 76. Please, if only so your oldest and dearest friend can live vicariously through you while she's stuck at a sink washing poop out of Avengers underwear!"

Cassie stopped as Jess's words sunk in. She wasn't dead. She was still young with plenty of life left in her. In this city of her bedtime stories, she had the choice. She could stay shut away and hide from the pulse of the night beyond the hotel.

Or she could step out and experience it on her terms.

Trepidation falling away, she smiled as excitement bubbled in her chest.

Chapter
Twenty-Seven

T he pumping music thundered through Cassie's body as she stepped
through the dark doorway of the club on Lucas's arm. Sweat, alcohol, cigarettes, and pot converged in her nostrils, spurring her eyes to water
and burning her throat as they moved through the blue-lit bar.

Lucas's imposing form remained a few steps ahead, lips to a cocktail
server's ear. Cassie blinked against the haze to keep him in her sights. People
pushed in around, swirling, and threw her bearings out of whack. She
concentrated on Lucas's midnight blue form ahead. He eventually stopped
and waited for her to catch up. His lips were moving, and she craned her
neck toward him, but the music blaring all around made it impossible. He
shook his head and put a hand on her lower back, guiding her to a roped-off
booth.

She climbed in, mesmerized by the scene. The booth was tight, and
Cassie had to sit with her legs to one side but it afforded a full view of the
dance floor. Crushing hordes jumping, gyrating, shaking forms illuminated for seconds at a time by the sweeping spotlights.

"What are you drinking this evening, Monsieur Dalton?" The waitress
bent toward them. Her painted-on barely-there black dress was unable to
contain her heaving chest spilling out, fully displaying her dark nipples.

"Macallan black. Neat." Lucas turned to Cassie.

"Uh, wine?"

"Bring a bottle of Montrachet," he said. The waitress winked at him before leaving.

Cassie tightened the black cardigan across her chest and smoothed the fabric down over her thighs. It didn't afford the kind of coverage she wanted, but it was her attempt at modesty. The teeny-tiny dress was designed for a petite figure, not her taller frame that was mostly legs. It ended a good five inches above the knee, so sitting proved challenging.

The sweater provided peace of mind, though. If something happened to the skinny straps across the bare skin of her back, she wouldn't be left with everything hanging out. She hadn't exactly packed a bra that would work with a backless dress.

Nipple Waitress returned and set down their drinks, giving Cassie's glass a quick pour before sliding to Lucas's ear, saying something Cassie couldn't catch. She lifted her glass and tried to stop her eyes from rolling out of her head.

When the waitress left, Lucas lifted his Macallan. "To Paris. And you." His gaze again swept her head to, well, not quite toe... "Look at you out at a club. Wearing a sweater."

She tilted up her chin and raised her glass. "Sorry, I didn't pack anything that highlighted my nipples." She tilted the glass to his, and then took a sip. The wine tickled her taste buds, sweet and rich against her parched mouth. She had to stop herself from knocking it back too quickly.

"Everyone has nipples, Cassie. I'm sure yours are just as nice as hers."

She eyed him, but his attention had already gone elsewhere. She followed his line of sight to two women standing opposite their table. The taller, a brunette, stared straight back at Lucas and dragged her tongue across her lips, while the shorter woman pressed against her, whispering.

Cassie scoffed and gave herself a full pour from the bottle of Montrachet that had been left on the table. She sat back and sipped the buttery nectar, letting its sweetness hum in her forehead. Her shoulders eased and her neck relaxed. She finished off her glass too soon and the buzz reverberated from head to toe.

Lucas moved closer and refilled her glass but continued his roving of the two women.

"Are you going to eye-fuck them all night?" A giggle squeaked from her lips. Lucas turned his icy stare to her. Something dangerous danced across his face.

"Eye-fucking sets the stage for the real thing, Cass." He sat back and expanded his arms across the back of the booth, tickling the few hairs loosened from her twist. A chill coursed down her neck.

"But which one will you choose?"

"Who says I have to."

"That's not against the rules?"

When Lucas leaned closer, the smolder of alcohol from his lips heated her nose and skin. "Not if they both leave at the same time."

His fiery eyes lapped her skin like flames licking a wall and forced her gaze down to the open buttons of his black shirt and the hint of blond hair escaping from it.

The spell broke when the two women entered his orbit. Lucas diverted his attention to them, and Cassie's gut unclenched in relief. She needed to walk away. Shimmying out of the booth, she peeled her thighs away from the plastic padded seat.

Once a few steps away, she turned back to survey the scene. Lucas held court in a tailored suit that likely cost more than what the two young women made in a year. His long body stretched casually in the booth, exuding the true nature of his role in all of this: he didn't need them or anyone else. People served him, not the other way around.

She floated away, putting some much-needed distance between them.

***

Cassie propped herself against the railing, in awe of the colorful characters crowding the dance floor. She cursed herself for leaving her phone behind because she'd heard some of the funniest pick-up lines, mostly around her height, and she wanted to send Jess the highlights.

"You must be here for fashion week."

"I bet you play basketball."

And Cassie's personal favorite; a very short man who simply stated, "I want to mount you like Everest."

But more than anything, Cassie wished her best friend was here. She wanted to share this night, this trip, with someone. The ache pelted holes in her chest. She got along fine by herself and she would make the most out of this visit, but the sacredness of this city, made mythical by the parents she yearned for, dampened her spirits.

Then there was Jason. What would he say if he saw her tonight, in this dress that garnered so many lusty glances and lingering touches?

She scanned the dance floor full of people living life in this moment, not the past where she tended to reside. She wanted to get there, too. Maybe this could finally be the place to do it. She shook her head, trying to get the world to make sense. The battle in her mind raged amid this place so full of life. Jason's deepening absence, his apathy toward her, and his passive disapproval of her work continued to weigh. Had it always been this way? When had things gone so wrong?

Frank.

His death took with it whatever life had remained in their marriage. Not only because of the financial burden it led Jason to bear but also because of the guilt that had carved a permanent place in their life.

Her stomach bubbled. The fresh pastries from her room proved insufficient to soak up the wine. She needed to go, get some food, and drift away from reality for a few hours. But first, she needed a bathroom. She clutched the railing for a beat before venturing toward the toilet sign in the distance, forging ahead one step at a time.

In the bathroom, she crumbled into the velvet settee. She stripped off the cardigan and leaned back against the cool tile wall. Women converged around sinks and mirrors, adjusting makeup, hair, and cleavage, swapping lipstick, cigarettes, joints, tampons, and condoms.

Even amid the noise, she heard the truth she had silenced for too long: she and Jason weren't going to make it. Sins committed long before this latest round of his financial mistakes rattled around in her head. His promises of a steady income. The questions about why she wore what she did. The suggestions to cut her hair. The sighs whenever she mentioned plans with Jess. The support for taking the restoration job that had signaled the end of her own painting, without once questioning if that was what she really wanted to do.

Divorce had whispered through her brain before, but Cassie hadn't dared give it space or air to breathe. But in this bathroom, it was hard for her to think of much else.

Waves of truth crash over and over against her heart. The clamor of the other women coming and going added to the symphony of noise rushing through her head, making none of them discernible from the other. Abruptly, one voice whispered with such clarity it was all she could hear.

This is not the life you're meant to live.

She jolted upright, animated by the message she'd muted for too long. This trip didn't have anything to do with Jason or her marriage. This was about her and all the dreams she had back-burnered for so long. Conscious choices she made to dismantle the very thing that made her who she was—and for what? Why did she give up on herself when her entire childhood was built around the opposite. Now that Cassie was here, she would set aside the right and wrong, good and bad, shoulds and shouldn'ts of her least supportive voice: her husband. And listen, for once, to her own.

Exiting the bathroom, she swayed one way and then the other in time to the rhythm rippling from all sides. Lights flashed, and bodies clashed as she made her way to the center of the dance floor. Smoke, sweat, citrus, and cedar swirled around, and she reveled in the renewed life that shot through her.

Someone moved in close behind her as she rocked her hips back and forth. Little by little, she let go. Large hands gripped her shoulders, moved with her, and a hard body met hers. When he pulled her back, she sank into him. Hands coursed all the way down the fabric of her dress, landing on bare thighs beneath the rising hem.

He was tall and the heat of his breath on the skin behind her ear prompted her to stand taller, willing his lips closer to her neck. He sucked her neglected skin. Shivers surged through her as the moment continued and his lips, hands, and body stayed on hers.

She rocked her hips back, prompting a moan from him that vibrated her skin under his lips. Eyes closed, she spun. Head back, she gave him full access to her neck. His head bent into that space and his mouth trickled from her left ear down to her collarbone. He cupped her bottom in strong hands and lifted her slightly, forcing the breath from her lungs.

She gripped the back of his neck as he moved his mouth and head away from her. His icy blue gaze devoured her whole as she gasped.

"Lucas!"

Chapter
Twenty-Eight

C assie ripped her body from Lucas's and made a break for the club door. She needed to get out of the building before she burned up.

The night air raked her steamy skin, prickling it. Her sweater abandoned, she shivered, but then something hit her shoulders. Lucas's jacket drenched in cedar musk and citrus surrounded her. It hung long and loose and she gripped it, accepting the offering and nestling into its warmth.

Then his car appeared, and he guided her in before shutting the door.

Please make him stay at the club.

When he climbed in the other side, Cassie turned her head and stared out the window for the trip. Things were different now. Very different. She had lost control, made the choice to do so, and now everything had changed.

That dance... His hands on her body... His mouth scorching her skin... The fire he had lit still raged in her gut.

"I don't suppose I can convince you to join me in my room."

Her back stiffened at his words. She shook her head, willing him to stop.

"Come on, Cass. You know it'll be worth it."

She relaxed her posture and closed her eyes. She still didn't face him, wasn't sure at the moment if she would ever be able to look at him again.

"No one has to know," he continued.

She opened her eyes as they turned a corner. Ahead was the hotel.

"He doesn't have to know."

The words slapped her across the face and sank to the bottom of her stomach.

"I would know." Her words were barely a whisper as she swallowed.

The car slowed to an idle. Then, as the one in front moved, it slid into the space at the hotel entrance to let them out.

"Cassie." His breath fanned across her neck. "You know it'll be good. That I'll be good."

When the driver put the car in park, Cassie burst out the door, unwilling and unable to remain in a shared space with Lucas.

Even at the late hour, the lobby teemed with people spilling out of eateries and bars. She made her way through, head angled to the ground. She felt the shadow of shame was firmly affixed and visible for everyone else to see. Maybe not so much for what she'd done, but for what she *wanted* to do.

The elevator stood open waiting, and she slapped the button as she entered. Before the doors could close, Lucas stepped inside, his midnight blue pants and black not-quite-buttoned-up shirt throwing gas on the spark igniting in her core.

They reached her floor without sound, only the pulse of the vacant space between them. She held her breath, waiting for the doors to free her from the desire surging from every pore.

"You know it's a one-time thing with me. I won't pursue you again."

When the doors tore apart, Cassie stepped towards the threshold, still holding his jacket around her. She inhaled the musk of it and closed her eyes hoping to see something, anything, that would propel her to her room.

All she saw was the want and the desire left by years of an unfulfilled life and love.

The elevator doors whispered shut before her, and just like that, Cassie made another choice.

***

Stepping into Lucas's luxury suite stripped every bit of breath from Cassie's lungs. Floor-to-ceiling sliders bordered the living room to the front, and the dining room to the right, giving a one-hundred-eighty-degree view of the Parisian skyline. The Eiffel Tower glittered just beyond the panes. The lights dripped, popped, sparked, and danced, capturing her in the tower's hypnotic splendor.

She stepped closer and the beauty squeezed her chest. This place was her origin story, and while she stood transfixed by the scene outside the window, the ghosts of the past hovering close, Lucas peeled the jacket from her body.

Cassie found his reflection in the glass. He was unbuttoning his cuffs, his head tilted and trained on her body. Her skin hummed and her insides quivered watching this distorted Lucas wanting her like he did. When the image stepped closer, his hands were in her hair, untying the messy twist and sending her loose hair rushing down her back.

He inhaled the smell of her hair and his hands raked down the messy tendrils. If she shifted backward ever so slightly...

As she moved, he clutched her shoulders and buried his mouth in her neck. He groaned louder than he had on the dance floor, or perhaps it only seemed so because here it was only them.

He gathered her in his arms, and the leanness of his muscles secured her to him. His breath tickled her ears, sending a fresh round of shivers coursing through her chest. He ran his lips from her left temple down to the curve of her shoulder. Her body grew heavy with anticipation and before she could right herself, Lucas spun her around and crashed his lips into hers.

The heat of that kiss melted all lingering hesitation. She threaded her hands around his neck and pulled him in closer, sucking, and nibbling his lips. His hands worked from the base of her head down her back, settling firmly on her bottom, pulling her into him, seeming panicked that some unknown force would separate them.

His hands found the zipper along the side of her ribcage. He eased it down and, without breaking their union, he slid the small straps away from her shoulders, pushing the fabric down until it pooled at her feet.

Lucas stared down at the naked flesh exposed by the loss of her dress. She watched his chest rise and fall as she unbuttoned his shirt. The gravel in his breath rubbed as his gaze absorbed every inch of her. When she had unclasped the last button, he stripped off the shirt and gathered her to him. Their flesh met for the first time with nothing between them. He ravaged her lips with his and her body molded into his hands.

Cassie fought to separate from him. The muscles rippling beneath his clothes were now laid bare and she moved her fingertips from the back of his neck down to the ridge of muscle between his pecs. His skin was smooth, except for the light trickle of blond hair fanned across his chest. Her mouth watered as she traced the line that split him from left to right, all the way down to his belly button and beyond.

She looked up at him and realized it was the first time they had made eye contact since the dance floor. The intense desire pulsing in his gaze pulled at her insides in a way she had never felt before.

Her fingers continued their journey down to his belt, and she loosened the buckle.

As she went about undressing him, she caught him tilting his head studying her. Lucas stepped out of his pants and reached for her again. Instead of holding her, he lifted her off the ground in one swift and easy movement. She wrapped her legs around his hips and clasped his back. It was as if they'd done this a million times before. He took one, two, three steps. Then her back was up against the glass, the cold pane making her gasp. He smiled against her mouth before pulling his away and trailing the softest caresses of his lips down to her bare breasts.

Within seconds, he peppered kisses around the fleshy mound of one breast and then the other. She moaned and tightened her legs around him. He swirled his tongue across one nipple, teasing her before he drew it into his mouth. The sensation of it tore through her, and she cried out, melting from the inside out.

Lucas carried her to the bedroom and laid her down and his mouth and hands resumed their magic. He hooked his fingers in her panties and pushed them down, sliding his tongue from her chest to her belly. When his body left hers, the bed sank as he moved between her legs. He parted them and whispered his lips along the inside of her right thigh as she raised up to watch him, each move further stoking the fire raging inside her core.

His gaze lifted then, capturing her, daring her to keep watching before again dipping his head and sliding his tongue over her. Cassie clenched at the covers as he worked her into a state of frenzied chaos.

"Do you want me inside you?" he growled against her throbbing skin.

"Yes."

He stood, reaching into a drawer by the bed. He slid off his boxers, then opened the condom and rolled it down over himself.

As Lucas loomed over her nakedness with his own for what felt like forever, Cassie was sure no breath came into her lungs. Then he spread her open and eased himself into her. His moan as she absorbed him entranced her. She reveled in him moving over her and inside her, of them moving together, fitting perfectly. Two halves of a broken whole.

She dangled on the edge of reality, the cliff, and her eyes watered as every nerve impulse fired, pushing her closer to going over. Breath built inside her chest as pleasurable pain grew between her legs. When Lucas lifted her legs over his shoulders, allowing them to move together even better, the sensation of his body pressing into hers was the last nudge she needed.

She tightened her legs, knowing it was time to release all that pain, pleasure, and joy she had kept inside for far too long. Her cry grew, along with the pressure housed deep inside her core.

Grabbing his arms and arching her back, she tore apart from the inside out. All the color in the world erupted at once from her. It was euphoric, something wholly new and unfelt, until now. All the years spent in her previous life had never come close to the pure feral bliss of this moment.

When Lucas's body moved away, her eyes sprang open. Before she knew what was happening, he was back on his knees, his head between her legs, and his tongue triggered an aftershock, prompting tears, and her thigh muscles tightened around his ears.

Breathless, her legs contracted and shivered when Lucas reinserted himself. He worked himself into his own frenzy. Beads of sweat dripped as he released himself into her, crying out. His eyes were closed and his hands balled into fists on either side of the bed about her. He seized and shivered, dropping his head, revealing the thatch of matted hair at the nape of his neck where she'd grabbed him not long before. The beauty of him overwhelmed her, as did a strange sensation pulsing from the pit of her stomach.

But it wasn't happiness or contentment. It was something quite different, equally as filling, but bitter. It sucked at her soul and gnawed at her gut until she knew this thing she'd done was anything but beautiful.

Shame railed at the happy flutters moshing about in her stomach, making her feel like she would vomit. Regret ravaged and compelled her to separate from Lucas, pushing him from her. She got up and staggered under the power of betrayal surging through her.

She moved quickly into the sitting room and gathered her dress from the floor. Pulling it over her head, she jammed her hands through the straps while moving toward the door.

Truth sounded inside her head as she ran from his room. She would not be able to come back from this, carrying a guilt no amount of penance would ever absolve.

She had chosen to do something she wanted. Like every other time, she'd now pay the price and her world would fall apart because of it.

Chapter
Twenty-Nine

The Parc Monceau's rising green canopies and brick-raised pathways speckled with colored flowers unfolded before her. Cassie had memorized its layout, studying it in print since her undergrad days, preparing herself to see it in person, walk its storied paths, and discover its whispered secrets.

"Do you mind?"

Cassie blinked at the camera extended toward her. She followed the length of the arm until she met the eyes of an older gentleman smiling and nodding at her. The broken English wasn't threaded with French, but another accent, German, perhaps. Either way, Cassie shook off the haze that had swallowed her all day and snapped a few pics of him in front of the black fence.

The man thanked her and moved along, allowing her a clear shot at the wrought iron gate. She stepped to it; nose pushed between the slats like a runaway dog trying to find a way back inside.

"Always on the outside looking in, Cassie," she whispered into the void.

Monet had come the closest to capturing the heart and soul of this English-style garden springing to life in the heart of Paris. And here she was, finally able to walk its famed bricks and breathe its mossy-sweet scent.

Except she couldn't. Like all the other public parks and monuments, it was closed during the strike.

Even so, just being here, standing in its presence, knowing Monet stood here at some point, sent a pulse surging to Cassie's fingertips where her right hand gripped the iron gate. She pressed forward and inhaled the peace and energy that hit her inside and out. It was different, and yet so familiar.

Her phone buzzed from her bag, interrupting her musings. When Cassie dug it out, the picture of Jess sticking her tongue out flashed across the screen. Cassie and Jess had exchanged a couple of short texts throughout the day, all centering around that damn phone call in the wee hours of the Parisian morning. Fresh out of a shower she had hoped would scald Lucas's smell from her, she had been stupid enough to leave Jess a voicemail, regretting it ever since.

"Hey." She cleared her throat and began idly walking along the iron fence.

"Jesus Christ, Cassie! You were supposed to call me." Jess's voice shrilled through the phone.

"Sorry."

"That message you left scared the shit out of me!" Her friend gasped for breath and sniffled.

"I never should've called that late. I guess I just..." She trailed off, not having a clue how to say the words.

"What the hell happened?"

Pressure rose in her chest. The regret she'd attempted to wall off from reality dripped in. She wasn't sure where to start, what to say, or whether she should say anything at all.

"Cassie?"

She inhaled and looked around, finally nodding.

"I had sex with Lucas last night."

A breeze rippled through the air, and Cassie let it wash over her. The energy pulsing as she stood at the fence was gone, replaced by unease, disgust, and every other close relative of shame. The airwaves between her and Jess deadened, along with Cassie's breath.

"Okay." Jess had used her let's-fix-this voice.

A chuckle mixed with a groan surged out. She stopped ambling and dropped to a bench along the roadway. "Yeah. So."

"And the message about something horrible happening that you will never get over was the sex with Lucas?"

"Yes."

Jess hummed low, a sign she was processing and formulating, to concoct that just-right answer.

"Did you tell anyone else?" Jess asked.

"Who else am I telling? It's not like I have a long list." But the implication snapped in her brain, connecting the dots.

"So no one knows but you and me? And Lucas."

"Yes."

"Good. Keep it that way," Jess directed.

A dog rushed by, his leash dragging behind him. A little boy squealed, chasing after, giggling, and calling out to the white fluffy pooch.

"Jess, I'm going to have to tell Jason. I feel awful."

"I understand that, but you're in the city of your dreams, and he doesn't need to know. Not yet. Maybe..." Jess paused. "...he never needs to know."

Cassie glanced around at the people filtering by in pairs or groups, all fanning out, meandering through the streets to eat, drink, dance, and any other measure of togetherness. She squeezed her eyes shut.

"I feel so guilty," she whispered. The pain in her chest didn't ease with the words.

"I know."

"I love Jason."

"Cass, that doesn't always mean what you think." Jess was an intelligent woman. Her years as a therapist had given her a wide range of exposure to every gamut of humans. The tales she told Cassie always fascinated her. Jess never outed her clients by name. But she shared enough that Cassie could form a complete picture of the pain that ate away at them.

One of those instances had been a man who woke up in the middle of the night to find his wife whispering to a lover on the phone. When he confronted her the next day, she shrugged and said she'd been out of love with him for years. When he asked why she stayed, she said she was too scared to leave and enter an unknown world. The man went to counseling to try and win his wife back, and Jess worked to bring him around to one simple line of thinking: not everything is worth saving.

"Fear and devotion do not equal love," Jess continued.

"I'm not afraid of Jason."

"I don't mean it that way. I mean fear of the unknown."

"But he's my husband." She scanned the crowd for some explanation as to how she could let things go so wrong. "I'm awful."

"You're human. And a damn good one at that."

"Good humans don't cheat."

"I didn't say it was ideal, Cass. But maybe now you know the thing you haven't wanted to admit for years."

Tears welled behind her lids as she let Jess's words fill the void in her head. A young couple fluttered about before her, him with his hands in her hair, while she bantered on with full pouty lips. It was a gut punch. What she saw in them she had never completely felt with Jason. A spark. Passion throbbed in the air between them.

Kind of like...

Lucas.

That had been the thing between them all these months. The energy—the vibe—that pulsed between them that she never quite understood. It hit her across a table. A train car. A sidewalk.

"I'm coming home tomorrow," she said, speaking the moment the thought entered her mind. Jeffrey could bid through a remote proxy. She could go home to set things right with Jason.

"That's not the answer," Jess scolded.

"It is."

"And what are you going to do? Come home tomorrow and confess your sins to your husband? You'll have to hunt him down at work to do it." Jess scoffed.

An unsettling urge to hang up on Jess needled its way into her head. "That's not fair. He works hard for us."

"Correction. He works hard for *him*, Cass. There's a difference."

Fire lapped at Cassie's earlobes and scorched her neck. What Jess was saying simply wasn't true. For all the wrongs that happened to Cassie, Jason had been there; he'd seen her through them.

"I know you're about to come up with a list trying to prove me wrong, but don't. Not now," Jess shot back as if in Cassie's head.

She sat devoid of the words she needed to retort as Jess shut her down.

"He's supported me, Jess. You know that."

"No, I don't know that. Everything he's done that you think is supportive has been for his own benefit."

Lava pushed up from Cassie's fiery core. That crossed a line, even for Jess.

"I had sex with someone else! That wasn't Jason's fault. Stop attacking him for something that's all on me. You don't know everything."

Cassie clamped her mouth shut, cutting off her words. She and Jess had only fought once before, on the night Cassie had told Jess that Jason professed his love for her after three dates. Cassie had thought it romantic, a testament to Jason's comfort and confidence. But then, like now, Jess was combative, telling Cassie it wasn't romantic, but delusional and toxic. A red flag unfurled and flapping in the middle of a calm spring day.

When Cassie jumped to defend Jason, Jess had leveled her with an unfair blow. She had brought up Cassie's dad, saying it was too soon to dismiss the possibility this was an attempt to fill the void left by a man Cassie had adored above all else.

She couldn't believe how Jess had acted then, and she couldn't now. The same defenses rose back in her throat, but they died before her voice could give them life. She didn't want to fight. She didn't have it in her bruised, battered, and nearly broken heart.

"Jess?" Cassie said.

Had she hung up? Did Cassie just lose another person?

"I'm here." Jess passed a heavy breath to Cassie's ear and relief washed through her, even if it was tinged with alarm. "I love you, Cass. And I want you to get that fire back. That love of life. The thing that's gone out little by little ever since your dad died. I want you to be happy. That's all I've ever wanted for you."

"What if it's too late?"

"It's never too late."

Her shoulders bounced up and down as sorrow drained away. Jess knew her heart like no one else. And right now, it was broken wide open and had been for a long time. The loss of her family, those from the past and those she would never have, chipped away at her heart, her spirit, her very essence. Then at the loss of her hand, a dream had ended which began in this city all those years ago when her parents' footsteps whooshed down the hall of the Louvre, the love made between them all but cementing art in her cells and soul.

The hand in her lap was no longer dead. Cassie moved the fingers, balled them up, and squeezed her nails into her palm, biting her lip against the sting. Her heart railed against her ribs, pushing, surging. Her story was not over. Not yet.

"Please, don't come home tomorrow," Jess said. "Just live. Reality will be here when you get back. And we can figure things out together."

Chapter Thirty

Lucas

Lucas took his drink out to the balcony. The frustration from the day washed over him, but the scotch would ease it. The meetings were done for now, though the deal wasn't.

His phone alerted him to a text from an unknown number.

She's on her way up.

He put the phone back in his pocket and took a long draw from his glass.

Cassie had been incommunicado all day. Though the auction had ended hours ago, she hadn't returned either his phone calls or texts. He entertained the possibility she flew back to New York, though Stephanie assured him that hadn't happened, at least not on the company's dime. But that didn't mean Cassie hadn't done it on her own. She could do so much.

The entire situation had been a distraction all day, which he didn't appreciate or need. He was on the brink of brokering his company's biggest single acquisition, and all Lucas could think about was a woman who was ignoring him. It was absurd, and even now, he admonished himself. Cassie was not his concern. His company was.

Yet, when he had returned to the hotel, he slipped the concierge some cash to intercept Cassie and direct her to his suite. Lucas shook his head against his stupidity. It didn't matter what she did anymore. He had accomplished with her what he set out to do all those months ago.

Six months. That was how long it took to get her into bed. Cassie had been his greatest challenge. Never before had a woman resisted him for so long. If he wanted someone in his bed, he simply had one. The point of this deal had been the chase, and he had liked it. Liked when Cassie's eyes lingered on his lips or moved to his chest. Liked the way she squirmed whenever he stood close. He hadn't been quite sure he'd be able to close the deal with her. Until that day on the subway. She had quivered that whole trip, making something so abhorrent to him quite satisfying.

While turning a woman to putty wasn't unusual for Lucas, his reaction to Cassie every single time they met was. His throat dried. His heart pounded. His sense of reason left his body.

The knock at the door jarred him out of his head. He took an extra beat before answering it and paused before the knob to affix his mask of indifference. He opened the door and came face-to-face with Cassie's beauty.

"You wanted to see me," she said without emotion.

He nodded and moved to the side so she could enter. She walked past him like he was a fixture or piece of furniture, her attention drawn to the view from the balcony he had graced moments ago. Peaches and jasmine lingered in the air that chased her. Lucas stepped in and focused out the sliders beyond her.

"What do you want?" She turned to him now with a look of indignation. But there was something else. Cassie usually walked with an air of invisibility, born out of a lack of confidence and humility. But tonight, she moved like she wore—or wanted to wear—armor.

"I wanted to see how the auction went," Lucas said.

"It was fine." She clasped her hands in front of her. Her hair had been hastily gathered back, and slivers of ashen highlights sprung out around her face.

"Good." It was all he could say. He moved toward the kitchen to get another drink. "Care to join?"

She politely declined with a subtle shake of her head. Lucas hated turning his back, afraid she would disappear.

"Anything else?" she asked as he finished his pour. Her tone was tight, biting, and short, all the things she wasn't usually. Lucas paused a beat, waiting for the charge in the air to dissipate.

"I wanted to give you something." He strode to the couch and grasped the paper handles of the bag he had set down a short time ago.

"What's this?" She eyed the bag and trepidation dusted the soft creamy skin of her face.

"Just a gift."

Her eyes reflected the conflict between him and the bag, but she didn't reach out.

"I thought you'd like it. If not, it's fine." He held fast to his neutral tone. This was like any other negotiation; he needed to strip any measure of emotion from his voice. So, utilizing the same strategies, he focused on the air expanding his lungs and his skin tightening when he inhaled.

Cassie conceded, took the bag, and peered inside. Her forehead crinkled and then went slack as she looked up at him through her long lashes. He remained in his spot, taking time to appreciate the cool glass in his hand and the way she swept the hair behind her ear before withdrawing the sketchbook and pencils.

"I didn't know what kind to get, so if they aren't right, you can toss them," he continued.

Her gaze darted to him and then back to the sketchpad in her hand. She peeled back the leather cover and caressed a page with long, lean fingers.

"No, it's right. It's actually quite..." Her sea-green eyes roamed the page. "...perfect. Thank you, Lucas." She clutched the leather book to her chest.

He dipped his head and ignored the tightening cleave in his chest. Her gratitude was painted across her face, her body, her entire being. He didn't often witness this in those he dealt with.

But Cassie wasn't like them. She wasn't like *anyone*.

When his phone rang, he stifled a grunt in his throat and withdrew it from his pocket. The screen showed "Stephanie." She was under strict orders not to intrude or allow others to unless it was necessary.

It must be important. He glanced toward Cassie. "I have to take this."

"Of course," she said, sliding the sketchpad back into the bag.

"Stephanie, hang on," Lucas said. He put the phone to his chest and looked at Cassie again.

"You can sit out there if you want. I'll be tied up in here for a while."

The air between them deadened. He had dangled a carrot he desperately wanted her to take, but the conflict in her face had returned. She turned away from him, toward the balcony and the Parisian world beyond it, but it didn't take her long to nod. The nibble at her lip was so telling and tempting.

When she floated to the balcony, he followed the shape of her until she was out of his view.

***

By the time the calls were done, night had wrapped itself around the city. The Parisian sky remained lit, only now from the ground up. Relief flooded Lucas's limbs, softening his tense muscles. Even though the phone calls had been unanticipated, they had gotten him much closer to the deal he came here to broker.

The beautiful woman on his balcony also brought contentment to his haggard mind. He kept stealing glances here and there during the calls. She started with her mile-long legs stretched over the chaise, head back, attention glued to the tower.

Another time she stood and stretched and his eyes ratcheted to her every move. She lifted up onto the tips of her bare toes, fingers kneading the back of her neck. He momentarily lost all sense of what the people on the phone were saying as his fingertips tingled with the recent memory of her skin.

He turned his back, finally, to get his head on straight and cleanse his senses of her body from the night before. Once he did, his focus returned until the details of the contract were all but hashed. He spent some time after clicking over the keys of his laptop and getting everything down for Stephanie to handle the final arrangements. The six-hour time difference put him ahead, which gave Stephanie time to make plans and finalize the documents before she retired for the evening.

When he turned back to the balcony, Cassie sat with her legs curled underneath her. Her hair had long since been unfurled and twisted down her left shoulder. Her head was bent to what he assumed was the sketchpad in her lap. The top of a pencil was visible over the bare skin at the curve where her neck joined her right shoulder.

He didn't want to break the spell the night had over her, but he couldn't help but wonder. For all the times he had tried to get her to talk about her art, she never did. He didn't even know if she was any good, though he really didn't care either way. But he was curious about what she might create if given the chance.

He opened the slider and she lifted her head from the pad.

"Are those pencils working?" he asked.

A crimson blush streaked across her cheeks.

"They're perfect, I'm sure. I just..." She dropped her gaze back to her lap. Her vulnerability was so real, so refreshing, it struck him square in the chest. "I haven't done much but doodle. If you can even call it that."

"It's a start," he said, his attention never leaving her face, following the curve of her cheek down to her full pink lips.

"I suppose you're right." She uncurled her legs and stretched her arms above her head, arching her back, sending her hair flowing down.

"You don't have to rush out," he said. His fingers itched to sift through her hair.

She stopped, mouth open. But then she shook her head, closed her mouth, and stood up.

"No, it's fine. I need to go. It's late."

Lucas followed her through the suite toward the door. The swing of her hips set off a hum inside his chest that grew with each step she took. He shook his head against the memories of last night knotting his stomach. She needed to leave so he could maybe get a modicum of peace.

Cassie stopped short of the door and turned. Hands gripping the handle of the bag in front of her, her shoulders were slightly rounded and her hair wild and long. Her eyebrows arched slightly and her lips were drawn down in that almost-pout almost-frown that made his gut ache. When she nibbled the corner of her bottom lip, that ache started to throb.

"I almost left Paris today."

He didn't ask her why; he knew. After she had fled his room, her scent and taste and touch had lingered, alongside the new rushing sensation of guilt. It was part of what drove his desire to see her. He had needed to make sure she was all right after coaxing her into breaking a vow she had made to a man who never deserved her.

"Why didn't you?" He plunged his hands into his pants, where he could ball them into fists and fight the twitch racing through every fiber of his body.

Cassie shifted, searching the air everywhere around him. Her shoulders lifted and her head shook.

"I guess," she started then paused. Their gazes locked across the three feet between them. "I'm not ready to leave the fantasy yet. What I did can't be undone, so I might as well avoid reality for a couple more days." Her cheeks flushed with that candy-apple red that rose from her neck when she got flustered.

He had never had a problem putting off any woman.

But Cassie Reynolds was different. Special. A force that drew him in, unlike anything or anyone he had ever contended with. All those months he spent wanting her, he had almost walked away from the whole fucking scheme more than once. She had turned his insides out from the minute they met. The phenomenon defied all the logic in his world.

"Anyway. Good night, Lucas. Thanks again for this." She turned and took the final steps to leave.

His mind raced. and he made a split-second decision.

Before she could open the door, Lucas reached above her head and kept it closed. When Cassie turned, she was inches from his face, eyes flickering and dancing like the lights on the Eiffel Tower behind him. He peered down at her.

The need to take her again was too hard to fight.

So, he stopped resisting.

He pushed her up against the door and kissed her hard. He was not surprised when she kissed him back with the same pressure, her hands gripping his biceps.

He tore himself away from her and stared straight at her kiss-swollen lips.

"I've already broken the rules for you, Cass. What's one more."

Chapter Thirty-One

His fingers followed her velvet skin along the curve of her supple back. She lay on her belly beside him, face turned to his, eyes closed, as the city lights outside fell across her in beams, highlighting her lust-drunk slumber.

"Tell me," she whispered, "about your parents."

He pondered the question, trying to decide how to answer it. He had made it known through the years, in articles and interviews, that his grandfather had raised him. He attributed all of his success to his the man's teachings.

"I didn't know my father. Still don't."

"You never met him?"

He trailed his fingertips in a circle in the middle of her back, relishing its warmth melting into him.

"I don't even know who he is."

She blinked and opened her dark green orbs inches from his.

"Not even his name?"

He shook his head, now following the curve of her shoulder to her neck.

"My grandfather said he wasn't worth knowing. Left my mother heartbroken when she was pregnant. It's why she..."

His throat tightened. Whenever his mother crossed his mind, he righted it and thought about something else. He needed to course correct. Now.

"I never knew my mother," she whispered across the pillow. He appreciated that she had caught onto his reluctance. She was intuitive, somehow always knowing what to say or do. It was a quality he had never experienced, like so much about her.

Her slight smile danced across the shadows brushing her face, and he dusted away a cluster of hair from her shoulder.

"Tell me about her."

"Her name was Helen. My dad said that before me, loving her was his greatest honor." The sadness seeped into her sleepy voice.

"What happened?"

"She was holding me right after they cut the umbilical cord. Her eyes rolled back, and she started convulsing. The nurses snatched me away and shoved my dad out of the room. Twenty-two minutes later, they told him she was dead, and we were on our own."

"That's awful," Lucas said. He never knew how to handle someone else's grief. It was rare he had to. "I'm sorry."

"Yeah, me, too." She shifted to her side and drew the sheet over her chest. Now they were face to face. "My dad talked about her every single day, so it felt like I knew her. She was an English teacher and loved to read and travel. He had a map in his study with red dots over all the places they'd been. I stared at that thing all the time and asked him over and over about everything they did. I made a list of all the ones I wanted to see. He told me he was going to set up the Cassie Mae Adventure Fund so I could travel someday. It wasn't until after he died that I found out he had." Her cheeks rose as she recalled the memories. "I never used it. Not for that. Not for anything."

"Why not?"

She closed her lids again and the ripples in her forehead sprang to life.

"The time never seemed right."

His stomach tightened. The trust Jason stole had been a gift from a devoted father and widower. A growl stuck in the back of Lucas's throat begging to be set free. *That asshole.*

"What was your mother's name?" she asked.

"Rosemary."

"That's a beautiful name. What happened to her?"

He looked across the pillow and into her eyes. They were sympathetic, empathetic—she was everything he wasn't.

"She got sick after my father abandoned her."

"I'm sorry."

His gaze dropped to her lips and then to the smooth skin of her neck under her ear. He wanted nothing more than to bury his face there to escape the demons driving in from the far recesses of his brain.

"My grandfather told me that's what love did. It made his daughter so sick she had to live in a hospital."

While other kids had mothers at class parties and field trips, his was locked away. He hated his father for that, without ever knowing the man.

After his grandfather died, he had learned it was much more than that. His mother had bipolar disorder and borderline schizophrenia.

When Cassie touched the top of his hand, its warmth drew him back.

"We went to visit her every Sunday," he said. "On my tenth birthday, she was different. She kept hugging me, stroking my head, telling me how much I looked like my father. How proud she was of me. How much she loved me. It was strange because she never did any of that stuff. She usually never said a word.

"The next morning, my grandfather woke me. She had slit her wrists with a broken mirror." The breath went out of his lungs as he said the words. The burden and weight of her death remained a bruise on his heart all these years, aching with all the questions that would never be answered.

He believed he must have done something that day to break her. Or perhaps his existence had been enough to do it.

He usually avoided this abyss because it led to other darker places buried even deeper.

Cassie enveloped his face with both of her hands. "I'm so sorry, Lucas. That must have been awful for you."

How did she do that? Know what she did. Feel what she did. How deep did that insight go? He inhaled deeply and the back of his throat stung. He could not stay in this place, where all the things he fought hard to forget were roaring back to life.

He took her in his arms and pulled her to him. Her naked flesh warmed every chilled part of himself. She didn't resist and rested her head in the crook of his neck. He kissed her head and she turned her lips up to meet his.

He released the grief, letting her take it into her because she was stronger than he was. Lucas took her over and over and over again until she fell into a deep sleep, ravaged by him and all the sorrow he kept locked away.

***

Lucas was buttoning up his cuffs outside the closet when Cassie's phone illuminated for the third time. It was on the floor in the hallway just inside the bedroom, alongside the slacks he had stripped from her the night before.

He grabbed his suit jacket from the hanger and walked toward the door, pausing to pick up her phone. He was greeted with the smiling faces of two young children, which he guessed were her friend's kids.

Cassie shifted in the darkness, and he slid the phone into his pocket. It was early, and he had pulled the darkening curtains shut so she could rest.

He couldn't sleep last night, not even after hours of sex. It was always a means to an end, a way to burn energy or regain focus. But with Cassie, it had instead brought him energy and clouded his head.

He took one more peek at her from the door, before shutting out the darkness and stepping into the growing light of the day.

At six fifteen the waiter greeted him at the door with his usual breakfast cart of coffee, eggs benedict, fruit, and bottles of sparkling water.

"Good morning, Monsieur Dalton," the man said.

He nodded, watching the man wheel the cart into the suite. When he paused for a tip, Lucas gave him a hundred euros. The man's face brightened considerably. The amount was nothing to Lucas, and he always made it a point to take care of those who worked hard to serve others.

No other words were spoken, for it was already well known among the staff Lucas didn't converse. He had established the rule a long time ago, not just here, but everywhere he went. A creature of habit, he stayed in this hotel every time he came to Paris.

The first sip of coffee bit his tongue. Arthur was awake and texting from a few floors below, reminding him of the final talking points they had put together over the phone last night. Arthur had been his grandfather's choice for vice president all those years ago. The man had never wavered in his support of Lucas's vision, though Arthur often warned him about being too aggressive. He had soon learned Lucas couldn't be any other way.

Uncovering the breakfast on the cart, he picked at the fruit while scrolling through the latest financials and reports. This was it. Today would solidify his foothold in the European market. Once he closed the deal, it would launch him higher on the lists of the most powerful and richest. He already had more money than he knew what to do with, but climbing ladders and lists remained almost as important to him as his reputation.

While he nibbled on a piece of pineapple, he saw the paper bag where Cassie had left it. He replaced the phone in his pocket and retrieved the leather sketchbook. A pang of uncertainty, that he might be intruding on Cassie's privacy, bounced from his chest. Brushing it off as ridiculous, he opened the book.

Splashed across the first page was her name written in swoopy letters. In the upper left, she'd dated it underneath the name of the hotel. The next page reminded him of something he might have done in high school on the margins of his papers. A series of dots, dashes, and lines first light then dark, danced about the page. Circles and squiggles snaked around, trickling down from the top. Turning the pages, he found each one like that. Doodles, just as she had claimed. No real shapes or forms, other than a flower bud here or a mountain top there. The rest of the book remained blank; a canvas he hoped she might fill at some point.

Another buzz from his pocket broke the trance, but when he withdrew his phone, there was nothing new on the screen. When he felt it again, he realized it was Cassie's phone.

He returned to the table and placed the sketchbook down as he looked at her screen. He couldn't unlock it, but he could read the messages as they came through. His chest heaved.

Jason: I hope you're enjoying Paris.

Lucas tightened his grip on the phone.

Jason: I've been working 20 hours a day since you left.

Jason: I miss you.

He scoffed and set down her phone. Even as the disgust poured into his mouth, he pondered the possibility Cassie might not tell Jason about them.

He never went back on a deal. But as he walked out of the suite, he decided he no longer wanted to help Jason succeed. Especially when it meant going through with something that gnawed his gut like this did.

Chapter Thirty-Two

Cassie

T he auction house buzzed more than usual that afternoon. After the break, news that the strike was ending made its way around. Public transportation and services would resume the following day, including reopening the museums and monuments.

Cassie didn't want to believe it could be true. With it being the last day of the auction, tomorrow she could play tourist. The timing of the compromise felt too perfect.

Tomorrow she could go to the Louvre. The Parc. The Eiffel Tower. All the places that made up the fairytales that starred her parents.

The prospect energized her exhausted limbs as she stepped out of the auction house and into the warm Parisian air. She took off the do-not-disturb from her phone, pausing to see what might greet her. The world stopped when Jason's name popped up with two missed calls and three more text messages.

People surged around Cassie as she stopped in the middle of the walkway. She hadn't returned any of the texts Jason sent in the wee hours of the New York night because she got out of bed late.

Lucas's bed.

What was she going to say? How would she keep herself from spilling her sins to Jason from across the Atlantic.

It was sins—plural now.

The ache in her belly pulsed as she thought about Lucas, his body, and the things he did that made her want to jump out of her skin.

Before she could change her mind, she hit Jason's name. It rang two, three, and four times. She pulled the phone away from her ear, certain he wasn't picking up when his voice echoed in the void.

"Are you there?" he asked.

"Hey."

He breathed into the phone, a giant exhale she could feel across the miles.

"I thought I answered the phone too late. I was downstairs." She heard his desk chair squeak. "Had to run up to hear you."

"You could've called me back."

"I didn't want to miss my chance."

She looked down at the patch of cobblestone beneath her feet. She'd begun walking away from the auction house. Now she stood in a courtyard outside a café dotted with people at metal tables enjoying beverages, treats, and lively conversations.

"Did you get my messages?"

Cassie found an empty bistro table with a solitary chair and sat down. The hesitation in his voice pulled at her chest.

"I did, yes."

He cleared his throat and the chair squeaked again. She pictured him leaning back, work boots on the desk, jeans spread long before him.

"I'm sorry I haven't been myself, Cass. It's just all this business shit."

She closed her eyes against the excuses. He always used the same ones, even years ago when they were happy. Back when she had used the front room as her studio because the light was perfect. Back when Jason and

Frank met for drinks every Friday night to swap stories about their individual businesses.

Back before Frank talked Jason into that first loan.

Back before Cassie started fertility treatment.

"Did I lose you?"

What a loaded question.

She gulped against the bitterness of guilt.

"I'm here."

"Anyway. I know we'll talk more when you get home. I just wanted you to know. I'm sorry," Jason said.

"It's okay. We've both been busy. There hasn't been much ti—"

"Yes, alright. I'll be right there."

She stifled a scoff. Muffled voices from his end indicated he wouldn't have heard anyway.

"So hey, Cass," he said. "I gotta run back downstairs."

"It's fine. I've got to call Jeffrey about something." It wasn't exactly a lie, but it wasn't the truth, either. She wanted to have something to run off and do. She was tired of Jason being the busy one.

"Sure, Cass. Listen, we're going to Brooklyn to pitch another company, so it'll be a long twenty-five hours for me."

"Good luck with that."

"But I'll be at the airport bright and early Friday morning to pick you up." His voice bounced as the background noise grew.

"You don't have to do that."

"I want to."

Silence fell. Even with all the miles buffering them, tension billowed. She hated it, but she was powerless to stop it.

"I'll see you then," she said.

"Sounds good."

The line disconnected, and she exhaled herself into the back of the chair. Peace filled the air around her, not because of anything that had been said, but because of what she didn't say. Two nights separated her and Jason. Whatever happened after that, she would face. But for now, for these fleeting moments, she would do her best to push it from her mind and enjoy herself.

The Louvre waited for her tomorrow. She would be damned if secrets and lies would keep her from soaking in this part of her past.

Her phone lit with a message from Lucas. His name across her screen sent renewed energy into that warm spot in her stomach.

Lucas: Closed the deal. Will you meet me in an hour to celebrate?

She considered the message, not sure how to take it. Was this another club excursion or a business dinner with a bunch of men in stuffy suits?

She didn't want to assume anything about Lucas's intentions, so she asked.

Is this a business dinner?

Lucas: Just us.

The thrill of the night ahead overtook any misgivings. Throwing her phone in her bag, she headed to a boutique she had passed every day to claim the shimmering cobalt and cream dress in the window she was tired of simply admiring.

Chapter
Thirty-Three

Lucas greeted her at the door to his suite, his eyes widening as they roved her from head to toe.

"You make that dress beautiful," he said, planting a kiss on her temple. It kicked off another heat wave in her core, a contrast to the cool Parisian evening billowing through the suite. Lucas ushered her inside and his cedar and citrus mixed with the spice of food wafting throughout the space.

"I thought it would be nice to eat outside tonight." He paused, allowing her to step out on the patio before him. A table for two, adorned with fresh flowers, flickering candles protected in lanterns, and fine place settings, afforded them both an equal view of the Eiffel Tower.

He stood behind the chair to tuck her in. While she sat, his lips grazed the side of her neck. Her skin was still buzzing when he unbuttoned his gunmetal gray suit coat and sat down.

"Good evening." A man clad in a tuxedo set out two glasses of white wine. "This evening, at Monsieur Dalton's request, our chef has prepared a menu dégustation with wine and dish pairings." He draped a white linen cloth over his forearm. "We'll begin serving now if you're ready."

When Lucas nodded his approval, the man bowed before taking his leave.

Cassie had no idea what it meant, but the wine was good, and she hadn't eaten a bad meal since arriving. Although come to think of it, she hadn't eaten many actual meals here at all. Everything was usually on the run or in between the auction and—

"Enjoying the wine?" Lucas asked, running his hand down the shiny black tie centered over his cranberry shirt. He gave a quick nod to the empty glass in her hand. Warmth—of embarrassment or alcohol—rushed up her neck.

"It appears so."

"You'll have to pace yourself. There are seven courses with wine tonight."

"I'll be dead before we get to the third one at this rate."

A chuckle escaped his deep pink lips.

"So, you finally closed the deal," she continued.

"Yes. It's done." His face darkened momentarily, or perhaps it was only the shadows cast by the twinkling tower lights.

The staff returned, setting down the first course.

"Leave the bottle," Lucas said. "Please."

Cassie's plate held a small piece of thick bread topped with finely chopped veggies drizzled with oil. She wasn't sure the most delicate way to eat it, but if she wanted to make it through the meal, she needed to put something in her belly.

"Just kick it back, Cass." Lucas picked up his piece and threw it in his mouth whole, but before he could finish it, an errant olive slipped his lips and fell somewhere on his lap.

"Classy." She giggled while he struggled to keep the rest in his mouth. A muffled laugh shook his chest and crinkled his eyes.

She leaned over her plate and took a large bite of the overflowing toast. The last thing she wanted was to send any of it careening down her silk dress. The food hit her taste buds, exploding in a flurry of rosemary and garlic and the bitter bite of olive nipped her tongue. The sweetness of the wine, still fresh on her palate, enhanced the seasoning prickling across her tongue.

She looked up to find Lucas studying her. The faint flicker of a smile remained on his handsome features.

"Tell me," he began. "If you could go anywhere, where would it be?"

The question surprised her. To gather a moment, she wiped a trickle of olive oil seeping from the corner of her mouth.

"Before this week, I would say here."

"This can't be the only place the Cassie Mae Adventure Fund was intended for." His smile widened across his face.

She sat back and looked out over the city. Her memory flooded with her dad, of afternoons and evenings coloring and sketching on the floor of his study while he worked. She would fixate on that map sprawled on the wall behind his desk. It had been, what, twenty years since she'd seen it? Back when he'd chuckled about putting it away somewhere safe for her.

Only she never found that safe place.

She gulped back the sadness skirting her heart and closed her eyes, allowing the image of it to paint her lids. The sprinkling of red dots marked all the places her mom and dad visited. She had stared at that map so many times, tracing a line with her fingertips between cities and continents, across oceans, and mountain ranges.

Rome. Lisbon. London. Paris.

A memory of a beach scampered across her brain. White sand kissed by water as blue as Lucas's eyes. A place so sacred, it was neatly tucked away in the back of a drawer, all but forgotten.

The clattering of the servers reentering swept away the memories. Cassie opened her eyes as a familiar French onion soup appeared in front of her. She inhaled the warmth, part sweet and part bitter. It was the perfect analogy for her heart. In the shadow of the tower that figured so prominently into her childhood, she sat across the table from a man who understood the depth of her grief more than anyone else. They were connected by a shared loss that burdened and shaped them. His made him tough and enabled him to take risks without worrying about consequences or failure.

For Cassie, though, it had done the opposite. Every subsequent loss only magnified the ones before, feeding into a belief that some choices were better left unmade. In that way, she could remain safe.

"Still no answer?" Lucas's voice beckoned her back to the moment, his gaze again heavy on her.

"My dad always talked about Paris and my mother," she started. "He talked about other places, but nothing compared to here.

"But there was a postcard I found shoved in the back of an old dresser drawer. It was a picture of a white beach and on the back, he had written 'our beginning'."

Her dad's face had fallen, and he'd gotten quiet when he plucked the postcard from her little hand. He ran his fingers over the picture like he could reach inside and touch it.

"That's when he told me it was a beach in Key West, Florida, where he met my mom." She recalled the excitement of a secret story that had coursed through her young body.

"I immediately ran to the map, but there wasn't a dot on Key West." Cassie would never forget how his face had darkened. "He told me not to ask again. That he would tell me when the time was right. The postcard disappeared after that."

Cassie had forgotten the way that postcard deepened the lines across her dad's face, bringing that haunted look in his eyes. It had rattled her so much she never did bring it up again. Anytime she thought to ask, the pit in her stomach put a stop to it.

"I suppose I would go there. Even if I never know any more about what it meant to my parents. Maybe when I finally break open the trust. Who knows."

The slightest flicker of something danced across Lucas's face, rattling her insides, but she washed it away with a sip of wine.

"What about you?" she asked, desperate to change the subject. "I mean, you actually can go anywhere and do anything. So maybe this is a silly question to ask you."

He chuckled and turned toward the lights dancing across the night sky.

"I would buy a boat and sail from New York to Vancouver."

"I figured you already had a boat." Lucas had more money than Cassie's brain could comprehend. He had a plane, so it wasn't a huge leap to believe he had a boat.

"This is different. I want to do it alone. Just me on a boat for as long as it takes to get there."

The lines on his face disappeared, his skin smooth and slack with the idea of it.

"Won't you get lonely?" Her chest echoed with a pang of sadness. For all his success and wealth, Lucas didn't have anyone to share it with. Cassie had Jess to share things with, but Lucas was truly alone.

The way his jaw tightened, clearly something weighed on him, trapping him, making it hard for him to get out from underneath. There were moments between them where he shed some of it, giving her a glimpse beneath the armor. How much more was there to this man peering back through troubled eyes?

"Do I look lonely to you?" The gravel in his voice sliced through her, forcing her to abandon her quest to dig deeper. He gave a quick wave at the opulence around them before reaching back for his glass.

"A person can feel lonely even in the middle of all this, Lucas. I just think..." But she stopped. He wasn't asking for an opinion. In fact, everything about him took her back to that moment after she had asked her dad about the postcard.

"So why don't you do it?" she continued.

Before he could answer, the waiter brought in the next round of food, though neither had touched the soup. Lucas remained trained on her, sending her a message. Something he didn't want to say but didn't want to leave unsaid. Then his gaze dropped down her chin and beyond.

Cassie swallowed at the ripple of heat pulsing in her core.

Lucas stood and took her hand, guiding her up from the chair.

"I think we're done. Do you mind leaving the rest in the kitchen for later?" he said to the maître d' who stepped aside. They did as he willed. Everyone did. The power he wielded over the world was impossible to resist. Especially for those, like her, who didn't want to.

The skin on her body tingled all the way to the bedroom, where he closed the door, shutting out the world beyond them.

Chapter Thirty-Four

Lucas

"Can I ask you something?" Cassie said from across the couch.

After they had spent the better part of the night tangled in bed, she had wondered aloud if the wait staff had left dessert. So they got up, her clad only in his button-down, while he pulled on a pair of joggers. Now she was licking the rest of the mousse from her spoon as her legs stretched long, feet perched in his lap, soft soles moving like satin under his thumbs. With her hair wild, the freckles dancing in the rim of pink highlighting her cheeks, Cassie was the embodiment of beauty.

"Sure." He looked down her neck to her chest at the fleshy mound of one breast peeking out from the half-unbuttoned shirt.

"Did you have a bad experience or something?"

"With what?"

"Did someone bite you? Like by accident. You know." She paused and waved her hand toward his lap. "Down there."

Lucas removed his hands from her as the pieces fell into place. He shifted away, burrowing further into the corner of the couch, her feet sliding away from him.

"No, nothing like that."

"Then what?" She folded her legs to her body, resting her chin atop her knees.

He needed her to let this go.

"Why did something have to happen?" He added a bit more tenor to his voice, hoping it would do what it normally did with conversations he didn't want to have: shut them down.

"Lucas, never in the history of my life have I ever met a man who didn't want a blow job."

"You can't say that now, can you?" That time, it was clear. The harshness worked, killing the curiosity that had sprung to life over her face. The silence soaked the air between them and expanded the discomfort in his chest.

"I want to reciprocate all that you do for me. Because you do everything." Her voice was timid as she peeked out between the strands of hair that trickled across her face. Those eyes of hers stoked an ache in him. The whole of her did.

He swallowed the wave of anger lapping at his tongue and instead, reached for her legs. Her delight deepened the pink of her cheeks and her bottom lip pinched between her teeth when he spread her legs apart, moving between them until his lips were inches from hers. He relished the chocolate lingering on her breath and the remnants of jasmine clinging to her hair. All the sweet of her mixed with the salt of him that clung to every part of her skin.

"You should know by now that I don't do anything I don't want to do." He moved his right hand up the outside of her thigh. "So let me do what I want and enjoy it." He kissed her lips, sinking his tongue into her sweet mouth. She rewarded him by tightening her legs around his waist, clutching him closer.

Her teeth against his bottom lip forced his head back from hers. A smile teased her lips. The fire in her gaze, the lust on her breath... He never wanted to give this up. He would never stop wanting her, and the prospect of not having her, not seeing her this way or any other, made his chest burst.

He dipped back to kiss her, but not before she grabbed his face to stop him.

"Why won't you just tell me?" she asked, tracing his jaw with the lightest of fingertips waiting for an answer.

He shook his head.

"Nothing you say is more awful than what I'm imagining," she continued.

He considered her statement while the world around him faded, replaced with flashes of a life long before her. The way everything had changed after his mother died.

"You'd be surprised," Lucas said more to himself than her.

"Try me."

He shook his head again and pushed away from her warmth. He stood, unsure of what path to walk. His steps were unsteady as defenses inside started failing for the first time in decades. The more he thought about his mother's death, and the year that had followed, the more the darkness and the pain expanded. Those things he kept in a box sealed and buried floated to the surface.

"The woman who cared for me since birth, Myrna, died less than a year after my mother. She was a good woman. Always there whenever I needed her. Always putting me in my place." The words stung crossing his lips, and he turned to the sliders, staring head-on into the darkness.

"My grandfather worked all the time. And even though I was almost eleven, he didn't want me to be alone at night. Which I was happy about since I still liked going to bed knowing someone else was home."

"Of course," Cassie said from behind him. "Being alone at night still terrifies me sometimes. I couldn't imagine it as a kid."

He nodded, half hearing her, half urging himself to go on.

"He hired a babysitter, a college student who needed the money. She'd be there when I got home from hockey practice. She'd let me eat whatever I wanted. All the stuff Myrna never would. And she talked to me like an adult, you know? Not like a little kid. She cared about what I wanted. What I thought. She never made me feel like she was babysitting me. More like we were friends, hanging out."

He gulped against the rising lump in his throat.

"One night, I woke up, and she was in bed with me. Under the covers. She was stroking my head, telling me how handsome I was. How much older I looked and acted. How she thought of me like I was in college, too."

It was all there, festering under the surface. Too available—too easy—to recall.

To relive.

"She asked if I wanted to touch her. Like a boy in college would. I remember feeling scared, but curious. So, I said yes. I didn't know what it would mean. She took her shirt off and put my hand on her breast.

"And so it went. Every night she would crawl into bed with me, and I'd be her boyfriend so she could show me. It wasn't long before she got naked and made me touch her with my hands and then my mouth. Then she said that since I'd made her feel good, it was her turn to do it to me."

He willed his mouth to stop, to close, and never open. For the words to dry up. Anything.

"After a few weeks, she had me take my pajamas off. She used her hand on me that night. Then her mouth every time after. Even when I cried and begged her to stop, she kept going. It felt wrong. I was terrified that people would find out and tell my grandfather."

He shut away the images that thundered in. They pounded at his head and gnawed at his chest. The thoughts of that woman, what he had done to her and what she did to him, unleashed a heat inside that cracked him open.

"It went on for months. And one morning before school, I looked at the mirror and thought about my mother. How she used it to kill herself. How maybe I should do that to stop what was happening without hurting my grandfather." The taste of shame rose against his throat. He always wanted to protect his grandfather at all costs.

"That night at hockey practice, I looked up from the ice and saw him sitting in the stands watching me. He never came to practice. He barely came to matches. But he was there, and I knew he found out what I'd been doing with her."

The disgust and disappointment of that moment filled him anew. His dread in the locker room. His reluctance to see his grandfather. How could he look the man he loved in the eye when he knew Lucas's disgusting secret?

"After practice, we climbed into the car, and he asked me what I wanted for dinner. That was it. From that night on, the car would take me to his office after school or practice. If he traveled, I would miss school to go with him. I never asked why. And he never..."

Lucas's vision shifted to his reflection. His stomach squeezed, his throat burned, and his mind raced with a single unanswered question: had the man he loved known?

In all these years, he had succeeded in shutting it out. Pretended it didn't happen. He had never spoken of it, not to any of the therapists or doctors his grandfather took him to. Not even aloud to himself.

Until now.

The burn in his throat poured over his face and tears streamed from an agony that tore him apart. His body shook as the cries of his younger self rang out into the room. The weight of his pain forced him to his knees and he covered his face as the shame melted out of every pore, pelting him mercilessly. He was alone with his guilt. His sins. His secrets.

Except he wasn't.

Arms drew around him, guiding his head to her. Kissing his face, her tears mixed with his. Whispering, she willed him to let it out—*let it go*—let her take the unbearable weight of grief and shame that had broken him into a thousand splintering pieces.

Just when he thought it would never end, his brain pulsed and his senses ended their merciless punishment. Stopped. Logic and reason and clarity illuminated every broken piece of the mistake he could not unmake.

What had he done? What was it about Cassie that made him feel safe enough to rip the callous from his deepest wound? The one he had buried in the darkest part of his heart with the intention it should never, *ever*, see the light of day.

He reared up, a monster no longer bound by the ropes of grief. Cassie jumped back as he seethed. The heat of his body evaporated the tears from his face.

"You," he breathed the word like fire.

"Lucas," she whispered.

Anger fueled by shame ripped his chest, flexed the muscles running out from his heart and down into his hands which contracted and clenched into fists at his sides. It willed him toward her, but something held his feet in place.

"You can never tell anyone."

"I would never. Luc—"

"NEVER TELL ANYONE!" The voice erupted from inside him, scorching his throat, and outrage ran down his arms and into his fists. They trembled and pulsed, needing somewhere to plant the overwhelming shame-fueled rage. "Even when you hate me. Even when you can't stand the sound of my name, you can never tell anyone."

"I promise."

The energy flowing through his body needed somewhere to go. The rage demanded he bury his fist into the wall beyond her tear-soaked cheek. He stepped forward, forcing her to glance down to the balls of rage at his sides.

When she dared slide her gaze back to his, what he saw in her was something he understood. Her fear penetrated him, mirroring his own from childhood when all he had wanted was that woman to stop. To go away and never come back. That fear rose again, shooting through him like lightning, awakening him to everything, including the words spilling from Cassie's mouth in a broken whisper.

"It wasn't your fault."

Her words pushed back against the rage demanding him to advance. To push her away. Scare her. Make her *pay* for unleashing this fury. His insides clamored, goading him to do it. Shut her up or she'll tell everyone. Ruin *everything* he built. Everything his grandfather created. She'll turn it to ash. Out the secret. The shame. There's always a price. Always.

She'll ruin you, Lucas. She already has.

He couldn't stop the voice, the anger. Tears poured from him, the shake in every breath rattling through him. It was all his fault. He *deserved* it. The pain. The hurt. The shame.

But Cassie didn't.

He couldn't hurt her. A woman broken from birth. A heart powered by fairytales and love. She believed in the good. That's why she stayed married to Jason. Even as he clipped her wings. Willed her into a cage. It's why she kept coming back to Lucas. Challenged him to see the world and himself differently.

She was the *hope*. She believed in redemption. In worthiness. In him.

He needed to act. Fast. Get away. Free her from this false hope she'd held that he was worthy.

He sprinted past her out the door of his suite. The rage pounded the muscles in his legs. Moving without thinking, he found the stairs. Down to the lobby. The ache in his chest heaved every breath. He couldn't go back to her. Not now. Not ever. He was no good. Never had been. Never would be. He stumbled past the baffled concierge before righting himself and pushing through the entry doors. He paused in the cool Parisian night air, barefoot and shirtless.

Then he ran through the streets as fast as the rage could fuel his muscles.

Chapter Thirty-Five

Cassie

C hoices have a funny way of screwing everything up. Or at least they did for Cassie.

On a bench outside the glass pyramid marking the entrance to the Louvre, the sun's rays kissed her face. Her sketchbook was nestled on her lap. The electricity of this moment should be shooting through her body, lighting her up inside and out.

But not today. Not after her choice to prod Lucas last night. She would never forget the fear and pain painted across his face just before he turned his back and left. She had been certain he would come back, so she stayed on the couch in the suite waiting for his form to broach the door so she could right her wrong. It was her fault he ran away. Her insistence had pushed him so far into the deepest recesses of pain, he had no other course of action except to run away.

If only she hadn't asked the question.

If only she hadn't insisted on an answer.

He might be sitting here with her right now, side by side, a fake couple amid the real ones strolling by hand in hand. She could walk through the

Louvre bolstered by his presence and strength rather than sit here with nothing and no one to hold her up but regret.

When would she learn that she could not make the right choice? That what she thought was right was assuredly not. Her choices had robbed her of so much over the years, and now they had cost her the companionship and affection of a man she'd grown close to over the last six months, right or wrong. Though she didn't want to face this fact head-on, she'd developed strong feelings for him far beyond what they should be. Chaos throbbed inside her, a battle between her head and her heart, and it spilled down her face, raining upon the sketchbook on her lap.

It made sense she would get it wrong. Look at Jason, how put together and solid he had appeared when they met. Now, after years of her choices hammering away at him, he was a fraction of the man he once was.

She had screwed it up—again. Not just for her but for Lucas, too. What if he'd been changing in some way, trusting her over the past few months, opening himself up, and her actions last night put the brakes on that, setting him far back. It rattled the cage of all the other mistakes she'd made that had resulted in the death of someone or something. Each one had taken more and more of her heart, numbing her. Until she had simply existed before Lucas offered her a hand out of the self-portrait of regret she had been painting her entire life.

The chatter in line to enter the Louvre echoed through her head. She'd been sitting here since before the famed museum opened, yet she still could not bring herself to enter. What would that be like, surrounded on four sides with the whispers of her parents and their love in light of her current situation? She had always believed coming here would be a joyous and momentous event. Before her dad had died, when she was readying herself for that fellowship, she had lain awake dreaming what it would feel like to stand face to face with the Mona Lisa, knowing her mother had done the same all those years ago.

Doing it alone back then hadn't seemed this hard or heavy. But then she'd had her dreams in her grasp, her dad's voice a phone call away. Her whole life spread wide ahead, bursting with colors and opportunities she couldn't fathom right now. Colors that had bloomed eternal back then no longer existed in her palette. Now, they were only shades of gray, watered down by loss.

How could she consider stepping inside the Louvre with the chaotic and crushed life her choices created? More than anything, she needed someone to prop her up and cushion the blow of the overwhelm stepping through the doors would surely unleash.

No, she couldn't go in. Her guilt choked the possibility out of her, goaded by the grief that skimmed just below the surface of her skin at all times. She stood and turned her back on the line and the loneliness waiting for her inside those hallowed halls.

Four steps away from the Louvre, regret reared its ugly head. She had come so close to being here once before. This time it was no longer only about having a moment with her mother. Stepping over that threshold, she would need to face her dad's death head-on, too.

His loss took so much from her, and Cassie had no desire to rehash it. The grief had encased her heart and kept her ensnared for too long. It squeezed that part of her spirit that made her whole. It quite literally had choked the art from her heart.

If her dad knew how his death had crippled her and knocked her so far off her course, it would devastate him. Would he understand why she was terrified to walk into that museum and confront their ghosts? She believed so, because once upon a time she found a postcard that had drained the color from his face.

Did she really come this far to fall short? To give up something she wanted because a choice she made last night took another chunk from her dwindling supply of hope? This time, if she decided to leave, the fallout might be the thing that took it all from her. She couldn't do that to herself. Not again.

She tilted her head up towards the sky, letting the air of this magical city wash through her, and asked silently for strength. Then she turned, blinked back against the sun glinting off the glass pyramid, put the lid back on her grief, and ventured inside.

***

Crossing the threshold into the museum, Cassie's skin prickled with goosebumps, and her throat was scorched. In those first steps inside, the sights and sounds railed her, overtaking her emotional brain and severing it from her thinking one. It's what she needed to keep from running away. She hovered above the surface of the floor, being willed, or pulled or pushed through the entry and down the hall. Everything else blurred until she locked eyes with that fabled woman and her mysterious smile, suspended under a mirrored sky.

The world around melted away, leaving Cassie connected by a cosmic thread to the face immortalized by Leonardo da Vinci. Every story her dad told about Paris started and ended with Mona Lisa. With each telling, every photograph and letter, Cassie had painted her own ineffable picture of her mother's favorite painting.

In the museum's sacred space, the beautiful and reticent stare of Mona Lisa bored into her. The smile so famous for ambiguity and mystery was crystal clear to Cassie. Compassion. Empathy. Resilience. Pride. The smile a mother would cast upon a child, one forged in unconditional love.

She didn't know how long she stayed in that room, sharing a moment that ripped the words from her chest and reduced her to tears. At some point, the grief morphed from despair to gratitude to hope. When she finally had her fill, she bid the Mona Lisa...and her mother...goodbye.

Room after room, light poured through Cassie's own cracked canvas, breaking open that long-ago locked-away part she had thought lost. Colors and shapes and beauty blossomed in her head for the first time in years. When she couldn't stand to confine them another minute, she found a corner to sit and opened the sketchbook from Lucas. She liberated the images from her head and heart and poured them out onto page after page.

Every scratch of the pencil resurrected another shape she had buried. Every smudge and shade reopened crusted over grief and pulled it out. Line by line, tear by tear, Cassie went a little deeper, and the old feelings washed through.

The flow took over and pulled the memories out from where she'd tucked them far away. Her dad's hand wrapped around hers. Jess holding the newborn twins to her chest. Jason's effortless smile from across the table. The ocean scene on that mysterious postcard. She worked with no concept of time or space, something that hadn't happened since her dad died.

"Vraiment belle!"

The voice jolted Cassie from the haze of the page. An older man in a security uniform hunched over her right shoulder, pointing at the sketchbook, the overhead lights reflecting off his silver head.

He slung more sentences at her in French, the animation of his hands and the upward lilt of his voice did nothing to make her understand.

"My apologies," he begged in broken English. "Your work is very beautiful. I see many here sketching as you, but none hit my chest like these." He punctuated this by placing a wrinkled and weathered hand on his chest. "This is the best you've done today!"

She shifted her surprised gaze from the man to the page where the latest image she'd been working on sprang to life. It took even her breath away.

The chiseled lines of his jaw, the anguish painted about his brows, and narrowing icy eyes. Even without the color, the light shading, and subtle crosshatching of the graphite had captured the iceberg stare of Lucas Dalton that had pierced her, pained by the agony and torment he had locked away from everyone including himself.

It rippled from the page and through her, reigniting the guilt sparked by last night's events. A firestorm surged in her head, rocketing her to her feet.

"Belle, what's the matter?" he said.

She wasn't about to stay any longer and defile that sacred space with her poisonous choices. The shame of her affair, of the way she broke Lucas. The reality she had once again chosen poorly forced her outside. She only paused to toss her sketchbook into the trash where it and she belonged.

Chapter Thirty-Six

"Please keep your seat belts fastened while we taxi to the gate. Thank you again for choosing Air France, and welcome to Kennedy International Airport."

The gray scenery rolling by her window matched her mood. She turned her phone on and sighed, waiting for the screen to come to life. The knot in her stomach, which hadn't dissipated since the Louvre, bounced like a rubber ball.

The man behind her cursed into his phone about how slow the plane was moving, but Cassie was only too happy to delay the inevitable. She expected Jason to be waiting somewhere nearby to swoop in and grab her at the curb, and now she would give anything for a text telling her to take the train home.

It would give her more time to think, as if an almost eight-hour plane ride hadn't been long enough. Between her exhaustion and heavy heart though, she'd had little opportunity for rest or productive thinking.

After the Louvre, she had returned to the hotel and inquired after Lucas. The concierge advised he had checked out, but informed management she could stay as long as she wanted. She dragged her sorrow and regret up to her room and packed right then. Within minutes, she was in a cab on the way to the airport. She could not stomach being in the city another minute longer than she needed to be.

On the trip, she had composed message after message to Lucas, all apologetic, and most asking for a response that he was safe. Somehow, she could not bring herself to send a single one, the guilt of what they'd done, and more specifically, what *she'd* done, wouldn't allow it. She decided to leave their relationship in Paris and return home as if it never happened.

It was the right thing to do. But it didn't make it easy.

Her phone buzzed on her lap, the return to service bringing a plethora of incoming messages. Two from Jess, three from Jeffrey, and one from Jason:

I'm in baggage claim! You can't miss me.

The plane stopped to a round of applause and seat belts clinking. Cassie closed the message and stole a final glance out the window. Back on the same soil as Jason, the gravity of what she'd allowed herself to do—to become—bubbled up from her stomach and into her chest.

All their time together, from the moment they stood in front of that Pollock was now cast in the light of the Lucas she'd come to know. Before Paris, her beliefs about him were skewed through a lens of Lucas's own making. But once that lens had broken, his true nature snapped into focus, and she'd found it far gentler and compassionate than the facade.

Then again, was it possible to really know someone? As transparent as she always believed herself to be, her own lens was distorted by her view of the world that choices are risky and result in disastrous consequences. And anytime she followed her heart, she got it wrong.

She hadn't been wrong about Jason. Not back then. But her choices—to move away from painting, to try so hard to have a baby, to ruminate in an apathetic life after her nerve damage—had changed him over the years, too.

Jason tried to love her the best way he knew how. Maybe that was good enough.

Maybe she was too hard on him. Maybe he wasn't capable of giving her the life she thought she wanted. But he could give her the one she needed. He was a kind and decent man. There was more to life than passion.

Devotion and trust, honesty and loyalty were all qualities Jason possessed, as misplaced as they'd been recently.

Choices have a funny way of screwing everything up. Or at least they did for Cassie.

Was she ready to leave him and walk down a path that had seemed so right days ago?

Or had that decision been based purely on discontent and lust?

When the plane doors opened, the passengers started filing out. Cassie was carried along in the wave of people pushing her from the sanctity of the plane's cabin into the unknown.

There was too much at stake. She couldn't start over now.

At the end of the day, she didn't want to lose anyone else because of her selfishness. If she ended her marriage now, she would be untethered. Jason was her only family, a safe haven. Cassie couldn't bear to leave because she was unhappy and weak. He didn't deserve that. Not after all these years.

She winced at the memory of Lucas trembling and running from the suite. None of it would have happened if she hadn't slept with him in the first place, hadn't looked to him for the passion and companionship missing from her life for so long. She couldn't go back and change things, but she could move forward.

She would make it work with Jason. She owed it to him. She would be the kind of wife he needed, one who supported him and didn't keep trying to live up to her delusions.

Cassie now had a purpose; her head filled with it. Tears stung as she paused to collect herself. She had to forget about art. She had to forget about Lucas. If nothing else, he had proved what she already knew to be true: when she did what she wanted, it ended badly. She could not let her choices burn down her world. Not again.

She inhaled and filled her lungs with resolve. When she exhaled, she let go of Paris, of Lucas. And never intended to give this secret another bit of air.

She continued her forward motion and with each footfall, she stepped back into the shadows of her former life toward the husband at the bottom of the escalator with a hand full of flowers. This was the man she had loved once upon a time. They would get back to the way it used to be.

***

An hour later, Cassie emerged from a much-needed shower to air steeped in maple syrup, cinnamon, and bacon. Jason's famous pancake breakfast. He had first made it on their third date. He'd never shared the exact recipe because he liked being the only one who could make it for her.

Her mouth watered as she used the towel draped around her shoulders to wring out her hair.

"I know you probably had crepes and croissants in Paris," he said with an awful over-the-top, not-even-close French accent. "I figured this was the perfect way to welcome you back." He flipped a pancake with the flick of his wrist.

Coming up beside him, she surveyed the feast, reaching for a piece of crispy bacon, which he playfully rejected.

"You gotta wait."

"I just want a little. I'm starving, and this smells so yummy."

He returned the pan to the stove and whisked her into an embrace. He dipped her against the counter, and his wood and leather scent filled her nose as his lips scraped hers. They remained pressed together, though it did little to move her insides in any good way. His tongue invaded her mouth, a fish flopping around, trying to find its way back to safety.

She separated and his dark eyes narrowed, puckering the skin. Something about it stabbed at her chest. For a second, she thought he recognized the betrayal lingering in her mouth.

Then, just as quickly, Jason's face returned to normal, and he planted a softer kiss at her temple.

"Is it almost ready?" she asked, the words shaky as his bitter taste lingered.

"It's done. Go sit and I'll bring it over."

She was relieved to turn her back on him for the few seconds it took to get to the table. She sat more heavily than she intended, but gravity was working differently on her body. Her head felt twenty pounds heavier as if it were crushing her neck.

"You okay?" Jason set her plate down.

She waved him away and sipped the orange juice. "Yeah, I think maybe it's jet lag."

"Did you get any sleep on the plane?"

She gulped the bittersweet juice and shook her head.

"You should go to bed after this," he said and dropped into the opposite seat. He refilled her orange juice before cutting all the food on his plate.

Her head sloshed as she nodded. She wasn't good at lying, and this secret was worse than anything she'd ever held. She cleared it out of her throat and sunk her teeth into a pancake. The sweet maple soured in her mouth. Just like Jason's kiss.

"You sure you're okay?" His voice came from three worlds away.

Her hands shook, her body weighted like she was walking through water with her clothes on. Everything was so damn heavy. The guilt. That had to be it. But that kiss. It was nothing like Lucas.

The fork rattled from her hand and clattered to the ground.

"Cass, you're shaking," Jason said, as she tried to steady the vibration gripping her entire body.

She chose to give up that fellowship.

She chose to stop painting.

She chose to take that last IVF shot.

She chose—

"I slept with Lucas."

—to confess.

No sound passed between them, not even a breath before his face morphed from concern to something much worse.

His stare burrowed into her with an intensity she had never seen in him.

"Jason..." Tears dropped like boulders.

He gritted his teeth and his lips curled up around them. He rose with such fury, his plate flipped to the ground. "I fucking knew it."

"Please. It was a mistake."

He walked away and she followed. "I couldn't keep it from you. It's killing me," she continued.

He whirled around inches from her face. "Am I supposed to be *grateful* that you have enough of a heart left that you had to tell me?"

She couldn't give an answer because in the end, she didn't have one. "I don't—I don't know." She broke and slid to the ground. "I'm so sorry. Please believe me."

"Why, so you can keep humiliating me?"

"No. It's done. I don't want him. I want you." The sobs made it hard to get words out, but she needed to try. For their sake, she needed him to know. "You're my husband."

Jason grabbed his keys off the counter and stormed to the door. Before opening it, he jerked his attention back to her. "Were you thinking about me when you let that arrogant asshole fuck you?"

He didn't wait for a response. He pushed out the door and slammed it shut, leaving her in a heap on their floor.

Chapter Thirty-Seven

SIX MONTHS LATER

"**M**aybe a size or two smaller?" the woman asked.

Cassie raised her eyes to the sales clerk standing behind her in the mirror. The woman took hold of the excess fabric in the back of the dress and pulled it tight, causing it to conform to Cassie's diminishing frame.

She didn't want a tight dress.

"No, this is fine. I prefer it baggy."

The woman's disagreement was punctuated by the high lift of her shoulders.

"As you wish." She unzipped the back enough that Cassie could slip it off, though really, it fell off without that extra step.

She didn't love the dress, but it was the only one out of the dozen or so she had tried that Jason would approve of. Black and unassuming, it was the perfect understatement to his handmade Tom Ford suit she had picked up from the tailor yesterday. He would be the star at the party tonight.

She collapsed into the fitting room chair, defeat weighing heavy. The mirror in the tiny room showed Cassie the same thing the saleswoman saw.

The strain of the last six months had left her small and slight, face sunken and swallowed by dark eye circles.

After confessing the affair, she had been certain Jason would leave. He stormed out and didn't return until the next evening. He surprised her when he agreed to try and make things work. Relief washed through her, and she vowed to do whatever it took to convince him she would never hurt him again. She was committed to him and would prove it any way she had to.

He presented his list of demands and conditions, which Cassie had to accept in order to regain his trust. She agreed to stay at home, with only their marriage counseling sessions twice a week outside the house. Jason's shadow loomed while Cassie made the two calls he demanded she make. The first went to Jeffrey, ending their working relationship. She'd had to fight to keep the tears out of her voice when Jeffrey's sobs hit her ear. He begged her to stay and offered her a sizable salary to do so. But she had to turn it down for her marriage. Jason believed working in the city with Jeffrey would give Cassie access to tempting people and situations.

The second call she made was to Jess. With shaky hands and silent tears, Cassie explained she needed to focus on staying home and working on her marriage, so she wouldn't be able to visit Jess and the kids.

Cassie had kept the conversation general, so Jason didn't know the extent of Jess's knowledge of her crime. The line remained deadly silent while Cassie spoke, and when Jess finally responded, it was nothing more than "I see" in her therapist voice, followed by a curt, "If that's what you want, Cass," before the line went dead by Jess's hand.

After that call, Cassie questioned whether her marriage was worth the high price she had to pay. But when she brought this up to the marriage counselor, Jason stormed out of the room, furious she was whining about giving up friends when she was the one who cheated.

He didn't speak to her for three days after that particular session. Silence was the weapon he wielded whenever she didn't go along with opinions he expressed at their sessions. The therapist told Cassie Jason was entitled to his anger and trust issues in the aftermath of her affair.

The therapist was right, of course. As was Jason. Only Cassie understood the catastrophic consequences she faced because of her choices, not only for herself but for others. People she cared about. Like Lucas. He remained even more out of the public eye in the wake of Paris.

A few weeks into her sentence, after Jason left for work, a knock came at the door. Cassie couldn't fathom who would be there at six a.m. When she opened it, Jess stood there, face flush with the mild fall morning.

"Before you tell me to get out of here, you need to know that your niece and nephew ask about you every single day." Jess's arms were crossed, unmoving and unwavering. "You can hurt me, Cass, but when it comes to my kids, I won't tolerate it."

"Jess, I didn't know." But didn't she? Cassie had been a part of Abby and Nicholas's lives from the first ultrasound to the last push that brought them into this world.

Cassie cleared her narrowing throat. "I'm sorry. I guess I didn't think—"

"No, you didn't. How could you give us up like that? Like we never mattered."

"That's not it at all, and you know it."

Jess moved a hand to her hip. "Do I? Before three weeks ago I thought we were best friends—sisters. And then you just threw me away all for..." Jess gestured toward the house behind Cassie. "...a man who is forcing you to kowtow to his every demand. All because he finally made you miserable enough to cheat on him."

The words slapped Cassie across the cheek. "That's not fair to Jason. He didn't make me miserable."

"Jesus, Cassie. Open your eyes. That man has been draining you of everything you were so he could feel superior."

She stepped back and shook her head. "How dare you say that. Jason always supported me. He never purposely made me feel bad about anything, even when I deserved it!"

Jess pushed the air out of her lips like a horse. "You really couldn't see it all these years? The campaign he's waged and won to keep you away from the one thing that makes you whole."

"I don't know what you're talking about, Jess. I think you should leave."

"When did he ever support your art?"

She huffed, the anger and sadness incited by Jess's challenge. "He always has."

"Bullshit. It was his idea that you not rush back into that fellowship after you met because it was *too soon* for you to leave him alone. Your adviser at NYU begged you to go the following year, but by then, Jason had won. He convinced you that you needed him too much and that he couldn't be without you. If he loved you like he swore he did, he would have encouraged you to chase your dream instead of trapping you here."

Jess's chest heaved. All Cassie could do was stare. Her mouth hung open. Her brain tried to process everything.

"He was right, Jess. I didn't want to leave him—"

"You think Frank telling you about that art restoration job was a coincidence? Pffft. Cassie, you have to know better. I saw right through it. Jason put him up to it."

"That's a stretch."

"If you went off in a studio and created your own art, it would have upstaged everything Jason ever did. He knew that the first time he saw an exhibit with your work at NYU. He couldn't have you outshine him, so he got Frank to push you to take that bullshit job."

A rumbling rose inside Cassie's gut and moved like rocks up into her chest where they scraped and chipped against her. Anger, aimed toward the one person she thought would understand what she needed right now. But rather than support her, Jess was chiding and goading her, challenging every decision Cassie had made, including this one to save her marriage.

Jason had always believed Jess didn't care for him; and that she would eventually come between them. Cassie had always reassured him none of that was true. Jess liked him. She would never do anything to drive a wedge between them. Now, Cassie finally saw things the way he did. Jess had been pretending all this time to like Jason only to turn around now and go on the attack.

"I won't listen to any more of this," she said. "I'm sorry I can't see the twins, but I'm sure you've told them it won't be forever."

Jess reared her head back. "Are you blowing me off?"

"I'm choosing my husband over you. That's not the same thing."

"To hell it's not. I came here to talk you out of this. To tell you that you have options. Greg and I want you to come live with us as long as it takes to get out from under Jason's tyrannical rule."

The anger pushed out of her chest. "Jason is my family, not you. You're here attacking him and expecting me to choose you over him. That's not happening, Jess. Not now. Not ever."

Fury flowed through Cassie's voice, fueled by hurt more than anger. Jess's face fell and tears cascaded from her face. The sobs racked her chest while she opened and closed her mouth three, four times to say more. But no words emerged.

Cassie reinforced her position. "This is where I belong, and I can't have you in my life if you can't respect my husband. This is my choice, not his."

She hoped in Jess's state she wouldn't notice the lie, though it fell from Cassie's lips like water through a colander.

Jess palmed the tears from each cheek and steadied herself. "I see. If that's how you feel, then I guess nothing I can say will make you see the truth."

"Guess not."

Her best friend nodded solemnly and left the stoop without another word. Cassie waited until she saw Jess get into a waiting cab and it took off down the street before she closed the door and collapsed on the floor behind it, already regretting yet another choice—to let her best friend walk away.

***

It had been five months since Jess had showed up at her house. Not a day went by that Cassie didn't think about her. Even now, stepping out of the car at The Met, Cassie wished more than anything that Jess was here.

Tonight was all about Jason. The museum was hosting some of the most influential small business owners in the Tri-State area. When Jason had received the invite, Cassie thought he was going to burst on the spot. Having spent so much of the last year and a half running a business like his head was on fire, this event reinforced his belief that, against all odds, he had made it.

The plan at first was for him to go alone. He said as much in one of their counseling sessions. When the therapist asked Cassie how she felt about it, she cast a glance at Jason and agreed it made sense. She was more than happy to stay behind and let him have his moment in the sun. In truth, she had grown numb to so much of the world that staying home was probably better.

Then a week ago, Jason came home from work and asked her to go with him. She took it as a sign her efforts over the past six months weren't in vain. Jason understood how much she wanted to make this work and that he was the only one she wanted.

Tonight, as she took the steps of The Met, optimism surged. Jason held her hand and told her how beautiful she looked. Everything was as it should be. She remained by his side and played the part she'd been rehearsing. She declined alcohol. She laughed at all the jokes. She averted eye contact from any man who held it too long. She fought like hell to remain present and conversational with those Jason wanted to impress, which turned out to be everyone.

Exhaustion pulled at her after a couple of hours. All the small talk and pretending sucked her energy like an overloaded outlet on the verge of surging out. She excused herself to the restroom for a few minutes alone. She turned to leave. Jason held fast to her fingers a beat longer than necessary. His dark stare held hers, blacker in the low lights like a night devoid of stars. When he did release her, he told her not to get lost.

She took a moment to refresh the under-eye concealer and slicked back the wiry baby hairs springing out around her face. Knowing they would not leave until Jason was ready, she took a deep breath and willed away the exhaustion.

On her way back to the party, Cassie cast a long look down the hall to her favorite gallery. Her body altered course without hesitation. A few more steps later, she stood before Monet's *The Parc Monceau*. She didn't dare get too close, afraid doing so would pull her back to when she had gripped the gates and peered inside.

The lighting was dimmer here, an attempt by the museum to preserve the priceless paintings and keep away the partygoers. At this late hour with so few people in the building, it cast shadows in every direction, projecting them onto every canvas. Monet's works appeared less whimsical and more mysterious in this setting. Were the waterlilies bursting out of the water? Or sinking under the weight of dew on the petals?

"Hello, Cassie."

Lucas's voice grabbed her by the neck, yanking her back to the present moment. Cold crept up her spine and gripped her throat, making it impossible to swallow. To breathe. Her lungs burned. Cassie stood stuck, unable to turn away. A voice inside her head whispered, telling her to get out, return to the party, and back to her husband.

Maybe this wasn't real. Maybe *he* wasn't real.

Then she turned toward him.

He remained on the fringe of the shadows. She didn't need to see him in full light to know his gaze was fixed on her. Those blinding azure eyes that saw so much of the outer world and kept the inner one locked up tight.

"Lucas," she whispered.

He shifted forward and a strand of light trickled across his face. Cassie's stomach dropped.

"I can't be here," she muttered. Her body responded to the alarm in her head, and she stepped backward. She needed to get out of this room and find Jason.

She stumbled as a weight crushed her chest.

"Cassie, wait." He stepped toward her. "You look unwell."

The concern painted across his face amplified the sirens in her head. She wasn't about to say another word to him. She wouldn't engage or make him think she wanted to. She continued to step backward, shaking her head.

"I can't. We can't..." She allowed her words to trail off as she turned. But before she could escape, a darker figure stepped out, blocking her exit. Cassie gasped, stopped in her escape by the smoke billowing behind Jason's black eyes.

Chapter Thirty-Eight

"Jason." Cassie pushed the word out but didn't think he'd heard. Rage poured over his face and thudded to the ground, shaking her insides.

"How did you plan this without me knowing?" Jason thundered.

"I didn't—"

"Do you have another phone?"

The question knocked her back.

"What? No. Why would that matter?"

"That's the only way you could pull this off. That or Jess. I knew it." Jason snarled; his fists balled at his sides.

"Jason, this wasn't planned. I swear. Please be—"

"She's telling the truth." Lucas stepped from behind her.

Cassie silently willed him to leave. Hoped beyond all reason they still shared some thread of a connection, and he could dip into her thoughts, hear her pleas to leave this space.

She turned sideways, aligning herself between the two men. Both were imposing forces more than capable of getting physical. Cassie was stuck, not wanting either to get dragged out in handcuffs or worse—a stretcher.

"Fuck you, Dalton. You think I'd believe a damn thing you say?" Jason turned his blazing gaze to Cassie. "And you. After everything I've done for you."

The air pulsed with the probability of violence as Lucas's footfalls echoed closer. Cassie turned toward Jason.

"Jason, let's go. Please." She begged him. The steps behind her stopped.

Jason silently raged, his eyes were lit up and wide. Something skimmed the edge of his glare that she couldn't quite identify. Then without a word, he grabbed her arm and pulled her toward the door. Relieved to have avoided a fight as his grip seared five fingerprints into her skin.

"What have you done to her?" Lucas asked.

She didn't want to stop, so she didn't. But Jason dropped his hold and turned back to Lucas. She pulled at his shoulder, trying to stop him, her strength nothing compared to his.

"Me? You destroyed her."

Lucas's gaze shifted to her, and she wanted to fall under their weight. He swept it up and down her body, but not in the way he once had. She wrapped her arms around herself and looked at the ground as a shudder shook her spine.

"He's punishing you. Why?" Lucas asked.

The words caught in her throat, but Cassie managed them anyway. Willing herself to look at him for a split second, she immediately regretted it. "You know why."

The rasp in her voice came from someone else. She looked away, unable to bear his concern.

Jason claimed her wrist, holding on a little less rough. He looked at her, appearing satisfied by something only he could see. She complied and moved again toward the exit, her chest full of breath that would not let go.

Only a few steps remained between them and freedom.

"You never told her." Lucas's voice forced her steps to stop. Jason's jaw clenched, and that thing Cassie had noted earlier skirting the edge of his eyes, now spread across his face like a wave lapping the sand: it was fear.

"Jason?" she asked.

"Tell her," Lucas demanded.

"Tell me what?"

Jason didn't move.

"The truth. But it appears he doesn't want to."

A chill in the air reverberated through her skin and cut down to her bones. She backed up. "What is he talking about?"

"Tell her," Lucas urged.

Jason snapped his head in Lucas's direction. "You shut up," he said, jabbing the air with his finger.

Lucas shook his head. "You're hurting her for something you wanted, hell, *needed* to happen."

"Jason?"

She expected Jason to look at her and brush the words away, but he didn't. He stood seething in Lucas's direction.

"Lucas?" She turned to him.

Lucas never broke his stare off with Jason as he answered. "We made a deal—"

"DALTON," Jason cried out.

But Lucas continued, his gaze sliding to her. "I paid him. For you."

The weight of those words knocked Cassie back, her brain working overtime, trying to keep her upright.

I paid him for you.

A quaking shook her insides, releasing a dam that sent fire scorching her throat.

I paid him for you.

"I don't understand."

"I gave Jason five million dollars. Half after I met you and decided I wanted you. And the rest after I had you."

The rush of heat and cold collided in the space between her toes and her head. It echoed as her brain roared to life. The painting. The diner. The job. The surgery.

Paris.

"You paid him?" she asked Lucas. But then she turned sharply to face her husband. "To have sex with me?"

Jason's fear washed visibly over him. His shoulders slumped and the skin on his face fell. His voice rose two octaves. "Cass, let me explain."

She stepped back. Put her arms before her. She had to stop the advancement of a predator. One she had trusted. One she had believed safe.

"It's true." Her voice caught as tears gathered. Every bit of disgust rising in her mouth concentrated on her husband, on the implications of what his next words would be.

"I was desperate!" Jason cried out, "Cassie, I did so many bad things with our money. And this bastard knew it." He jabbed again in Lucas's direction, but Cassie didn't tear her eyes away from him.

"Why didn't you tell me how bad it was? Even after I got the foreclosure notice. You swore that was the worst."

Jason pulled his hand across his forehead. "I couldn't tell you everything, Cass."

"I would have forgiven you."

Jason shook his head, his dark eyes somber and glassy. The dim light now did nothing to shade the bloodshot streaks coursing through them. "No, you wouldn't have. I stole your trust fund. All of it. Is"—he drew a breath—"gone. I made this deal for us. For you."

Tears streamed down her face.

"Selling me to a stranger was better than telling me?"

Jason sunk further.

Cassie left Jason twisting and turned her disbelief to Lucas, moving to him for the first time. The air between them displaced as she cut through it. "Was any of it real?" she whispered.

Lucas appeared defiant. That rigid mask firmly affixed across his face.

"It was a game, and I did whatever it took to win." He thrust back his shoulders and plunged his hands into his pockets. "You don't think you're the first married woman I've seduced, do you?"

That shallow tone. Aloof. Smug. Awful. It put an end to the temporary hope that sprung inside her chest in the seconds before his answer. The air crushed in on her all at once. The tears that had fallen in sadness, desperation, and shock evaporated under a heat stoked just beneath the surface.

Looking away, Cassie tried to gather all of these shattered pieces inside of her. The truth, *this* truth, she hadn't expected.

She turned back to Jason, seeing him for the man he'd become. Or had he always been this way?

Jess's voice clamored in her head, words she whispered to Cassie in the seconds before the six-minute ceremony that made Cassie a wife: *You don't have to do this so fast. This won't make you whole. It won't bring your dad back.*

Her dad.

That trust fund.

She cut her glare back to Jason.

"You knew what I did before I came home," Cassie said. "And you let me suffer."

"He didn't know," Lucas interjected. "Until you told him."

Her brain sputtered, trying to make sense of something that would never—could never—make sense.

"But if you paid him after we had sex..."

"I was supposed to, but I didn't. He called after you got home and demanded it."

The weight of it fell upon her. Words coming from Jason burned up somewhere in the air between them. Lucas remained silent, and it was this void she chose to rage against.

"You," she said, closing the distance toward Lucas. The cold wafting from him did nothing to stall the heat radiating from her. "You think everything and everyone is for sale. You think because you can own anything that you want, you should. You are an awful human being."

Lucas didn't flinch in the face of her assault. He was a fully fortified presence. Cassie waited for a sneer to tease the corners of his mouth, but it never manifested.

"And you," she said, turning her fury upon Jason. "You're my husband. The man who's supposed to protect and love me. Instead of telling me the truth about the money, you pimped me out like a fucking *whore*."

Jason's eyes glistened, droplets falling over his lashes. Through all the losses during their thirteen years together, he had never shed a tear until this moment. But it did nothing to pacify the anger exploding through her body.

"I gave up so much for you," she continued.

The heat melted and cracked her from the inside out as she reframed her entire marriage with this new insight.

"You put me through hell." She seethed. "And I took it. Because that's how sorry I was. How heavy my shame was about what I did. And the whole time, you wanted it to happen." She paused, knowing this was a choice from which she would not come back and didn't want to.

"Him," she said pointing at Lucas. "I understand. But you. How could you?"

She asked the question without wanting an answer. The burden of guilt she had carried since the night she met Lucas. The guilt over tears shed in secret for a man who thought of her only in terms of a conquest, a commodity. All of it to save a marriage that turned out to also be a lie. Money and greed and winning were things she never thought were important to Jason, but she was wrong about everything.

The silent room closed in around her, so she turned her back on Monet and the two men. She didn't run. Her actions were not controlled by fear or grief as they had been in the past. Instead, she walked pushed by anger and rage pent up by a lifetime of mistakes and regrets combined with choices gone horribly wrong. Of unbearable loss.

For the first time in her life, Cassie let every piece of pain she'd pushed away scorch through her like molten lava to leave nothing but ashes in its wake.

Chapter Thirty-Nine

ONE YEAR LATER

"Noah! I told you to stay out of the way." Ned Lainey chased his toddler around the bottom of the stepladder where Cassie perched, as the raven-haired boy baited his father.

"Sorry about this, Cassie. I'll have him out of here in a jiff." The game ended when Ned pretended not to care about Noah. When the toddler drifted too close, Ned snatched him up and slung him over his shoulder amid a chorus of screeches and giggles.

"It's not a problem. My niece and nephew play this game all the time."

"Yeah, but I'm guessing not while you're trying to do that." He gestured to the mural on the wall.

"Not exactly, but they do manage to get into some rather tight spaces."

She stepped down and placed her brush and palette inside the plastic bin at her feet.

"It's perfect. I'm so glad I let Jeffrey talk me into it." His exhausted tot flopped over his shoulder.

"I'm happy to hear it." The mural had been her idea. During the consult, she caught on to Noah's love of the zoo between the tower of stuffed animals and the elephant sheets on his bed. After touring his tiny room with the single elevated window, too small to provide light or a view of the park below, she got the idea to bring the zoo inside.

Greenery and towering trees formed a backdrop to an animal habitat with monkeys swinging on vines, elephants showering each other in the water, and tiger cubs playing hide and seek in the brush below.

Ned was a conservative man who had been very clear about his budgetary constraints and preference for minimalist design. She wasn't sure if he would go for it, but after sketching her idea, she had handed it over to Jeffrey to sell him on it, and he did.

The entire renovation took twenty-three days to finish. It wasn't the most complicated redesign and hadn't required knocking down walls or purchasing copious amounts of furniture and decor. It had demanded creativity and a lot of legwork repurposing items Ned already owned, but those were the two things Cassie loved most.

The mural she had saved for the last few days, once everything else was finished. After using a light gray charcoal pencil on the wall to outline the landscape, she let her brushes and sponges fill it in little by little and bring her vision to life.

"I can't wait for people to see all that you've done here. It's beyond anything I imagined."

Ned's words swelled her chest.

"I'm so glad," she said.

They stood together in comfortable silence as Cassie roved the wall for any place in need of a touch-up. When she was satisfied it was complete, she picked up the bin and tucked it under her arm.

"I should go. It looks like Noah here is ready for a nap." She stroked the boy's cheek. He rewarded her with a sweet smile from under heavy lids.

"Give me one second, and I'll walk you out." Ned placed his toddler into bed and Cassie withdrew from the room to give them space.

A moment later, Ned reappeared. They exchanged smiles, and Cassie took another step toward the door, Ned moving ahead to grasp the handle. He hesitated before opening it and directed his attention back to her.

"Now that you're all done, maybe we could have dinner sometime?" He swayed before her.

Cassie bit her lip as the words settled with a thud in her stomach.

"I'm flattered, but—"

"Hey." He offered a dismissive wave. "I get it. You're probably seeing someone. I'm all thumbs when it comes to this sort of thing."

His awkward chuckle bounced off the still-shut door. A faint pink rushed up into his olive cheeks all the way to the tightly cropped dark hair required by his former military service.

During their consultation, Ned had talked about how much he loved the military and hated to give it up. But two years ago, when a Mississippi court informed him a baby boy bearing his name on a birth certificate had been surrendered by the mother, he walked away from the service and never looked back.

Cassie admired someone who could walk away from something they loved because it was the right thing to do.

At the same time, she wouldn't consider getting close to anyone anytime soon. She had spent the past year rediscovering and fortifying herself. In that time, she also concluded she didn't have any interest in becoming entangled with a man. Because what if a do-over led to a do-everything-the-same?

She didn't trust herself yet to recognize a man who wasn't good for her. She'd failed before and, even though so much of her life—of her—had changed for the better, she could not take the chance with her fragile heart.

"No, that's not it. I'm just not looking for anything like that right now."

"Sure. I get that. I do." His smile remained plastered in pretend understanding.

"I should go."

"Of course. Sorry." He shook his head as he opened the door. "Thanks again. I'll let everyone know how wonderful you are...uh...you and Jeffrey."

She left the apartment and exhaled only after the door closed behind her.

Waiting for the elevator, her gaze dropped to the shades of green, orange, and black staining her hand. It reminded her of a whole other part of her life—of herself—she was still keeping shut away.

***

"I'm making a coffee run. Need anything?" Derek asked from her office door.

"No thanks." The younger man bobbed his head, sending his mop of dark blond curls flopping. As he started to duck away, Cassie asked, "Is Jeffrey due in?"

"Any minute. Which is why I've got to run out now before he sticks me with a project." The man's brows arched high.

She nodded, knowing all too well what it was like getting trapped by Jeffrey, especially when trying to do anything but.

"You should probably go."

He gave her a thumbs-up and took off. The younger man's quick steps snapped across the tile, fading until all that remained was silence.

Derek was the newest addition to the business. His youthful exuberance, dedicated work ethic, and the single dimple that pitted his right cheek had won them over. He was a jack of all trades, part assistant, part designer, and part laborer. He did whatever was asked without objection.

She jotted a few more notes on the cover page for Ned's reno and then closed the binder. Jeffrey's constant ribbing this past year over Cassie's old-fashioned filing system had done nothing to make her want to change.

She got up and moved to the cabinet against the opposite wall. Jeffrey had gifted it to her the day he offered her a partnership. The French display cabinet was an original from the 1890s Belle Epoque or Beautiful Period of French society. Jeffrey said it was the perfect way to brand their partnership. With fresh tears on her cheeks, Cassie hugged him and accepted the offer.

She ran her fingers across the other finished binders lining the shelves. They had been quite busy already this year. With a steady string of consultations, the pace would only continue for the foreseeable future.

"Derek around?" Jeffrey's voice sang from the doorway.

"Coffee run."

"It figures. I need him at the Pearson's to tell me what shade of mauve he thinks the wife wants. The painter put six different samples on the wall, and I'll pass out if I look at it another second." He flung his coat at the rack and trudged to the loveseat under the window, flopping down in a fainting position.

She nestled into the opposite chair. "I swear you get more and more dramatic by the day."

"How are there even that many shades of mauve?"

She chuckled. "I'll go take a look this afternoon and sort it out."

He sighed, slinging his arm over his eyes. "So, tell me. Was it dinner or coffee?"

"What are you talking about?"

"Ned." He slid his arm away. "Did he ask you to dinner or panic and go with coffee instead?"

Her jaw dropped. "What did you do?"

"Nothing! I can catch a vibe, is all." He kicked his legs off the couch and pushed upright.

"It was dinner—and before you ask—I said no." She crossed her arms over her chest, not wanting or needing to have this conversation.

"I never doubted your ability to turn down a good-looking man." He settled back and fanned his arms across the back, his lips pinched.

She swatted the air. Jeffrey feigned offense, but the pucker at the corner of his eyes said otherwise.

"I'm not interested. You know it's—"

"Too soon. Yes, you've said that many times. Many, many, MANY times." He bobbed his head to accentuate each word. "It's been a year since your D-day, Cassie, and Ned isn't a bad pool to dip your toes in."

She balked and pushed herself back in the chair, as if widening the space between them could push the suggestion away. "I like my life now. It's easy. I have zero interest in complicating things. It turns out I like being alone."

Jeffrey sighed and scrunched his nose, dismissing her with an extended eye roll.

"I talked to Sadie, my friend who's getting divorced." He picked at his nails.

"Right. How's it going?"

"Not awesome. I told her that maybe she could swing by and see you. She's in the weeds, and I don't know how to help."

She nodded, understanding all too well what it meant to be in the thick of such a life-altering event.

"Sure. I can take her to lunch or something."

"That's perfect. Even though..." Jeffrey looked down again to his nails. "What?"

"Well, I think she's going to want to know how yours was over so soon."

Most divorces didn't finish as fast as hers. It was three months from her first filing to the judge's signature. Then again, most marriages didn't end quite like Cassie's had, either. Plus, they hadn't had much to settle. She and Jason agreed to sell the house and put whatever they got from it into the debt. Jason took the remaining debt because it was all his.

Jeffrey's eyes never left her face.

She often wondered if he knew more about the events that led to her divorce. It was a question she expected would come, but it hadn't yet. Not the morning after The Met when he showed up at Jess's with an entire plan to extract her things from the house "without incident." Nor in the weeks that followed, when he asked her to help him out with a few jobs. Instead, Jeffrey forged ahead, supporting her without question or consideration of the details that had led her there. He was always giving Cassie space when she needed it and pulling her back from it when that space got too big.

She sat back and let the bitter truth hang. Once she had seen Jason for the man he was, it became impossible to see him any other way. Though scared to death to be alone, she also believed leaving Jason was one choice she would not live to regret.

"Once Jason finally believed that he could no longer control me, all the pieces fell into place."

Jeffrey nodded and twisted his mouth. Cassie braced herself for whatever he launched next because, at the end of the day, the past was just that. She had spent so much time healing, accepting, and finally letting go—the shame, the guilt, the weight of unrealized expectations. With all of that work, nothing Jeffrey would say or ask in the coming seconds would hurt.

"You see that thing about Lucas Dalton?" he asked.

Then there was that.

"Not recently." She wasn't sure how the words left her mouth.

"No one's seen him in months, which I guess makes sense in a way after what happened at the groundbreaking."

She had no idea what Jeffrey was talking about. She purposely avoided city gossip even though she lived here now. Even Jess, her go-to source, had remained mute on the subject of Lucas in the past year.

Jeffrey raised his brows, obviously understanding she didn't know.

"He committed to building a clinic for victims of sexual abuse last year. Turns out, it's because he is one."

Her heart sputtered as the shock of this revelation landed squarely in her chest. She shook her head and leaned back in her chair. She hadn't breathed a word of Lucas's disclosure to anyone, not to Jess, not even to her therapist.

"He was giving the dedication speech and just came out with it," Jeffrey said. "Totally shocked everyone. I can't believe *we* didn't talk about this then."

She ignored the whirling in her head and shrugged. "We've been super busy."

He tilted his head and nodded. "Anyway, it's part of the reason people think he's gone M-I-A. The guy in charge said Lucas is running things remotely, but apparently, shit is hitting the fan. Lots of nervous rich investors are freaking out because the man has quite literally vanished." He punctuated this last statement with an O-shaped hand moving with every word.

Cassie focused on evening out her breath and preventing the lines from breaking across her forehead.

"Wow," she mustered.

Lucas talked about his abuse publicly and now he's gone.

She planted her feet underneath her, the ground no longer solid, and walked back to the desk. Busying herself at the computer, she sent a clear signal she felt the conversation was over.

"Another theory floating around is that he met a woman and ran away with her."

She stiffened in her chair and swallowed the sand in her throat. The prospect Lucas had found someone he cared enough about to walk away from his business suffocated her in a way she didn't want to acknowledge. She nibbled her lip, trying in vain to focus on anything but this.

"But I don't buy it," Jeffrey said as he walked to the door and grabbed his coat. "I think it's more likely he met a woman he's trying to forget."

When she met Jeffrey's gaze, he held fast to it. A moment later, he took mercy on her and left. The silent message screamed in her head long after.

Chapter Forty

"Remember, you're taking the Van Alstyne consult at three." Derek bobbed into her office and placed a cup on Cassie's desk.

"Thanks for the reminder. And the coffee."

"No worries. And your appointment is in the lobby."

"What appointment?" She hit the keys on her laptop, and it sprung to life, bringing up her calendar. Other than the Van Alstyne meeting, Cassie didn't have anything else blocked off. "Did they say what it was for?"

"No, just that he's here to see you." Derek started retreating. "I can get more info if you want."

She stood and waved him off. "It's fine. I'll go." She followed Derek out the door but turned toward the lobby. As she rounded the bend, she was met with the back of a man.

"Can I he—"

His turn in her direction halted her as suddenly as if she'd hit a brick wall.

Jason.

She hadn't seen him since they signed the divorce papers almost a year ago.

Now, here he stood, in the lobby of the place where he once forbade her to work. In his hands was a large envelope, and he appeared something between timid and nervous. Perhaps both.

"Hey, Cass." His voice was quiet, subdued. "Sorry to barge in."

Movement eluded her, as did a response. He looked every second of his fifty-two years and then some. The gray had overrun his once dark head, and lines cracked across his face. His once solid form seemed softer, his shoulders stooped.

"Do you have a minute?"

She blinked herself back to life.

"This way," she said, her voice flat and monotone.

He followed her into her office and shifted from one foot to the other while she sat behind the desk. Only then did he lower himself into the chair across and a grimace flashed across his face. He shifted back a bit before settling down with the nondescript parcel in his lap.

"Your back's gotten worse?" she guessed.

He nodded. "Bound to happen after beating my body to death for so long." He paused and looked around. "This is a nice office, Cass. You've done well."

In spite of all your efforts.

She nodded but kept her vitriol within the confines of her head. She worked hard to keep herself neutral, not wanting anything to bubble to the surface. She refused to go down this road again. There was never a reason to revisit it.

"What can I do for you, Jason?"

"Right to the point. You never did like small talk." He chuckled, an attempt to dispel the tension. "I made the last payment to the trust. It's all back."

This revelation surprised Cassie.

"That was fast."

"I didn't want to make you wait. It wasn't right." He shifted in the chair. His voice subdued, he said, "None of it was."

She gulped back the discomfort rising in her chest.

"No, it wasn't." She cleared her throat as the bitterness of those last months of her marriage threatened to reinfect her.

When she reflected back on those turbulent times, she never downplayed or excused her role. While the events surrounding her affair were set in motion without her knowledge, she had cheated of her own free will. It had been her choice, her consent to the act that brought about the end result. No one had forced her into it.

But she never deserved the hefty sanctions he had imposed on her in those months after, especially given he wasn't an innocent party. While she couldn't lie about what she'd done, Jason had no problem doing so.

"You didn't have to come all the way over here to tell me." She regarded how different he looked. This was a man burdened with demons, past mistakes that cost him everything, while she was, for the first time, free of her own.

"I sold the factory." His voice broke, and he cleared his throat.

"I'm sorry to hear that. I know how much it meant to you. For Frank."

It had meant everything, as it turned out. When Frank took himself out of the equation and left Jason with the possibility of success, it was all he'd needed to forge ahead with his own desire to enter the business elite. His ambition had been greater than she believed possible. The taste of notoriety, of doing something so big, had changed him from the man she fell in love with to the toxic and bitter one she divorced.

He nodded but looked down at his lap.

"I wanted to tell you in person because I thought you'd like to know. Things will be different now for me. It makes me think about how they could've been different...for us."

His tone and the upward turn of his eyes now struck Cassie differently. He punctuated his words with a self-deprecating grin, the same one he had used so often to pull her in after a fight. But now, she saw these things for what they were—ploys. He was trying to stoke her empathy by pretending to have some of his own.

"I doubt that." She leaned back in her chair. "I have another appointment due any minute."

His face fell and he placed the envelope on her desk.

"This is actually why I stopped by."

She looked at it, not daring to touch it.

"What is it?"

"It came in the mail after I first opened the trust. I shoved it in the utility closet at work and forgot it was there until I cleaned it out." He looked from her to the envelope. "I'm guessing it was part of the disbursement."

She picked up the envelope. It wasn't heavy, just thick. She couldn't imagine what the financial firm would send.

"Sorry it took me so long to get it to you." His voice dropped again, and he struggled to stand.

Her attention returned to the unopened envelope, and a flash of pressure squeezed in her chest. Her heart thumped as she turned it over in her hands.

Her intrigue over the contents was interrupted by Jason's movement. Her first reaction was to walk him out; she would do so for anyone else. But not this time. Jason wasn't anyone else.

"Guess I'll find my way out." When Jason grinned, the easy smile she had fallen in love with was dimmed by time and regret.

"Thanks for bringing this by." She fought to keep any hint of emotion out of her voice. She would not let him get any sense she felt anything for him, even though their years together had granted her some understanding of him. There was absolutely no going backward. Ever.

Before crossing into the hallway, he paused.

"Thank you, Cassie. For giving me the best thirteen years of my life. I'm only sorry I ruined it." He turned away and limped out the door.

Chapter Forty-One

"Do you want me to read it?" Jess's quiet voice bounced around in Cassie's head.

After Jason had left her stunned in the office, more over the package than anything else, Cassie had called Jess at work. Somewhere through her tears, Jess cut her off and announced they would meet at Cassie's apartment in two hours and *not to touch that envelope* before she arrived.

The two friends looked at that package for a solid twenty minutes like it was going to spring to life or explode, or worse, simply disappear.

Then, after a full glass of wine each, Jess handed Cassie scissors. A few seconds later, a letter on some financial firm letterhead greeted her, explaining *per the terms of the Cassie Mae Adventure Fund Trust*, the enclosed package was being transferred to her.

She reached back in, and the two friends inhaled simultaneously while she ever-so-gently withdrew the mysterious contents. The map, waxy in her hand, set Cassie's throat on fire as she pulled it free of its encasement.

Something floated to the ground, freezing her. Dancing across that light gray envelope were the words "Cassie Mae," scrawled in her dad's familiar hand.

She bent to pick it up and the room blurred as she stood back up.

"Cassie?" Jess's hand covered hers. She realized then that she was shaking, the anxiety and nerves taking control. "Do you want me to read it?"

She shook her head as terror climbed up every vertebra of her back, using each like rungs on a ladder. Her fingers caressed every letter of her name as he would have written them. She imagined him sitting at his desk late one night with nothing but his green banker's light to illuminate the surface. Did he write it after she went off to college? Was she tucked into her canopy bed or out on the stoop painting on a rainy afternoon?

The spit in her mouth thickened as she sniffed back the grief. Jess placed a just-right palm across the middle of her back. Cassie looked over at her friend, and they nodded in unison, speaking wordlessly through the air between them. Whatever this was, they would figure it out together.

They had shared the same look on Jess's front stoop the night Cassie went running from The Met a year ago. Jess had been the only person she wanted to see, though Cassie understood her friend had every right to turn her away. The minute the front door opened though, Jess bounded out and hugged her so tight it almost knocked Cassie over.

Now she trailed her finger under the crease, cracked the seal, and withdrew the single sheet of matching gray bonded stationary. Dad had loved the heavy paper always in light gray or bright white. Never any shade in between.

As she unfolded it, her breath locked inside her chest. She peeled back the second flap unveiling its secret treasure tucked in the center. A postcard with blue crystal waters and a white sandy beach. Her heart thundered against her ribs.

My Dearest Cassie Mae:

I can still see your face when you found this postcard, the brightening of your eyes when I told you this is where Mom and I met. And just as clearly, the confusion and disappointment when I refused to tell the story.

By the time you read this, I'll be ready to have the conversation, but here goes the short version.

Mom and I didn't have a fairytale beginning. For one, I was a self-centered asshole willing to step over anyone who tried to get in the way of my corporate climb.

And two, your mom was on her honeymoon.

Or rather, she was supposed to be.

The night I watched your mother slip her bare toes across the sand and into that bar, it took every bit of the air from my chest.

Within minutes, she told me she'd run away the day before her wedding because she couldn't stomach settling.

So, I told her I was only in Key West because I stole a client from a co-worker.

She told me her almost-husband wanted her to keep working as a secretary even though she wanted to teach.

I told her that the only thing that made me happy these days was the balance in my bank account, and even that wasn't doing it anymore.

She admitted that she never wanted kids, and her thank-god-he-wasn't-her-husband did. She didn't want to be tied down and made a prisoner by kids ever.

I agreed because who the hell wanted to be saddled with a kid anyway? They were messy. You couldn't go out and do what you wanted. You had stuff all over your clothes, your apartment, who wanted that?

She laughed so hard she snorted.

And so it went. Back and forth, we aired all our worst fears and deepest secrets. We didn't hide our demons. We pulled up stools and offered them seats. Bought them drinks. Let them sit right out in the open.

And that's how we started. Two damaged strangers, united by the weight of our collective baggage. Confessing our sins like we were on death's door. Unburdening our souls because it felt safe. It felt right.

The man I was when I walked into that bar would never believe I could fall in love ever, let alone that night.

Or that the beautiful woman in the turquoise dress, alone on her honeymoon in Key West, would move to New York and marry me.

For eight years, we worked and fought and loved and traveled and lived. It was so hard. But it was so worth it.

Six weeks after we came home from Paris, that life fell apart on the bathroom floor when two lines appeared on that stick. Everything changed in an instant. My insides crumbled while your mother cried and cried. I was so afraid I was losing her. Losing us. Because this was the thing she never wanted.

And then, she turned her emerald eyes to mine and smiled. And laughed. And sprang up into my arms. We spent the next eight months in a whole other circle of love. One we didn't know we wanted and couldn't fathom existed before.

I never thought it was possible to love another person more than I loved your mother.

Until I met you.

She taught me everything I thought I needed to know about what it meant to love someone else.

Until I met you.

Things change. People change. We didn't try to change each other. But we loved our way through it. When you do that, things work out as they should, even if it's not the way you think they will.

If your mother hadn't been brave and stepped away from a wedding, had she not taken the chance on me, on us, and moved across the country a week after meeting my sorry ass, I hate to think what my life would have been like.

In her, I found my own courage to change. And in you, I found my purpose. Because being your dad has been—and will always be—the greatest honor and achievement of my life. Nothing will ever come close.

Once upon a time, a young, bitter, miserable, too-ambitious-for-his-own-good man sat at a bar in Key West. And a beautiful, fiery, and too-stubborn-for-her-own-good woman swept in out of nowhere, and it saved them both.

My hope is that you opened this trust to chase the thing that your heart wants most right now. Whether that's in Paris, a beach in Key West, or somewhere else.

Follow it.

And don't stay in a place where you don't fit. Don't be afraid to take that leap because even if you fall, you have the strength and the courage to get back up and find a new path just like Mom. It's never too soon or too late to change.

I love you, Cassie Mae Bergen. To the furthest parts of the world and back. Always and forever.

Love,

Dad

She stared at the blurry words on the page. Her insides trembled like an elbow bang on the edge of a table. She inhaled until her lungs crackled and burned. The pressure morphed into a warm wave of energy seeping into her chest, then down into her belly and limbs. Her stomach contracted and pushed the air back up into her throat and out into...a laugh. Uncontrollable, convulsing, hysteria.

"My mom was a total mess!"

She wept tears mixed with sadness and laughter and every emotion in between until she finally managed to hiccup and slow her breathing.

Jess nodded and pinched the page right out of Cassie's limp hands. "Reminds me of someone else."

"Why wouldn't my dad just tell me?"

Jess shrugged. "Probably because he knew you'd only hear the part about them not wanting kids."

Cassie reached for the postcard on the edge of the counter. All the time she spent trying to unravel the mystery of how her parents met and why her dad didn't tell her. The actual story was far less awful than anything her mind had conjured. But Jess was right. The part that would have stuck with her would have been the one that didn't matter.

Now older, she could appreciate the story and the message much more. Especially after spending so long trying to fit into a place she didn't belong.

"Your mom was brave." Jess turned her wide eyes to Cassie. "Can you imagine canceling a wedding at the last minute?"

Cassie shook her head.

Jess said, "And then she didn't look back and dove into the relationship with your dad."

"Don't forget the part about her moving across the country—"

"To a place she didn't know."

Cassie nodded. "To a *man* she didn't know."

"Who apparently was an asshole? *Your* dad?"

She shrugged, trying to reconcile the man she loved with one who once stole clients to get ahead.

Jess raised her light blond eyebrows. "It's kind of—"

"Psychotic," Cassie finished. Because it was. Stepping back and looking at what her mom had done spun Cassie's compass. Her family and friends must have thought her mom was insane to rush into a relationship like that. Jess had thought Cassie's marriage was fast, and she and Jason had a relationship before taking that last step.

Jess cleared her throat. "I was going to say liberating. Your mom took a chance instead of staying in something that didn't work for her." She took the postcard from Cassie and turned it over in her hands.

"But what if it failed?" Cassie asked.

Jess wrinkled her forehead.

Cassie continued, "What would you say to a patient who walked in tomorrow and said she was considering doing this?"

"Well..." Jess shrugged. "It depends on everything else. Like if she said she had a safe space to land if it all went sideways, then it might be worth a shot. Because not trying might leave her with a whole load of regret. More people regret the choices they didn't make, the chances they didn't take, than the ones that failed."

Cassie moved closer to the counter, to the map. For a moment she was sitting in her dad's chair, spinning, and giggling while he stood by watching, making sure she didn't get hurt, but letting her swirl and twirl until her stomach buckled and turned, and she cried *enough* and he swooped in to steady her.

Dad had always been like that. He encouraged her to try and learn and fail and succeed on her terms. Through it all, he had been her safety net, always poised to give her that place to land when she needed it. Since his death, she had lost that, but instead of grieving it, she had jumped into a marriage with a man she believed could replace him.

"This really does look beautiful," Jess whispered to the postcard between her fingers.

Cassie regarded her friend, and only then did she understand. *Jess* had become her safe place. They spent the last twenty years catching and bracing and supporting and cheering each other through every joy and sorrow life threw at them.

Even at her lowest. Even when she thought no other human in this world could understand her, Cassie was never abandoned or alone. She never would be. Not only with Jess and her family, but with Jeffrey, too, and even the everlasting presence of her parents. She could feel them at times now, ever since she broke her settled life apart and went her own way.

She slung her arm around Jess's shoulders and pulled her in. "It looks like the perfect place to take a few days and think."

"I'd say. Especially for someone with a supportive business partner and a fully funded trust."

When Jess smiled up at her, Cassie finally let the shackles of her past fall away.

Chapter Forty-Two

SIX MONTHS LATER

C hoices have a funny way of screwing everything up. At least that's what Cassie used to believe.

The only thing screwed up now was her stomach. Her nerves made it impossible to eat for the better part of twenty-four hours. Her knees shook beneath the satin emerald gown with the slim silhouette and long slit as she waited for her invitation to step into the spotlight.

"Cass, it'll be okay, I promise." Jess's hands were on her shoulders. "It's totally normal to be nervous."

She huffed as heat poured off her in waves and mirrored Jess's nodding head.

"I can't do this." The words shook as they passed her lips.

"You can and you will. You've been through worse, and I'll be right here." Cassie bit her lip.

"How's she doing?" Jeffrey whispered as he came around behind her.

Jess shook her head. "Not great."

Jeffrey stood next to Jess, who released her grip on Cassie's shoulders. Cassie rocked a bit but managed to remain standing.

Tilting his head, Jeffrey studied Cassie.

He reached up and smoothed back a wisp of hair at her temple. Cassie didn't know why she had let them talk her into wearing her hair up. She should have left it down so the red creeping up her neck and filling her earlobes wouldn't shine like a beacon.

"Hey, Cassie. Listen, I really need you to pull it together," Jeffrey said. "*We* need you to pull it together. Because if you don't, our business is going to go down faster than a hooker on 42nd Street. Understand?"

Jess swatted his shoulder.

"That's the best pep talk you could come up with. A tough-love hooker analogy?" Jess bobbed her head at Jeffrey. He grimaced and shrugged.

"It's not like I prepared a speech!" Jeffrey rolled his eyes at Jess, who returned it with one of her own.

Cassie couldn't help but smile at the two of them. Her friends. They were doing their best to keep her together. For a split second, it worked. Until the stage director stepped in.

"They're ready for you, Cassie."

Cassie's knees quaked. The lights in the makeshift backstage flashed and the announcer's muffled voice boomed. A round of applause erupted from somewhere beyond the curtain.

"I'm going to throw up," she muttered. Jess clasped her right hand and Jeffrey grabbed her left.

The stage director pointed to Cassie, the sign that she was to make her way out front. Jeffrey and Jess squeezed her hands, then dropped them and melted away. Somehow, she took the first step sluggishly as though the floor was wet cement grabbing at her heels. Then she was blinded by a spotlight, emerging to claps and cheers.

Moira, the program's hostess, clapped from the center of the stage, a microphone in her hand. Cassie smiled and hoped like hell she didn't look like a deranged patient escaping from an institute. She walked to her spot just like they had practiced earlier, but this time she was flanked on either side by painted canvases—both hers.

She stopped moving and bowed her head. Unable to see anyone in the crowd, she clasped her hands tightly together and put a practiced smile on her face.

"Cassie, thank you so much for being here. This is a big, big night." Moira's tattooed eyebrows arched and folded.

"Thank you for having me and not putting any pressure on me."

The crowd laughed, which did nothing to draw her attention from the bead of sweat trickling down her back.

"I told you she was charming, didn't I?" Moira had turned to the crowd, which answered with another round of applause. Then she turned back to Cassie. "We appreciate you agreeing to open this local artists' exhibit at our little museum."

"The Met is anything but little, Moira."

Moira bowed and the onlookers rippled with agreement.

"Tell us what it feels like to have two paintings included in the exhibit."

Cassie scanned the canvases. Two of *her* paintings. In The Met. How was she even supposed to remotely encapsulate what it meant to her?

"It's a dream come true." She forced back her tears. "I grew up coming here with my dad." She couldn't cry. Yet. It was too soon. But how could she not with the bubbles of sorrow and joy about to burst in her chest? "I'm grateful beyond words."

"Tell us a bit about these incredible paintings."

Taking a deep breath, she turned back to the canvases behind her. It was easier to talk looking at them than either Moira or the audience. The paintings were a complementary pair she had titled *Once Upon a Time* and *Happily Ever After*. The first portrayed a man holding the hand of a woman in a turquoise dress and the two stood on a beach of white sand. The second was a Parisian cityscape. That same man and woman now stood outside the Louvre, holding the hands of a little girl between them.

"My parents met in Key West at the lowest points in their lives. My mom was a runaway bride, and my dad was on a path paved by greed. They were two damaged people who made choices, good and bad, that led each to the other. For reasons that defied logic, they came together and lived a life beyond what either imagined."

When Cassie finally made a trip to Key West six months ago, she would never have believed it would lead her back here to The Met. But sitting on the beach memorialized in the postcard, a vision had danced across her brain and through her heart. A way she could return to her true self and honor the two people who had made it all possible.

She had sketched that day on the beach until the sun went down. The next morning, she went right back to it. She settled on the warm sand, letting every bit of the grief flow through and out of her for the first time since her dad died.

"I never knew my mom because she died after I was born. But my dad raised me on the stories of their fairytale love and adventures, so in many ways, I felt her in my life growing up. When he died, I had a hard time dealing with it, especially because they were both gone. But after I made the trip to Key West, I realized that my parents will always be together and that even though they aren't here, we'll always be a family. These paintings are my attempt at honoring them in some small way because, without them and their choices, there would be no me."

By that night, when she went to the tiki bar further down the beach, the same one where she liked to believe her parents met, her body had tingled. She had been lightened, accepting the idea all pain need not hurt forever. Not every shame needed to remain a chain around her heart.

Instead, she let herself go. She even let a man from Detroit buy her a drink. He, too, was divorced and trying to find his way through a very different world. She had enjoyed their conversation. Though, when it came time to leave and he asked if they could meet for breakfast, she declined and continued to go her own way.

It had felt good to do what she wanted without regret. It solidified that growing confidence and belief that not every choice she made was so wrong. It might not turn out to be right, but every mistake added to her arsenal of life lessons. She could change at any time and do something else, become something else, without reproach or regret.

Key West provided the end of a chapter that remained unfinished for too long. The last colors of a painting she started decades ago and left unfinished in the wake of grief. But Cassie's story wasn't over—it was only just starting, and it filled her with both excitement and peace.

"I'm sure your parents are extremely proud of you," Moira said, leading the room in a round of applause.

Cassie bowed her head in gratitude for the kindness of the crowd.

"I hear you're multitalented," Moira continued. "And that you spend a fair amount of time as an interior designer."

"Jeffrey Tanner is the designer. I just help out, whether it be art or furniture, to compliment his brilliant vision and bring it to life for our clients."

The eyebrows arched high again, clearly impressed by the answer. Cassie followed the familiar gasp from the front of the crowd to where Jeffrey and Derek stood. The light was no longer blinding, so bodies and forms beyond could take shape.

Jess stood there, too, her arm slung around Greg's waist. The twins were dressed in fancy clothes to match their parents. Grateful didn't even begin to express the waves of emotion and love flowing through Cassie.

"Is there anything else you'd like to say before we drop the ropes and declare the exhibit open?"

Cassie cast another look at the crowd, scanning the faces of those she loved most in the world, the ones who would and had always been there, whether it was decades or years. Her gaze fell to a shadow standing on the outskirts. It evoked the name that still whispered across her heart when she painted or sketched.

"I spent a long time avoiding the pain of loss, like my dad's death. I went to unbelievable lengths to shut out that pain instead of giving it space to breathe. Keeping that grief locked away is harder than letting it out; it led to the graying of the world and made it hard to experience the good parts of life, like joy, art, and love.

"Sometimes, all it takes is one person who listens and understands to set you free of the pain. So even though it was hard, once I started letting the grief out, the colors began to spring back to life." Cassie leveled a shaky glance toward the back of the room.

"It didn't just allow the art to return, but it balanced out my irrational belief that all of my choices were bad. Now I know, there is almost no mistake or choice that I can't come back from. No matter what, it's never too late to change."

"I can't think of a better way to open this exhibit!" Moira said amid the thunderous applause and dropped the rope that undammed the swelling crowd. Her friends, her *family*, wrapped their arms around Cassie. When her gaz moved to the back of the room, the shadow figure was gone.

Chapter
Forty-Three

C assie's bare feet cascaded through the lobby of the museum; her shoes discarded so she could maintain the silent reverence a bit longer. When she arrived at the Abstract Impressionism exhibit hall, she had no trouble stepping over the velvet rope. She continued toward the figure in the back corner, no doubt standing before the same chaotic piece she, too, had come to see. Familiar cedar and citrus gathered around as she drew closer, triggering a whole host of memories.

"Hey, Cass," he said. The grit of his warm voice seeped through time and space, wrapping itself around her chest.

"Lucas," she responded, giving a nod. She was a different version of the woman she had been once upon a time. She'd spent the better part of a year and a half working through her issues, fortifying her boundaries, and managing the messy feelings associated with him.

She turned toward the blue eyes that still haunted her and realized she wasn't the only one who'd changed. Her heart lurched at the sight of him, his tight blonde beard with sprinkles of gray, the skin across his forehead kissed and creased by the rays of the sun, and the highlights dripping through his longer hair.

"I thought you were gone," she finally said.

Lucas nodded. "I was for a while. But I'm back now."

"Did you take your boat trip?"

His bearded cheeks raised on both sides, boosted by a grin. "I did. It was just what I needed." He looked back at the Pollock painting like he was searching for something in the drips and lines. "It feels like it's come full circle, standing in front of this painting."

"It does." She took in his dark gray suit, the black button-down, and the absence of a tie.

"I heard about your exhibit, and I wanted to see for myself." He returned his gaze back to her. "You do amazing work, Cass. Those paintings are beautiful."

She nodded and took a beat to wrangle the thoughts racing through her head. She had spent a lot of time unpacking the part Lucas played in her unraveling. While Cassie had made peace with things, she still had many unanswered questions.

"Tell me something," she said, unsure why this conversation felt so hard after all the time had passed. After all the work she'd done. At the same time, she knew it was too important not to have. "Why did you make that deal with Jason?"

He dipped his head and then brought it straight back up. "Honestly? I was a miserable person." His gaze remained fixed to hers. "I made that agreement never planning on going through with it until I met you in front of this painting."

"But why me? It's not like you didn't have your pick of women, married or single."

"I can't give you a rational explanation because there isn't one. My therapist said that sometimes we're drawn to people for unknown reasons. I guess I needed to know you."

"I didn't know therapists went on boat trips with patients." She scoffed. She'd worked on this so much, but now that she could finally confront him and get answers, the imminent closure kicked off a chain reaction and forced some unpleasant feelings to surface.

"They don't. But they can meet with clients online. Sometimes every day if that's what it takes."

She waited for a sign he was lying. Why was it so hard to believe Lucas had gotten the help he needed just as she had?

"You know," he said, breaking into her thoughts, "I am so sorry for everything, Cass. I've learned to let go of a lot of things I once regretted. But that deal is the one thing I can't forgive myself for."

She shifted back to the painting. The first time she saw it, she had no idea how much her inner turmoil had aligned with the chaos rippling through it. Since then, she, too, had worked to let go of regret. Moments she held so close had worked in concert to tear her apart. Things like bugging her dad about the postcard. Turning him down for dinner. Sacrificing art so easily after he died. Struggling to get pregnant and the eventual outcome.

She had allowed her fear of being alone to blind her for years to Jason's true nature. She'd learned to release the regret and stop the loop of alternate endings that had hijacked her for years.

Except for one.

"Did you lie to me the last time we were here? About it, about *me*, being a game."

A sadness pulled Lucas's eyes. "Yes."

"Why would you do that?"

"Look how far you've come, Cass. None of it would have happened if I said what I wanted that night. You didn't need me or anyone else—"

"You lied to save me?" She crossed her arms to try and contain the wave of anger raking her ribcage.

A shadow passed over his face, a slight flinch. She'd seen it before, in Paris when she prodded the truth out of him.

"That's not what I meant." He looked down to his upturned palms where callouses had hardened his smooth skin. "If I would have told you the truth—that I love you—would you have left with me?" His icy blue gaze burned into her.

If only Lucas had told her the truth that night.

It was the last if-only she'd never quite let go. Her therapist had asked several times what Cassie believed would have happened if Lucas told her he was in love with her that night at The Met. At first, she remained adamant it wouldn't change anything. She would have turned her back on both men and forged her path to independence and happiness. She didn't need or want any man.

After the initial flares of anger and pain subsided though, she finally had admitted that was probably a lie. If Lucas had said he loved her, she would have fallen into his arms. But he didn't need to know that. Not then, not now, and not ever.

And yet.

She shook her head and nudged the tile floor with her bare foot.

"Probably. And if not, I would have looked for you. I still had a key to your apartment after all." She chuckled at herself and heaved out a rush of air, releasing that final piece of regret.

"It's good to see you still can't lie."

"Some things haven't changed," she said. "But a lot of others have."

Her gaze jumped back to his, catching the smile that dashed across his face. He wasn't the same, not in any of the bad ways. They had both changed, had both been changed by a sequence of events Lucas set in motion more than two years ago. But their journeys weren't finished, and Cassie doubted their transformations were complete.

Things work out as they should, even if it's not the way you think they will.

"You're the one who saved me, Cass."

Words flooded into her mouth, but she didn't speak.

"Until that night in Paris, I didn't know how my past affected me. When I came home, I tried to go back to the way things were. But, between the weight of the past and leaving you like I did, I couldn't. I was heartbroken. Then when I saw how Jason punished you..."

He fell silent as he pushed one thumb into the other palm.

"I lied because I was no good for you the way I was. You didn't need another project to fix. You deserved better than me."

She bit her lip as the implications of this rattled inside her chest. All the time she spent worrying she'd broken Lucas that night and it turned out she was right. But it was more of a breakthrough. One that helped liberate him from the baggage of his past like her dad's letter had done for her.

She looked back to the painting as her mind returned to the first time they had met.

"You've come a long way, Lucas. I hope you keep moving forward because you deserve to be happy."

"That means a lot from you, Cass. Considering what I did."

Yes, what he did was awful. But she now understood and accepted that mistakes can serve to redirect a person when life has taken them far off course.

"I forgave you a long time ago," she whispered.

He narrowed his eyes, his face painted with half surprise, half skepticism.

"We all make choices," she continued. "Some turn out to be good and some don't. We can't unmake the wrong ones, but we can learn from them and move forward. Forgiveness frees us from the burden of those mistakes."

He tipped his head. He looked at the painting again, plunging his hands into his pockets. Side by side, they stood together. For how long, Cassie didn't know. There was comfort in sharing the same silent space with him. They had a deep-seated understanding of each other that defied logic, both then and now.

The curator came to find Cassie and stopped dead in his tracks when he discovered Lucas Dalton standing in his museum after hours. He stammered and apologized, but Lucas stopped him with a single wave of the hand.

"It's okay. Cassie was just telling me how much she loves Jackson Pollock."

She laughed. They had shared a story once upon a time. It had ended in flames but, ultimately, allowed these new versions of them to emerge from the ashes.

She was the first to break the bond between them as she dipped her head in a quiet goodbye. He returned it with a broad smile and a hint of hope gleaming in his beautiful blue eyes.

As Cassie walked out of The Met, her shoes dangling from her fingertips, the nighttime city air enveloping her, the time felt ripe for a new story to write itself, a new painting to emerge from the secret parts of her heart. One about forgiveness and peace, possibility and second chances.

Once upon a time, a powerful, broken, and hardened man made an awful deal that brought him together with a lost, grief-stricken, and too-honest-for-her-own-good woman. But the pair were shackled to their losses, the shadows of which loomed large in their hearts. And the only way they could save each other was by falling apart—and saving themselves first.

THE END

Thank you so much for reading There's Always a Price! Please consider leaving a review on Amazon, Goodreads, Barnes & Noble, etc. Even a single sentence can help make a book successful. Sign up for my newsletter or visit jensinclairwrites.com to stay up-to-date on the latest news and be the first to find out about my next book coming in early 2025.

Acknowledgements

I t wasn't too long ago that I stood poised on the precipice of giving up on this dream of publishing a book. The road from a blank document to a published book is a long one, pitted with rejection, disheartening feedback, and crippling self-doubt. By February 2023, I was ready to shelve it all and walk away.

But then in early May, my brother Tim died unexpectedly. Along with the grief his death ripped open came the resurgence of my writing life. In the following months, I wrote because I loved doing it. I wrote because I needed to do it. It was part therapy, part escape. Soon after, I decided I was unwilling to give up on publishing and, more importantly, I was unwilling to give up on myself. Life, as I had been reminded, was too short. And I have many stories to share.

I'm also incredibly blessed to be surrounded by people who support me. I joined the Women's Fiction Writers Association a few years ago and received an invitation to join a local in-person meeting. Out of this evolved a core group we dubbed the Writer Hikers, who met weekly to walk together. These four incredible women have given me guidance, advice, and above all else, friendship. I cherish our time and conversations more than you will ever know. Thank you for everything you do for me.

They introduced me to Zoom Write-Ins and thus began my almost daily practice of meeting with amazing women online known as the Write-In-

Mates. These women and the members of my BTTD Brainstorming Group have been nothing short of a Godsend on this journey. Thank you all for being a Zoom click away every day.

I connected with my critique partner over the very first draft of this book, and she very quickly became a best friend. Thank you, Rachel Stone for being such a loud champion of this book and me. I would have given up on it or torn it to shreds if it hadn't been for your unwavering support. I love the path that led me to you, and I can't wait to keep riding this rollercoaster together. ILYSM!

Marta Lane's Trust Your Words workshops not only got me through the early stages of grief, but they also gave me the ultimate gift of a talented writer sister in Marta. Thank you for your friendship, support, and honest feedback. I am forever grateful.

Two others helped make this book what it is today. Book Coach Kenda Lee guided me toward crafting an arc and ending for Cassie that I love. My copy editor, Lara Zielinsky made this book shine. Thank you both for your support, guidance, and hard work. This book wouldn't be what it is without you!

My very first beta reader is my real-life Jess, Aimee Van Alstyne. We really were randomly matched freshman year of college decades ago and have weathered the many storms of life together ever since. Thank you for being my soul sister. I love you, and I would be lost without you in my life.

My in-laws, Tim and Peggy, and my sisters-in-law, Kelli and Jodie have been an enthusiastic cheer squad during this process. They've checked in on my writing and publishing progress, let me fumble over all attempts to describe this book, and most of all made me feel capable. I won the lottery when it came to you. Thank you for being nothing short of wonderful. I love you.

I was blessed to be raised by three of the strongest women in the world: my mom and my sisters, Kathy and Laurie. You always stoked my creativity and imagination, even if that meant watching plays in the living room and leaving a chair empty at the table for Tracy. You are the definition of unconditional love and have given me every opportunity to chase the dream that calls to me. I love you all!

I have three amazing kids. My sons, Ethan and Maddox are always happy to listen when I talk about my writing, and maybe even think it might be cool. My daughter, Kaylee has done so much for this book. She brainstormed, helped me design the cover, read it, and gave me her brutally honest opinion, which made the book better (even though it meant deleting my beloved Epilogue). You three are my heart. I love you beyond words.

And last, but certainly not least, I wouldn't be doing this without my husband, Chris. You've given me unwavering support, honest opinions, and a shoulder to cry on. Through it all, you always believed in me and gave me the faith and confidence to keep going when I had none. We are proof that second chances happen, and that love is always worth the risk. I hope that I can make you proud. I love you. Always and forever.

About the Author

Jen Sinclair is a freelance writer who lives in Saint Augustine, Florida, with her husband, kids, and spoiled puppy. When she isn't working out story elements, belting out songs from one of her many Spotify playlists, or having conversations with imaginary friends, Jen enjoys spending time outside, paddling the waterways, or driving around with the top off her Jeep. *There's Always a Price* is her first novel. Visit jensinclairwrites.com for more information, sign up for her newsletter, and follow Jen on Facebook and Instagram.

Made in the USA
Columbia, SC
25 September 2024

43020729R00190